THE RECKONING

THE
RECKONING

Ted Allbeury

Hodder & Stoughton

Copyright © 1999 Ted Allbeury

First Published in Great Britain in 1999
by Hodder and Stoughton
A division of Hodder Headline PLC

10 9 8 7 6 5 4 3 2 1

British Library Cataloguing in Publication Data
A CIP catalogue record for this title is available
from the British Library

ISBN 0 340 75093 6

Typeset by
Phoenix Typesetting, Ilkley, West Yorkshire
Printed and bound in Great Britain by
Caledonian International Book Manufacturing Ltd, Glasgow

Hodder and Stoughton
A division of Hodder Headline PLC
338 Euston Road
London NW1 3BH

With this novel I should like to say thanks to Derek Priestley who published my first book with Peter Davies and to Alewyn Birch and Mark Barty-King when they were at Granada. They all did so much in those early days to put me on the map and I'm very grateful.

Such wilt thou be to me, who must

Like th'other foot, obliquely run;

Thy firmness makes my circle just,

And makes me end, where I begun.

A Valediction Forbidding Mourning
John Donne

Part One

Chapter One

The brass plate on the solid wooden door of 37–41 Gower Street said, simply, Blake Friedmann Literary Agency. It was, in fact, one of the several SIS safe-houses in central London. It was Cooper who had devised the name and the description and he sometimes wished that it was true instead of just a cover for informal meetings away from the files and computers of Century House.

He detested the Janus meetings. They had no purpose apart from keeping people quiet. Waring and Shapiro would say very little because they knew what was really going on. Rimmer would air his suspicions about Max Inman and find some way to drag in Inman's girl's life-style. Potter would, as Cooper's deputy, fend off the criticisms and divert the suspicions. Cooper wondered if the KGB had similar meetings about their men, questioning their good faith and digging holes for them to fall into.

Security at Gower Street was discreet but efficient and the Royal Corps of Signals sergeant showed him the long list of ticked-off bugging checks that had already been carried out. He signed the form and the sergeant countersigned it. Operation Janus called for top security. It had grown from a rather amateurish experiment into what was almost the only up-to-date source of information SIS had on what was going on inside East

Germany, the self-styled German Democratic Republic. The operation functioned and depended almost entirely on the character and talents of one man – Max Inman. His cover was as a freelance journalist writing on politics and economics. It wasn't just cover, his pieces were accepted and used in a number of magazines and newspapers.

It was Cooper who had spotted the young Cambridge graduate who was still at Trinity taking an extra year. The student debate had been about the virtues and drawbacks of democracy and Max Inman had amiably but effectively showed democracy to be a 'fool's paradise'. Speakers had been given ten minutes but they had made Max Inman talk for almost an hour. They had loved it. When Cooper had spoken to him afterwards and congratulated him on his arguments which had undoubtedly won the debate, Max Inman had smiled and said, 'That doesn't make the ideas right of course. It just means I'm a better arguer than the others were. Just winning the argument doesn't make you right.' When Cooper learned that Max Inman spoke fluent Russian he lost no time in trying to recruit him.

People in SIS always described Frank Cooper as having 'a safe pair of hands'. He had never been quite sure what it meant but he sensed that it was some kind of approval. He had been recruited into SIS after six years in Field Security and the Intelligence Corps and he had served successfully as an agent in Australia, Israel, Italy and New York. He had achieved a reputation for establishing good working relationships in difficult situations without 'going native'. Both ASIO and the CIA had made passes in his direction and still maintained a good relationship with him when he diplomatically declined their offers. He lived in a pleasant flat in one of the side-roads off Kings Road, Chelsea. For almost ten years he had lived alone after his wife had left him for a merchant banker. An older man. The divorce had been uncomplicated and he saw the man from time to time at the Reform Club. They would nod if one caught the other's eye.

Cooper was one of the very few SIS directors who was trusted and respected by both layers of the organisation. His record as a field agent made him aware and tolerant of the pressures of an agent's life. The loneliness, the uncertainties and the constant suspicion that could temporarily be diverted by boozy oblivion or the proverbial tart with a heart of gold.

Nobody was sure who had recruited Paul Rimmer into SIS. He had done quite a long stint on the other side of the fence in MI5 and had a reputation for suspecting everyone of being guilty of 'activities against the State'. And the fact that a small proportion of them actually were, had given him a reputation for being uncannily perceptive. It was said that he had kept up his connection with MI5 and that they were the source of most of the information he used against his chosen suspects. He was respected but not liked by his colleagues in SIS.

Cooper's right-hand was Potter. He had a law degree and had practised law for two years before someone in SIS had realised that Chris Potter was the nephew of a former DG of SIS and when they had looked him over they had offered, and he had accepted, a job as a senior in the Legal Secretary's department responsible for giving guidance to officers considering the legal niceties of searches, surveillance and assembling evidence that would stand up in court. He had worked with Cooper on six or seven cases and Cooper realised that the young man was grossly underused in terms of his obvious talent as an administrator. He had been Cooper's assistant for four years and they had become a highly efficient combination.

Cooper walked over to the windows. It was beginning to snow. Just light flakes blown about by the wind. With a bit of luck the meeting would be over in half an hour and he could get a taxi before the evening rush started. He turned as there was a knock on the door and Rimmer came in with Potter, nodding to Cooper as he pulled out a chair and put his notes on the table. No minutes were ever taken at meetings about the most highly secure operations and Operation Janus was one of them. A few moments later Joe Shapiro came in, apologising for being late.

Cooper settled in the chair at the head of the table.

'There's not a lot to report since last month's meeting but Max Inman has passed me the names of all the staff at the Berlin Stasi HQ including private addresses and the telephone numbers at the offices. He also told me in a meeting we had in Berlin that there was a lot of tension between the Stasis and the KGB people at Normannenallee. He gets the impression that there is an equally frosty relationship between the East German politicians and Moscow. He's also built up a good relationship with the Stasi guy in charge of their operations in West Germany.' He smiled and shrugged. 'They're both football fans.'

Rimmer said sharply. 'What's he passing to them?'

'Just the bits and pieces we give him. Some of it true, some conjecture.'

Rimmer shook his head. 'I've said it before and I'll say it again – I don't go along with this operation. Never have.'

'Why?'

'First of all, double agents' operations always break down sooner or later. It starts with both sides trusting the guy and ends up with him being suspect on both sides. Janus is suspect for me.' He paused. 'I've listened to his little talks on his views of Soviet attitudes concerning Germany and he's always got some excuse for whatever they've been up to.'

Cooper intervened. 'When we started this operation we knew nothing about what was going on on the other side. We now get a picture of public attitudes to conditions, to politics, and the security set-up.' He paused. 'We accepted that only somebody who was genuinely open-minded could get anywhere. Janus was just right for the attempt. His cover as a journalist seems to work and it's genuine. His stuff gets printed and they've noticed that he gives them a fair crack of the whip which no other journalist does from this side. He's made a lot of contacts and he's more or less being accepted as genuine.'

'I wouldn't trust anyone in that situation and I don't trust him either.'

'Why?'

'His attitude. Ready to criticise us but only praise for them. I don't like the circles he moves in over here. All those bloody intellectuals.'

Cooper smiled. 'You ready to give some examples?'

'Yeah. The girl he lives with. What's her name – Felinska – have you seen her photographs – all anti-war – all starving kids and corpses. I've done some checking on her and she's a security risk by anybody's rules. They've been together for years and they live in separate places. Why don't they get married?'

'You sound like some agony aunt, Paul.'

'Do you know why they've never married?'

'No.'

'Why not?'

'Because I've never asked him. It's none of our business.'

'Everything's our business especially on an operation like this. Did you see that big piece she did about Russians in New York who missed the old country?'

'They were refugees, Paul. They'd fled from the Soviet Union. But they missed their old lives. The Brit ex-pats in the South of France do too and the Poms in Sydney miss Liverpool and Manchester but they still left.'

Rimmer sighed. 'It's up to you, Frank.' He pushed across a brown file. 'But read that stuff.' He paused. 'By the way they're both subscribing members of Amnesty.'

Cooper smiled. 'So am I, Paul. So am I.' He looked around at the others. 'Anything else?'

But nobody responded. When Rimmer had left, Joe Shapiro said, 'Don't dismiss what that idiot said entirely. He's paranoid about Reds under the bed but if Janus falls apart, which it easily could do, then friend Rimmer has put down his marker for having been agin it right from the start.'

'What do you feel about what Janus has produced so far?'

'It's all useful background material and it'll take time before he really makes headway. He's already saved my people from two potential cock-ups and that's enough for me.' He smiled 'By the way the Felinska girl is on TV tonight. I think it's BBC 2.'

Chapter Two

Cooper poured himself a glass of Saint Emilion as he settled himself in the armchair in front of the TV. He looked at his watch. It was five minutes before the start of the programme he was going to watch. He reached for the *Radio Times*. Her picture was on the front cover. Just her face and her finger on the shutter-button of a Leica. She was very beautiful, there was no doubt about that, classic Garbo or maybe Rossellini, and when he talked with her he sensed that she was well aware of the effect that her beauty had on men, but was not impressed by their attention. If you are that beautiful, he thought, you must get used to it. When he saw the title of the programme come up on screen he reached for the remote control and brought up the sound. The title just said, '*Katya Felinska — master photographer*'.

The interviewer, Patsy Soames, had a style somewhere between Sue Lawley and Libby Purves. Not aping the interrogation of *Face to Face* nor the amiability of Libby Purves.

'Katya Felinska . . .'

Felinska smiled and interrupted. 'For heaven's sake — let's make it Katie.'

'But Katya is such an unusual name and it *is* rather romantic.'

'Maybe. But only my parents still call me Katya.'

'Your background is Polish, isn't it?'

'My father was Polish originally but my mother is Italian and I've never lived in Poland.'

'But you speak Polish don't you?'

'Of course,' she said as if surely everybody could speak Polish.

'Do you see much of your parents these days?'

'Not often enough. My father is always somewhere else working on a film and my mother is the only one of us who's mainly in the same place.'

'Your mother writes those lovely children's books.' She paused. 'You're a very creative family. Why do you think that is?'

'I've no idea.' She hesitated. 'I think maybe it's because we have lived in so many different places that we've absorbed a lot of other people's characteristics and cultures. We don't belong anywhere and yet we're at home everywhere. I was born in Vienna. I grew up in France and Italy. I went to school in California and to university here in the UK.'

'But you're now a British national yourself. Why did you choose to be British?'

Katya Felinska smiled and shrugged. 'That's a long story. It would take too long to explain.'

'OK. Back to the photography. What made you want to be a photo-journalist?'

'At first I just wanted to be a photographer. News photographer, portraits. Anything that involved a camera.'

'With your father a very successful film director, did that influence you?'

'I don't think so. Subconsciously maybe. He was always looking at everything. Watching how the light fell on faces and scenes.'

'You specialised in your early days as a photo-journalist in the world's trouble spots where the fighting was going on. Why did you change?'

'I was sickened by the film and video footage, and the stills for that matter, of men in uniforms killing other men in uniforms, and civilians too. I found it impossible to be any part of it, even as a witness. Despite what they say, there is an underlying glamour in war pictures. Bravery, even gallantry, men being men. So I decided to leave that side alone and take pictures to show the misery that they left behind them. Homes destroyed, dead bodies, starving old people, women and children and all the rest of it. The part that women have to play in clearing up the mess. The physical mess and the mental mess.'

'Are you a feminist?'

She laughed. 'If you mean do I hate all men. No way. What I hate is destruction but . . .' she shrugged '. . . that's mainly men's work.'

'Do you enjoy it or feel a bit proud when people refer to you as "a master photographer"?'

Katya laughed. 'Forgive me for saying so when it's the title of this interview but I think it shows a complete ignorance of the world of photography. There are a few people – Ansel Adams, Weston and maybe a few portraitists like Cecil Beaton and Karsh – who could be loosely described as master photographers because to them the photograph, the finished product, is what matters. Focus, definition, tone range and all that. But for me I just record a moment in the life of some people or somebody and to me it's the emotion that matters.'

'Can you give us an example of the kind of photograph you find moving?'

'Yes. The photograph of the young girl in Vietnam running down the road towards the camera, naked and on fire from napalm. That haunts me. And it always will.' She paused. 'And there will be more like it until we get rid of politicians and diplomats.'

'Why diplomats?'

'The Foreign Office, our embassies and consulates overseas, won't lift a finger to help you if you're in trouble in a foreign country. They don't want to displease what they call their "client" countries.'

'Have you had personal experience of this?'

'Many times.'

'What should they do?'

'Raise absolute hell to ensure that you get a fair deal. When I read that bit in my passport that says I should be allowed to travel "without let or hindrance" it makes me very angry. Such hypocrisy.'

'According to the press-cuttings you're forty-two. Is that right?'

'Yeah.'

'And you've never married?'

She smiled. 'You're right and to save you the trouble of trying to work out some subtle way to ask if I'm a lesbian, let me say – no I'm not. But I *do* prefer women to men.'

'Any particular reason?'

'Women are the same all over the world. Like I show in my photography, they clean up the mess the world makes. They deal with fundamentals. A female is a woman the moment she's born. She just grows a bit bigger. But men are all bits and pieces. They're never certain what they are or even what they want to be.'

'You sound rather cynical. Are you?'

Katya frowned, thinking. 'I'd say realistic. Just facing the facts. And hopefully showing the facts in my pictures.'

'Your photographs are frequently of children. Would you have liked children of your own?'

'No. My photographs all too often are of children starving, dying for lack of food or medicines. After what I have seen I couldn't take the responsibility.' She shrugged dismissively. 'And

I've got a job that's twenty-four hours a day. Looking and thinking. Admiring real bravery — women's and children's bravery.' She shrugged almost impatiently as if explaining should be unnecessary.

'Do you have a special man-friend, a lover, at the moment?'

Katya laughed, obviously genuinely amused. 'I guess the answer is yes but he'd hate being described as my lover. Lover is the kind of word that the *Sun* uses when the libel lawyers won't let them go the whole hog.'

Patsy Soames smiled. 'Fair enough. So back to your work. What sort of camera do you use?'

'A Leica. Way back it was a IIIb but for the last few years it's an M3.'

'Where's your next assignment?'

'I'm going back to Somalia, to Mogadishu, to see what's happening there. And after that I'll probably spend some time in Addis.'

'Are you ever tempted to get involved — to be a campaigner rather than just an observer?'

'No way. In my experience campaigners cause almost as much trouble for the survivors as the politicians do.'

'Why's that?'

'For the general public to be told that two thousand people, civilians, have been slaughtered by some tin-pot army is meaningless. But show them a picture of the sad, pleading face of a mother holding a child that's long dead up to the camera and they can begin to understand what is going on. It's up to the public to take action or make the politicians and dictators stop what they're doing.'

'How can they do that?'

'That's for them to decide, not me. If I get involved I lose my credibility. I'd be rooting for one lot or another. For me they are all as bad as one another. Savages.'

'What about the United Nations?'

Katya shrugged almost angrily. 'Forget it.'

'It's not a very happy picture you give us of the world, is it?'

'It's how it is. You can always not look. Not wonder what it would be like if it was you in the picture with the dead baby.'

'How do you keep sane after all this?'

'I spend my time with ordinary people and you'd be amazed at how nice most people are, but unfortunately niceness won't beat guns and psychopaths.'

'What sort of people do you spend your free time with?'

'Creative people. Artists, theatre people, musicians, writers. People with imagination. Emotional people. People like my parents.'

'And when you're alone and not working, what do you do?'

'Read and listen to music.'

'What kind of music?'

Katya smiled. 'Romantic stuff. Violin and cello concertos. And blues jazz.'

'Any advice you could give aspiring photo-journalists?'

'Sure. Get out there with your heart on your sleeve and take pictures.'

'Katya Felinska – thank you for coming on the programme.'

'Thanks for having me.'

Cooper used the remote to switch off the TV and half-filled his empty wine glass. He'd read somewhere somebody's comment that she was a very 'feisty' lady. He had never really understood what feisty actually meant but she was an extraordinary person without a doubt. So incredibly beautiful and yet so absorbed in what she was doing. So feminine in her observation but so harshly masculine in her judgments. She and Max Inman made an odd pair and he wondered what she found in a man like Inman, a man whose trade was deviousness and personal courage made tolerable by a great deal of charm. But she must be used to charm, both real and phoney. According to the files they had met at

Cambridge and that was a long time ago. Still a pair but no sign of marrying.

He stood up slowly and awkwardly. Right now it was time for a last cup of tea before bed and a few pages of Ethel Mannin's *The Golden Road to Samarkand*.

Chapter Three

Cooper took Paul Rimmer's file from the safe and opened it as he walked to his desk and sat down. There were only two pages of typing, single-spaced and from the layout obviously typed by Rimmer himself. Cooper read both pages carefully and then reread them. When he had finished he leant back in his chair and closed his eyes. Rimmer was a strange man. He wasn't really an SIS type. His colleagues had nicknamed him 'Ferret' and the two pages of notes were a prime example of why he was shunned by his fellow workers.

The notes were a litany of niggling criticisms, none of them individually significant but giving a picture of undesirable contacts and associations by the standards of a rather mean-minded critic. Inevitably there was the reference to the girl and the man being at Cambridge together. There was no need to remind a reader in SIS of the other well-known alumni of the university – Philby, Burgess and Maclean. Even Maclean's brilliant academic record was held against him. Katya Felinska's contacts were a damning array of union leaders, Amnesty International, *Médecins sans Frontières*, Save the Children and the Red Cross all being rated as extreme left-wing organisations by Rimmer. There was a bitterness, an acidity, running through the diatribe of criticism that gave an impression of recrimination rather than information.

But Cooper had spent time with Rimmer on several social occasions when he'd been invited down for the day at the cottage in Sussex where Rimmer played for the village cricket team. And that was a very different Rimmer. A man at ease with his surroundings with a very pretty wife who obviously adored him. Drinking tea and eating cream buns in such company it was possible to see Rimmer in a different light. As the defender of the faithful and the defenceless. Or was he more like a nagging wife who only looked for the worst in the defence of her man. He couldn't just dismiss the information that Rimmer had assembled. All he had to remember was that it was a rather distorted picture of one person's life-style. Joe Shapiro's comment that it was just Rimmer putting down a marker to show that he disagreed with the operation if it eventually went wrong was just as biased.

Joe Shapiro was SIS's special coordinator of all information on the Soviet Union, including the Warsaw Pact. There were few people in the Kremlin who knew as much about what was really going on inside the corridors of power as Joe Shapiro did. There were layers of Janus's information that Cooper passed on solely to Joe Shapiro.

Cooper and Shapiro had never served together in the field but they felt instinctively that affinity that old soldiers have for one another. Shapiro's past service was never discussed and all that Cooper knew was that Shapiro spoke fluent Russian and German and had operated on the border between the two Germanys. Cooper assumed that Shapiro had been running a line-crossing network of some sort. Shapiro took a great interest in what Janus was sending back and had spent a lot of time talking to him before the operation started. When Cooper had asked Max Inman what Shapiro had talked about, he had smiled and said, 'I'm not sure but I think he was just trying to assess my views for and against the Communist Party.'

'What do you think his views are?'

'He doesn't give much away. I'd be guessing.'

'So guess.'

Inman sighed and shrugged. 'He's not anti-Russian but he is anti-Communist. He thinks they betrayed the people.'

'And what do you think?'

'First of all I think you've got to see them as people. Just trying to earn a living and get by. When you look at the Kremlin you're in a different ball-game. No statesmen, no real leaders, just icons.' He shrugged. 'It would take hours to explain and I'm not sure that I could do it. It's inside my head.'

Cooper watched Shapiro read through the Janus report and then leafed through the internal telephone numbers of the Stasi HQ. When he pushed the papers to one side he looked up at Cooper.

'You didn't get me across here for this stuff, did you?'

'No.'

Shapiro shrugged. 'OK. What's the problem?'

'You remember that for some time Max has been reporting that there is growing tension in the general population?'

'Yes. And I think his analysis is right.'

'He told me that the tension between the East Germans and Moscow was because the Stasi and the politicians are blaming the civil unrest on Gorbachev and *perestroika*. They think that maybe unintentionally he's given the green light to the protesters.' He paused. 'The second item is that Inman's well in with a group of activists who are preparing for an uprising. They've got information that the Stasis have put together a special unit that is prepared to go all the way to prevent a merging of the two Germanys.'

'How far is all the way?'

'He's not sure but he thinks it could be political assassi-nations.'

'Which side of the border?'

'Ours.'

Shapiro looked interested. 'Why, for God's sake?'

'Max thought they could make it look as if the assassinations were initiated by Moscow.'

Shapiro was silent for several moments and then he said, 'It fits some of the signals traffic that my people have been moni-toring in the last couple of months.' He paused. 'Did he say where it was based, the group?'

'Berlin and Dresden.'

'It fits, Frank. Encourage him to find out more. And keep me in the picture.'

Katya found the interviews an irritation but they were part of the job and she knew that Joanna, her agent, had made tremendous efforts to arrange all the publicity she could prior to the launch of her book. It was part of the job. Magnum were her photo-graphic agents and Joanna looked after her journalism.

She was expecting Roy Martin to discuss the cameras with her and that at least would be a pleasant relief.

Roy Martin was the owner of Camera Gear in Tunbridge Wells, where she had always bought her photographic equip-ment. He had let her use a Nikon F90X for a month and she'd laid out the proofs on her light-boxes. Black and white negatives, Fuji and Kodachrome slides and Fujicolor colour negatives. She had looked at them dozens of times. There was nothing to choose between the two cameras so far as the lens quality was concerned. They'd blow up to 20 × 16s with no problems.

When Roy Martin looked them over he agreed. There was nothing to choose between the two cameras. When she said she was going to change to the Nikon he seemed surprised.

'Aren't you going to miss the Leica after sticking to them for so long?'

She shook her head. 'I don't think so. Once I got used to the Nikon I found that I was using it all the time. I didn't have to worry about focusing and exposure and with the 24–120 zoom lens I didn't need any other lenses.'

'But it's a lot bulkier and heavier than the M6.'

She shrugged. 'Not if you throw in two more lenses.' She smiled. 'You're a bit of a Leica snob, aren't you?'

He smiled. 'You're right. Do you want to do a part-exchange deal?'

'No. I'll hang on to the Leica for old times' sake.' She smiled. 'You know for years I've always believed that Leica lenses gave a special kind of look to Kodachrome slides. A sort of Canaletto atmosphere but I've come to the conclusion after the tests that it was a delusion. The subtlety was in the film not the lenses.'

'What do you really want from a camera?'

She hesitated for a moment and then said, 'I want to be able to think about nothing but the picture I'm about to take. It's what I'm looking at that matters not the camera. How the camera works doesn't interest me.'

'I think I can get you a good deal with Nikon if you make the change.'

'How much?'

'If you don't mind them using you in their publicity, at least a fifty percent discount on the body and the lens. Maybe even a little more.'

'OK then Roy. Let's go ahead. Can I keep the camera and lens that you lent me?'

'Of course.'

She laughed. 'I'll get a lot of flak from the old boys at Magnum who all swear by their Leicas and Contaxes.'

'At least they'll take comfort from the fact that you haven't traded in your Leica.'

She laughed. 'I'm sure they've got dusty old Rolleiflexes tucked away in their studies. And to give them their due there's no two ways about it, just the whisper of a Leica shutter is kind of beautiful.'

Roy Martin stood up. 'Where are you off to next?'

'I'm due to go to Somalia but things have got a bit held up at the moment.'

'I see in the *Radio Times* that you're doing *Desert Island Discs* on Friday next week.'

'Yeah, but I'll be recording it tomorrow.'

He held out his hand. 'What it is to be famous.'

She laughed as she walked him to the door of the flat. 'There's a world of difference between being famous and merely well-known.'

'You're too modest,' he said. 'I'll do my best for you with Nikon and I'll send you the paperwork.'

She had put the Leica away in its original box and put it on the shelf in the dark-room. For some inexplicable reason people would pay more for a camera in its original box.

She phoned Magnum to warn them that she needed more time before she want to Nairobi and then up to Mogadishu. There were no problems so long as she gave them two weeks to gather up visas and documentation. Automatically she went to her desk, opened the bottom drawer and checked the date on her passport. It had just over two more years' validity. But as she leafed through the pages she saw all those red and blue and black entry and exit stamps that marked her travels. Why the hell should anyone have to have a stamp in a passport just to visit some other country, with all the opportunity for hundreds of bloody-minded officials to make it more difficult than the journey had already made it. But she knew all too well why they did it. It was to hide their government's corruption or repression of their own people. Repression of all freedoms, to express their opinions, to travel outside the prison bars of frontiers, killing because some tattoo or tribal mark made you a helpless victim. How in hell could you tell a Croat from a Serb when they all wore Marks and Spencer's sweaters? How did you bring yourself to killing the family who had lived for years four doors down the street? The one whose eldest son played football for Arsenal but who all went to the wrong church. Not regularly. Just Christmas, Harvest Festival and Easter. And you conveniently forgot that you'd been to that church when Milos got married. But whatever they'd done wrong it meant you could kill the parents and rape the daughters and call yourself a freedom fighter.

Chapter Four

⬦

They'd had a pleasant lunch together and then gone up to the recording studio, sitting facing one another with the microphone in the middle between them, the producer and recording people behind the big glass window that took up a whole wall.

Sue Lawley pointed at the pile of records and CDs. 'We've got several versions of all your choices so you can choose which one you prefer.' She paused. 'We won't just do that chat. We find it's best if you hear the music after each choice.' She smiled. 'Puts you in the mood of the music.' She turned to the internal mike. 'We're ready.'

Somebody in the control room gave a thumbs-up sign and Sue Lawley became the professional.

'My guest today is frequently referred to as a master-photographer – a title she modestly denies. She has achieved world recognition as someone who records humanity as it really is after the dogs of war have passed through some area. Not a brave new world but a plague of sadness and suffering. She has one advantage that most other photo-journalists don't have – she's very beautiful – and getting down to earth again, she speaks half a dozen languages. And so she should. She has lived in many countries as a small girl, a young girl and a young woman.' She smiled across at Katya. 'So Katya Felinska your first record please.'

'Thank you.' She paused. 'I was born in Vienna . . .' she laughed '. . . and those are the opening words of my first choice. '*Wien, Wien, bist du allein . . .*' The music came in smoothly and when, a couple of minutes later, it was faded out Sue Lawley said, 'Tell us about when you were a small girl in Vienna.'

Her father had been standing by the window looking at her mother who was looking back at him, smiling.

'*But why shouldn't we go to the cinema, papa?*'

'*Because it's July 15 today. We should remember that.*' *He paused looking at his wife.* '*Don't be taken in by the "Blue Danube" and all that Austrian "kissing the hand" and "may I have the honour". That's not what Vienna's really all about.*'

'*So what is it really all about, my dear?*'

For a moment he had hesitated and then he said, '*Put your summer coat on and the same for Katya. I'm going to take you both for a little walk. You can go to the cinema afterwards.*'

She was only five years old but she could tell that whatever it was all about it was very important to her father. She could sometimes sense his moods even better than her mother could.

He walked them down to the Palace of Justice then stopped, pointing with his walking-stick to the square. '*On July 15 1927 the Austrian Nazis fired into a crowd of defenceless civilians, the Palais de Justice was on fire and the Nazis went on firing until they had no more ammunition. Thirty people died in the attack.*

'*In February 1934 the workers went on strike because of more murders and the Austrian Nazis did what they were told to do. They went down to the blocks of workers' flats in Ottakring, Florisdorf and Favoriton. But this time they used artillery, howitzers, machine-guns and mortars. The blocks were full of the people who lived there and they were shelled until the blocks were just heaps of rubble.*'

She saw the tears on his cheeks and his voice trembled as he said, '*They weren't German Nazis, they were Austrian Nazis. Some of those workers' wives went* mad. Literally mad. The death toll was enormous.' He paused and wiped his nose with his handkerchief. 'So don't ever be fooled by hand-kissing or sugary compliments . . .' he looked at his pretty daughter. 'Especially you, Katya.'

'Were you here at the time, papa?'

'No, my love. But my father was. He told me about it like I'm telling you. The only difference is that he'd heard the screams of women pleading for mercy at the windows of the workers' flats. He could never forget it. I can't forget it either. Now . . .' he said, taking a deep breath, '. . . what are we going to see at the cinema?'

'It's Jacques Tati, dada. Mon Oncle.'

'Ah yes. Let's take a taxi and I'll join you.'

It was the first time that she had seen her father cry.

They were sitting apart from the others who were eating from a picnic basket on the banks of the Cam, not far from Clare Bridge. It was May but summer seemed to have started early in 1972. The others were arguing about the Americans in Vietnam. The two American students were having a bad time. But the couple by the bridge were talking about themselves. The girl was well aware that the young man was interested in her but she was used to all that.

'Tell me about when you were a kid. When you lived in Vienna.'

'It was strange really. My father was originally Polish. Jan Felinski . . .'

He interrupted. 'I thought your name was Felinska with an "a".'

'It is. In Polish men's names end in "i" and females' names end in "a".'

'It's a beautiful name — Katya Felinska.' He said it slowly and lovingly.

She shrugged. 'My Mama was Italian. Very beautiful and, unlike my Papa, was totally reliable.'

He laughed. 'In what way was he unreliable?'

'He was just beginning to make a name for himself in Hollywood as well as Europe so he was always rushing off to places to talk about scripts and budgets and raising money. He was more like a very welcome visitor than a father. But she loved him and he loved her.'

'Did you love him?'

'In a way but I think it was more admiration than love. Mama I loved and

Mama was there. Of course when he was home the house was full of marvellous people. Poets, writers, musicians, painters and a few professors. It was a real madhouse.'

'Was he political, your father?'

'I don't really know. He never discussed politics but there were things that made me think that he was more aware of politics than he pretended to be.'

'What sort of things?'

'He took me for a walk one day and he pointed at some buildings and said that they had been workers' homes but the Austrian Nazis had almost completely destroyed them with artillery. I can remember being upset because I saw tears in his eyes.' She smiled at him, encouragingly. 'Tell me about your family.'

'Nothing much to tell you. Father is a stockbroker. Makes a lot of money. My mother is just a housewife. Does a bit of charity work, bridge-parties and all that sort of crap.'

'What made you take Russian?'

'I guess it was just reading Tolstoy, Dostoevsky and Pushkin.' He laughed. 'They made me wish I was a Russian and one of the masters at school encouraged me to take Russian for my "A" levels. I became obsessed by the language and the country and the people. And, of course, I fell in love with Anna Karenina until I saw Julie Christie in Zhivago.' He smiled. 'What did your father think of Zhivago?'

'Loved the photography and the music but felt it didn't do justice to the book.'

'He's right you know. He's right.' He smiled. 'The difference between a layman's view and a professional's.' He paused. 'What did you think of it?'

'Loved it. Lara's song still haunts me.' She paused. 'Have you ever been to the Soviet Union?'

'Yes, twice. Once on a school trip and once on an exchange for a term with a Russian student.'

'Do you speak colloquial Russian?'

'Of course.'

She laughed. 'Don't sound so shocked. Most Brits who take languages see them as education rather than communication. Experts on using the past historic or defining a genuine gerund, but can't ask a girl out for a cup of coffee.'

He smiled. 'You're a bit of a cynic, Katya Felinska.'

'When do you take your finals?'

'I've taken my Russian finals and I'm doing an extra year on a Creative Writing module.'

'How did you get on with your finals?'

'I got a two point one.'

'Clever boy.' She paused. 'Tell me, what kind of job does a Russian degree get you?'

He shrugged. 'Most people try for the Foreign Office or high-grade interpreting like the UN.'

'Which do you want?'

'I don't really know. I've had a Foreign Office interview but that was two months ago and I haven't heard a peep out of them since.' He paused. 'How about you? What do you want to do?'

'I'm taking Psychology and History. My father thinks I'd do well in the film business but I'm not impressed by all that hassle. I've no qualifications for it but I'd like to be a photographer. Stills not ciné. There are several universities that do Creative Photography courses. My father thought they were a waste of time.'

'In what way?'

'Too much emphasis on the mechanics and not enough on what you photo-graph. He thinks just using a camera is the best training.' She shrugged. 'I'll wait till I've finished my finals and think again.'

'How old were you when you left Vienna?'

'About seven or eight.'

'What do you remember best about it?'

She thought for a few moments and then said, 'I had a feeling that I was part of history. So much had happened there. But I guess I remember best going to concerts with my parents. Brahms concerts, Strauss concerts and the New Year's Day concerts because Dada could always get tickets because he was by then a little bit famous. Or at least well-known.' She paused. 'And I went with them to see all sorts of films. Gigi. Hiroshima, Mon Amour, and Look Back in Anger.' She laughed. 'And when we got home we'd have coffee and have to give him our impression of the films. And he'd remind us of scenes, camera angles and lighting problems. It was good training. He always used to say,

"Remember one thing. Most people look without seeing, when you look you must look with your mind as well as your eyes".' She shrugged. 'He was right of course. He usually was. But it was very annoying.'

'Where's your home now?'

She laughed. 'Wherever Mama is. London at the moment.' She stood up. 'I need to get back and do a bit of work. Walk me to the bridge.'

She picked up her mail from her pigeon-hole and went up to her room. She found Max Inman strangely attractive. He was certainly physically attractive with an amiable disposition and a good sense of humour. It was obvious from several things that he had said since she first got to know him that he was fond of his mother but resentful of his father and the way he dominated the family. She guessed that Max was at least two years, probably three years, older than she was. The charm was real not phoney, and it seemed to work with men as well as with girls. He was genuinely interested in other peoples' thoughts and lives. Plain girls as well as pretty ones.

Chapter Five

It was just over a year later that they were sitting in Max Inman's room. Katya had been relieved at her second-year results and Max had successfully finished his module and was packing his things to take back to his home. There were a lot of books, an Olivetti Lettera portable typewriter and a small case full of clothes.

She was sitting on his unmade bed watching him scouring the room for anything more that had to be taken. He seemed to be disturbed about something.

'What's the matter, Max? What's troubling you?'

'The matter? Nothing's the matter.' He shrugged. 'I tried to get on another module but they wouldn't play.'

'Why another module?'

He stood looking at her as she sat on the rumpled bed. 'Because I'm going to miss you, Katie. I just wanted an excuse to be here for your last year.'

She patted the bed beside her and as he sat down she reached for his hand. 'So stay, just get a job in the town.'

He brightened up instantly. 'You wouldn't mind? I thought of that but I was afraid you'd think I was being too . . .' he searched for the word and settled on '. . . too much taking you for granted.'

She smiled. 'You're an idiot, Max Inman, you really are. Let's go to my place and have a decent cup of tea.' She swept her arm around the room. 'This place is depressing.'

As they walked to Clare they both knew that despite the banal words they had put down a new marker in their relationship.

Chapter Six

'Do sit down, Mr Inman. I'm glad you could come.' Cooper waved towards the chair alongside his desk. When Inman had settled himself Cooper got down to business.

'After the first interview I mentioned to you that if we were interested we should need to make a few enquiries.' He smiled briefly. 'Took us a bit longer than we expected.' He paused. 'Am I right in thinking that you're still interested?'

'Yes, sir.'

'Good, good.' Another official smile. 'Just a few questions. You'll understand I'm sure how careful we have to be.' He paused. 'We felt after that first interview that we might consider asking you to join one of our more confidential sections. You have a number of qualities and qualifications that we could make use of.' He paused. 'Have you heard of MI6?'

Inman hesitated. 'I think it's to do with Intelligence. The Secret Service.'

'Fair enough. MI6 is responsible for providing information for the government about what foreign governments – and sometimes friendly ones – are up to that could affect the security of the UK.' He paused. 'We have a wide variety of personnel. Academics, historians, linguists and chaps who can ferret out what we want to know from foreign parts.' He paused and looked across at Inman. 'Do you have any feelings about an organisation like that?'

Inman smiled. 'No. I've not given it much thought.'

'But you're not agin such an organisation?'

'No. Certainly not.'

'Right. Well now we've cleared the decks let's get down to the details. How do you feel about the Russians?'

'You mean Russians or Communists?'

'Either. Both.'

'The Russians I'm rather fond of. The music, the literature, the arts in general. When we come to the Communists we do have to remember that fewer than ten per cent of the population are members of the Party. And of course they've never had the chance of finding out what Communism is like. They've always been ruled by a handful of despots. A pity really. For all of us.'

'Why for all of us?' Cooper sounded genuinely interested.

'Well if you read their Constitution it's very like the United States' Constitution. In fact there are a number of similarities between Russians and Americans.'

'How interesting. What similarities do you have in mind?'

Inman was on his home ground now and he smiled. 'They admire size. Big men, big buildings, preferably the biggest in the world. They are both basic family people. Home, kids. They like winners. Football, athletics, swimming, acrobatics. It's always those two picking up the medals.'

By now Cooper was smiling. 'OK. Let's forget the Russians and look at you. Tell me about Katya Felinska.'

The previous passive acceptance of questions changed instantly. Inman said frostily. 'What's Katya got to do with you people?'

Cooper shrugged. 'Relationships can be important. And then there's the Polish/Russian name.'

'Katya's British and she's my girl-friend. Her father is the well-known film director, Jan Felinski.'

'How does she feel about the Russians?'

'You'd better ask her, Mr Cooper. I don't gossip about my friends behind their backs.'

Cooper laughed and although it was brief it was genuine. 'OK. Let's abandon Miss Felinska.' He paused. 'If you didn't end up with us what would you like to be?'

'A foreign correspondent.'

'Why that?'

'I just know I could be a good one.'

'Not very different from the job we had in mind for you. Are you interested?'

'I'd like to know more about the job.'

'You'd have to be one of us before I could go into that. But let me say that for general purposes you would be a freelance journalist specialising on the politics and economics of the two Germanys and the Soviet Union.' He paused. 'You would be expected to earn a good income from the writing in due course.' He waved a hand dismissively. 'You would, of course, always get your salary in full from us. As a matter of interest your MI6 salary is tax-free. At the moment you'd start off between fifteen and twenty thousand. And expenses of course.' He paused, eyebrows lifted. 'So what do you say?'

'In principle, yes. Sounds just what I'm looking for.'

'When could you start? You'd have a couple of months training before we launch you on the unsuspecting German public. You speak some German don't you?'

'Yes. I guess I could be available next week. I've a few things to settle up.'

'You'd be in this country for at least six months after your training.' He took Max Inman's arm. 'Let's go and have a beer.'

Cooper had taken Inman to the pub across the street from SIS's old HQ at Broadway. Despite their new quarters at Century House, the old China hands still preferred the Victorian environment that had been their territory for years. Nobody seemed to feel that the nearest pub just across the road from SIS HQ, patronised by dozens of its officers, might be a special target for the Queen's enemies.

It was left that Inman would have forty-eight hours to think it over and if he accepted he could expect to be based in London for at least the first year, although there would almost certainly be short trips overseas. He would also be expected to improve his German. When he pressed a little more firmly about what his duties would be, Cooper had said that he would be in plain clothes and would have genuine work as a journalist covering political subjects. Cooper, when asked, said that there would be no problem if Inman wanted to maintain a base in Cambridge. His quarters in London would be paid for by SIS. Most week-ends would be free until he was posted overseas.

He had relayed all that he could remember of the interview to Katya who was amused that they had asked about her. It didn't take them long to decide that the job sounded a perfect match for his qualifications, and interesting too. He would take a decent room in Cambridge and would come down every weekend or she would come to London and stay with him or with her mother. He had phoned Cooper the following morning and had accepted the offer of the job.

A letter on Foreign Office notepaper had confirmed his appointment two days later. He was to report in on the first of the next month in just over two weeks' time.

Chapter Seven

'"*Wien, wien, bist du allein*" with von Karajan and the Berlin Philharmonic . . .' Sue Lawley paused. 'How old were you when you went to the United States?'

'I think I was about seven years old when we moved to Paris and a year later to Rome.'

'These moves were because of your father's film-work?'

'Yes. Rome became very important in the film business and Cinecitta was the centre of activity. They had just finished Mankiewicz's *Cleopatra* and Visconti's *The Leopard*. I've forgotten what my father was working on.'

'Was it a good time?'

'Yes. I loved Rome and we had a lovely apartment right on the Via Veneto, and Italians are so wonderful with kids.'

'And the French and Paris?'

She screwed up her face. 'Paris beautiful – the French I didn't go for. Rather phoney but my father loved the films they made. The so-called "*Nouvelle vague*".'

'How about your next record?'

She laughed. 'Something to remember Italy by, so I'd like "*Parla mi d'amore*" sung by Tino Rossi.'

When the music eventually faded and Sue Lawley had repeated what it was, she turned to Katya.

'I've almost got you to the USA. You must have been ten or eleven by then.'

'I guess so. First of all we had a place in LA. Very palatial and lots of well-known people. Then we had a year in lovely Carmel. Dada needed a rest and was working on several scripts. Then another move. This time to San Francisco. We lived not far from the Berkeley campus and I went to the High School. I was there until I was sixteen and did quite well at school. I applied for a Rhodes scholarship but at that time you could only be a Rhodes scholar if you were a man. But my father had an unexpected windfall from work he'd done on *Un homme et une femme* and he put it all to supporting me to go to Cambridge. They accepted me at Clare and Mama and I moved to England. Mama to London, me to Cambridge.'

Sue Lawley smiled. 'Is that why you chose your next record – "I left my heart in San Francisco"?'

Katya laughed. 'Yes. And apart from that I'll always love San Francisco because that's where I got my first camera. My father found it in a junk shop and he had it checked out. It was an Olympus and I've still got it.'

The music came up and Tony Bennett's deep, honeyed voice started his lament for San Francisco.

A lot seemed to have happened in the year since they became a couple. Katya had taken a series of photographs of a Speakers Union meeting that had caught the attention of the editor of the college magazine. The wide-open mouth of the MP guest speaker showing his terrible dentistry, the sneer on the face of his leading opponent, and a don quite obviously asleep. The local paper had used that and paid her five pounds. They had also given her a press pass for the local by-election. Her shot of the main candidate's obvious distaste as he kissed an uplifted baby had gone across four columns and had been taken by a national newspaper.

She'd made £75, and even better she had been offered a job on a London suburban weekly. £25 a week and extra for shots that were used. The paper was one of a group of suburban papers and after two months she had been interviewed by the group's news editor and had been promoted to cover important local events for all three papers. She was regularly making between £75 and £100 a week.

She moved to a pleasant flat in Pimlico and Max Inman had given up the place he had in Cambridge, and just used his official accommodation in Lower Sloane Street. They had accumulated a lot of casual friends and acquaintances and they were the acknowledged centrepiece of the discussions and arguments about creative and political things. Not always agreed with but that didn't matter, they didn't always agree themselves. They neither joined nor supported any political party and looked on 'joiners' as having no confidence in their own thinking. With the girl's real beauty and the young man's easy charm they were a formidable pair.

Instinct told them that Max's people would not go along with them sharing his official quarters so they spent most of their evenings and a lot of their nights at Katya's place.

She was amused that despite his fluent Russian Max Inman was now working hard to improve his schoolboy German and she insisted that they both used German for at least an hour whenever they were together.

Inman had spent a week at each of several embassies: Bonn, Madrid, Rome and Athens, to learn how the diplomats did their work. He already had a press card and had written several articles about the economies and politics of the countries he had visited. None of them was ever used but his superiors at SIS had praised them.

After a year of training he was interviewed by a man named Shapiro who he learned later was the head of the Soviet desk at Century House. Responsible for initiating and evaluating all intelligence gathered about the Soviet Union. When he spoke Russian it was fluent but with an accent that Inman thought was Ukrainian. He sometimes spoke German but Inman's German wasn't good enough to recognise accents.

'D'you feel you know your way around the organisation now?'

Inman smiled. 'As much as I've been allowed to learn.'

'How long have you been with us?'

'Fourteen months.'

'They tell me you've done considerable research on Soviet affairs.'

He shrugged. 'I guess I have one way and another.'

'Did you wonder why we've made you brush up your German when you speak perfect Russian?'

'Not really. There's a lot that goes on in the organisation that one doesn't fully understand. I guess it's part of the security – even among the people who work for it.'

Shapiro laughed. 'We sometimes get so obsessed with security that we don't know half of what's going on ourselves.' He paused. 'But that doesn't apply in your case. We had something specific in mind for you when you were recruited.' He paused and then went on. 'A few of us in SIS realised a couple of years back that we, and the Americans too, had very little first-hand information about what was going on in the Soviet Union and its satellites – particularly East Germany. We decided we ought to do something about it. We get reports on grain harvests, scientific advances, budgets . . .' he waved his hand '. . . most of it is inaccurate and almost all of it is useless. It doesn't give us even the faintest idea of what those people are thinking and what ordinary people are thinking too.' He paused. 'You are going to be our first tentative step to putting this right. So let me explain what we were looking for – somebody who got on well with all kinds of people, who spoke fluent Russian and some German, who could, under the guise of being a foreign correspondent, meet and talk to all sorts of people on the other side of the fence.'

He paused. 'That wouldn't be too difficult to find but we needed something more. It had to be somebody who understood the other side and rather liked them. Not committed to our views and actions nor theirs. A genuine reporter but one who is exceptionally well informed. That will be you. How do you feel about it?'

'It would take a long time to establish those relationships and it would have to be a two-way traffic. I'd have to say what I thought about our side.'

'No problem. You could say whatever you thought.'

'One of the lectures I attended, the lecturer said that when you were being briefed for an operation you should look to see what the sub-text says.'

'Sub-text. Another bit of jargon. What's it mean?'

'It means that sometimes the briefing you get is a cover for something else that the operation will involve you in.'

Shapiro leaned back in his chair, barely concealing his annoyance.

'I wouldn't recognise a sub-text if I saw one. Those bloody lecturers have never been on an operation themselves.' He shook his head dismissively. 'Forget it. How about we meet again tomorrow, same time, here?' He looked at Inman, eyebrows raised in query.

'Right, sir.'

As Inman made his way to his flat he had been in the world of intelligence long enough to wonder what his 'sub-text' actually was. The operation itself seemed strangely diffuse. Maybe he'd learn more at the next day's meeting. He was rather impressed by Shapiro with his magnificent head from a Roman coin and his reputation inside SIS as knowing more about what was going on in Moscow than the Kremlin did. Max Inman didn't go in for hero-worship but he knew the significance of the self-confidence and self-assurance that was Shapiro's trade mark. It meant you'd been around SIS for a long time and that you'd been right more often than you'd been wrong. Shapiro, he felt, was a man to be admired but not necessarily trusted.

After the meeting the following day, Max Inman was even more impressed by Shapiro. The preparation of the operation was so thorough that he realised that it was more important than he had imagined.

There would be a small gathering to bid him an apparent farewell from his year's secondment to SIS from *The Economist*. A rather vague letter of accreditation from the magazine appointing him as its economics stringer in Germany. No mention of pay or his expenses which were in fact to be covered in full by SIS direct to an account in his name at a merchant bank. He was virtually to be what he purported to be, a freelance correspondent in Germany, with a connection to a well-known magazine. He remembered that when SIS had got rid of Philby he had been given a job as the Middle-East stringer for the same magazine. Not a good omen. Not too elaborate arrangements had been made for communication with SIS which would be direct to Joe Shapiro and Cooper. The only thing he intended to ignore was Shapiro's insistence that he should tell nobody, repeat nobody, about his connection to SIS. They both knew what was meant by 'nobody repeat nobody' but Max Inman had every intention of telling Katya Felinska more or less the whole story.

They had eaten that night at a small Italian place in Frith Street. It wasn't a celebration but it was going to influence their relationship for the rest of their lives. Neither of them realised the significance of the question she casually raised.

'Where will you be living?'

'I'll have a pad in West Berlin but I'll be back here for a few days most weeks. I'll fix myself up with a place over here before I go.' He smiled. 'Somewhere near to your place.'

There was another question embedded in that first question.

Max Inman knew that. And Katya's response was going to be more important than she probably realised.

'There's a two-bedroom flat a couple of blocks from my place that's got a sign on it.'

They saw the estate agent the following day and Max Inman signed a twelve-month lease. He had wondered what he should say if she offered to share her place. Shapiro would not have been best pleased. But as Katya had said — they could choose where they wanted to spend their time. And Katya didn't offer to share her place for she already understood some of the rules of the game that Max was involved in.

Chapter Eight

———◆———

'I think you and your parents lived in New York for some time – is that why you've chosen Ella Fitzgerald singing "Manhattan" as your next record?'

She laughed. 'No. Not really. I love it but when we were in New York we lived in Brighton Beach where my father was making a film about Russian refugees and I'd bought myself a Walkman and my father gave me an Ella tape because she was his favourite. As I only had that one tape I played it every day on the train back to Manhattan and school and it kind of reminds me of my father and him taking us in the evening to Coney.' She laughed. 'I can smell the sea right now.'

'Wasn't it a piece you did on the people of Brighton Beach that gave you your first big break?'

'Yes. In a way it was. It certainly taught me a lesson.'

'What was the lesson?'

'As you know Brighton Beach is the subway station before Coney, and Brighton Beach is often referred to as Little Odessa because there are so many Russian refugees there, and Poles of course. They have their own daily paper and the whole place rocks with religion and politics. There had been several articles about it before but they had all been about refugee politics. My piece was about the families. What differences they found . . .' she laughed '. . . not all that many. And what they missed from their old countries.

'The New York Times used it in a four-page spread and two months later the whole piece including text and photographs was used in a Soviet magazine. And I got a letter from the Soviet Ambassador in Washington praising the piece because it wasn't anti-Russian.' She laughed. 'The Times paid me two hundred dollars but I didn't get paid by the Russian magazine.'

'You said it taught you something – what?'

'Ah yes. It taught me that you don't have to have an "angle". You can just write it as you, personally, see it. It's what *you* see that matters, not what some editor or newspaper tycoon would like to pretend it is.' She paused. 'What I do is what women do, and talk about, over the back-yard fence. They aren't talking about who gets to the moon first but how to get rid of lice in your kids' hair.'

Lawley smiled. 'A great start. So let's move on and hear Ella and "Manhattan".'

Chapter Nine

Max Inman was not surprised when the Stasis picked him up at the coffee shop in Alexanderplatz. It was standard thinking for them to see all journalists and foreign students at the university as 'spies'. For an organisation that treated all its own citizens as possible 'spies' any foreigner was a reasonable suspect.

They took him to one of their houses near the gasworks, an old-fashioned house that had been rebuilt exactly as it was before it was bombed.

There was no rough stuff and when they showed him into one of the rooms they offered him a coffee and apologised because there was no sugar.

They checked his passport and press-pass and read the letter from *The Economist* before they got down to a fairly amiable inter-rogation. They mentioned three pieces of his concerning the Democratic Republic and commented on his even-handed approach to the shortcomings of the regime.

It was the big blond man who got them started.

'How do you feel about the party now you've seen it in action, Herr Inman?'

'You mean the Communist Party?'

'Of course.'

Inman smiled. 'A great idea. Maybe somebody'll try it out one day.'

'I don't understand. The GDR is a communist state.'

'Calling a state communist doesn't make it communist.' He smiled. 'I guess it all depends on what your views on communism are.'

'And your views?'

'Communism was a great idea. So is Christianity. But unfortunately no state has ever put either philosophy into action.' He paused. 'Less than ten per cent of the GDR's citizens voted for communism. And most of them don't even know what communism is.'

'So why did you write that article praising the GDR's crèches for workers' children?'

'Because it's an excellent idea. I hope other countries will copy it. It wasn't initiated by communism but by women who have jobs and young children.'

'According to our records you were a member of the Party when you were at university. Were you spying on members for the secret service?'

Inman laughed. 'You mean that I could only have joined for some such reasons not because I was impressed by Marxism?'

'So why did you give up your membership?'

'Like Marx himself said, about realising as he grew old that he no longer agreed with Marxism.'

The Stasi man looked shocked. 'I can't believe Marx said that.'

The young Stasi man said softly. 'He's right. Marx did say that.' He looked at Inman. 'I suspect that you've read Karl Popper. Am I right?'

Inman smiled. 'Yes. I agree with most of what he wrote and said.' He paused, still smiling. 'And he'd be interested in your government having the word democratic as your state's official designation.'

The young man smiled. 'We must argue that some time.' He paused. 'An ideal subject for a post-graduate debate.' He paused again. 'By the way, my name's Bekker, Otto Bekker, and my colleague is Helmut Weiss. I look after political problems and Helmut is counter-intelligence.'

'Which category was I in?'

Bekker laughed. 'A bit of everything. We thought we'd better have a closer look at you. You seem to cover this side of the Wall quite a lot and some of the people you spend your time with are not our best-loved citizens.'

'Anything more you want to ask me?'

'Just one question.' Bekker said softly.

'So ask it.'

'Who are you spying for?'

'I write about economics, trade, and politics. Is that what you call spying?'

'Maybe. But what do you call spying?'

'Information on weapons, the armed forces, military units, communications, et cetera. I know nothing about those subjects so I would be a pretty useless spy.'

Bekker stood up slowly. 'OK, my friend. Enough for now. But take the hint. Take the warning.' He paused. 'D'you want a lift?'

'I'll get a taxi.'

Bekker smiled. 'You must be kidding.' He paused. 'I'll drop you back at Charlie, OK?'

Inman shrugged and nodded. 'Fine, thank you.'

Bekker's car was an elderly black Citroen and as the Stasi man headed for the checkpoint, Inman said, 'How long have you been in the Stasis?'

'Six years. I was in the police for two years. And you? How long have you been a journalist?'

'Straight from university.'

'Where do you cover?'

'Technically anywhere but I stick to Germany because I speak a little German.'

Bekker laughed softly. 'The modest Brit. You speak excellent German. But why the close interest in the GDR?'

'There are dozens of writers covering West Germany and it's not easy to get editors to print anything about the GDR that's even-handed. The GDR is kind of dead territory. Even the citizens don't seem like real Germans. I guess that's what interests me. And what gets my stuff accepted.'

'What did you take at university?'

'Russian and German.'

'Why Russian?'

'The music, the literature and wonderful people.'

'Have you ever been to Russia?'

'Two trips from school and university. I had three months in Moscow on a student exchange.'

'You speak very openly about liking your country's enemies.'

'What enemies?'

'Russian communists.'

Inman laughed. 'They're like your GDR commies. They couldn't tell you what communism is. It's just what you have to join to get a good job.'

'Ah, a cynic.'

'No. Just a realist.'

'What's the difference?'

'When you've got a spare hour I'll tell you.'

As Bekker pulled up the car alongside the guard room on the GDR side of Checkpoint Charlie, Bekker said, 'I'll see you through the checkpoint.'

As the guard checked his currency and documents Bekker scribbled on a scrap of paper and handed it to Inman. 'My office and home numbers. Contact me if you have any difficulties.' He shook hands. 'I've enjoyed talking to you.'

'Thanks. I will.'

The Military Police redcap glanced briefly at his passport and waved him through.

As he walked towards the Tiergarten Inman realised that the sun was shining. It must have been shining the other side of the Wall but somehow you never noticed it over there.

He had been stopped and checked several times before by police or Stasis but today's episode was different. They had obviously been checking on him. He must have one of those brown files with his name on. His name probably spelt incorrectly. Stasi records went for quantity rather than accuracy.

The man named Weiss was typical middle-rank Stasi. In his late thirties and ready to be aggressive. But Bekker was something else. Obviously senior to Weiss and much better educated. More like senior KGB than Stasi. Cool and self-confident and obviously enjoying the conversation. No hint of violence, no warning, no threats. But on occasion the smile had melted away a little too quickly.

Back at his flat he settled down at his typewriter and did a page of notes on the encounter. There was a message on the answering machine. *Der Spiegel* would like him to call them to take part in a TV discussion on life in the GDR. He called the number but the producer had gone home.

When he answered the phone the caller said, 'You should go to Café Vaterland tonight. You'll see how it's going to be.' And the caller hung up. He'd recognised the voice. Its owner was the driving force in a neo-Nazi group calling itself the Viking Youth. Extreme right-wing thugs who were beginning to take over some of the poorer areas of West Berlin. The caller used the name Franz Leiche. Inman had seen him and spoken to him briefly several times at political seminars at the university. Leiche saw himself as the philosopher of the new thinking, in fact, there was nothing new about its thinking, it was crudely Nazi. Anti-semitic and anti-foreigners. It cashed in on the public resentment of the foreign immigrants who had quickly taken over most of crime in the city, abusing the system of generous support for refugees claiming political asylum.

Inman had gone to Café Vaterland with Pete Heron, a stringer for Reuters.

The place had been full of podgy youths in black leather jackets and jack-boots. Well covered with tattoos and standing around stolidly eating bread and greasy Frankfurters.

There were several other journalists there but nothing worth reporting. The violence lay under the surface but was limited to shouted obscenities at two particular journalists.

The man who was the centre of attention was a Frenchman named Henri Duras who was introduced as the leader of an extreme right-wing organisation based in Paris but with groups in several other countries. He advocated violence against the left including assassination of leading public figures. He suggested that they would see soon from the media that he and his followers were not bluffing.

Heron and Inman left about 10 p.m. and went for a coffee and a game of chess at the café near the Europa Centre. He heard on the midnight news that a journalist had been attacked on the street outside Café Vaterland. The police were investigating the assault which had necessitated hospital treatment for the victim.

The *Spiegel* TV programme had meant flying to Frankfurt and staying overnight. The subject was considered to be highly undesirable for the panel were to discuss the differences between the two Germanys. But the panel had been chosen carefully. One committed propagandist from each side and five so-called independents. They had two minutes each to say their pieces and after that it was to be questions from the studio audience. Inevitably, as a Brit, Inman was seen as being unbiased and most of the audience's questions were directed to him. The first question from a man on the front row of the audience.

'Would Herr Inman tell us what, from his experience, are the pluses and minuses of the two Germanys. Preferably not in the jargon of economics or political slogans.'

Inman smiled. 'I'll do my best but it's a bit like asking Einstein to explain his Theory of Relativity without using arithmetic or algebra.' He shrugged. 'Remember that I'm using only my own impressions and I could be wrong. It's easy to be wrong on this subject.

'But here goes. In East Germany you have a roof over your head – a place to live. You may not like it much but it's more than some people have in West Germany. And you have a job. You use out-of-date machinery and equipment but quite frankly you don't work very hard. And the rewards are very poor. And the state controls your life and decides what you can think and do. You get by.

'In West Germany the rewards are there in the shop windows. All you need is money and you can get money by working hard. You live in a kind of miniature United States. You can criticise in public the Chancellor, the President, the police, the BND and the train service. And if you haven't got what it takes – too bad.

'It's like choosing what kind of mother you want. One watching everything you do but not expecting too much from you, and the other encouraging you to go out and win in a race where the rules are lax but the rewards are great.'

He smiled. 'It's the old, old story. Is freedom of speech and life-style worth the risk of failure?'

There was a moment of stunned silence and then, slowly, people applauded.

His fellow members on the panel continued answering questions but they had axes to grind and party lines to defend. The questions were all too obviously 'planted' and the answers were dusty.

Chapter Ten

Inman was surprised when, a week after his encounter with the Stasis, he found a message on his answering machine asking him to telephone Otto Bekker. He gave a telephone number that was neither of the numbers he'd given to Inman at the checkpoint.

When he called the number it was a woman who answered. When he asked for Otto Bekker she seemed to hesitate and then said she'd see if he was around. Bekker came on the line a few moments later.

'Bekker.'

'Herr Bekker. Inman. You left a message for me to phone you.'

'Thanks for calling back. I wondered if we could meet.'

'Tell me more.'

Bekker laughed. 'It's not a continuation of our meeting a few weeks ago. More a personal chat. I think we could help one another.'

'So we could meet this side of the Wall. Yes?'

'Sure. No problem. When could you make it?'

'When would suit you?'

'How about tomorrow about four at the Savoy?'

'Why the Savoy?'

Inman could sense the smile in Bekker's voice as he said, 'I know you use it regularly and it's near to your place.'

'OK. That suits me. See you tomorrow.'

'I'll be there.'

Inman found Bekker sitting in the bar at the Savoy, casually dressed and perched on a bar-stool drinking a whisky.

They shook hands and Bekker said, 'I've booked in for the night. Let's go up to my room.'

Bekker paid for his drink and they headed for the lifts. As they went up Inman said, 'Do you come over this side often?'

'About once a month.' He smiled. 'Makes a change from my usual routine.'

Bekker's room was, in fact, a quite luxurious suite and Bekker opened up the drinks cabinet.

'What d'you fancy. There's everything here.'

'Just an orange juice will do me fine.'

Bekker smiled and raised his eyebrows but made no comment.

There were comfortable armchairs set around a low, circular coffee table.

'I suppose you're wondering why I wanted to see you.'

Inman smiled. 'I guessed it wasn't my charm at our last meeting.'

'It's odd you should say that. That is exactly why I wanted to talk to you.'

'Tell me more.'

'Is it OK with you if we make our chat strictly off the record?'

'That's OK by me. Anyway I don't write personal interview stuff.'

'I've never met anyone from your side of the fence who had an impartial view about East Germany and the Soviet Union. I'd better explain a few things. Is that OK with you?'

'Sure. Go ahead.'

'First of all I'm not Stasi. I'm KGB. And I'm not German, I'm Russian-Polish. And Bekker is my working name. I was the reason why you were picked up by Weiss who *is* a Stasi man.' He smiled. 'By the way your Stasi file is only two pages. Mostly details of people you meet on the other side. Just routine rubbish.'

'Why did you want me picked up?'

'I've read quite a bit of your stuff and was impressed and I got my colleagues in London to check on you.' He smiled. 'I love that girl-friend of yours. She's so beautiful but so tough. And like you, she says what she thinks.' He smiled again. 'There's a lot of Polish blood rushing around those veins. How does she get away with it?'

Inman laughed. 'If I looked like she does even I could get away with it.'

'You both seem to have the same attitude to things. Is that what attracted you both in the first place?'

'I don't know. We were at university together. We just sort of grew up together.' He smiled. 'We argued a lot. We still do. It broadens one's perspective to hear the views of somebody who's intelligent and bright but thinks differently from you.'

'Why haven't you married?'

Inman shrugged. 'We never felt that legalising our lives would be of any benefit. We've talked about it but we don't need the state's blessing.' He paused. 'Tell me about you and why you pretend to be a German.'

'Let me tell you a bit of the background. There are a lot of internal problems in the GDR. The politicians are blaming Gorbachev and *glasnost* for the rising discontent of the East German public. There is a lot of tension between Moscow and Berlin at the moment. And there always has been tension between the KGB here in Berlin and the Stasis. Right now even the KGB in Moscow are unsympathetic to the problems of the GDR.' He paused and sighed. 'It's my job to give Moscow a true picture of what's going on in both Germanys. Warts and all. I don't have to be diplomatic, like you, I can say it as I find it. Good and bad.'

'Do the Stasis know that you're KGB?'

'No. Neither do they know that I'm Russian. Or what my role is in Berlin. My official posting is as liaison between the Stasis and the KGB in Berlin. The KGB in Normannenallee don't know that I'm KGB either.'

'Isn't it dangerous to tell me all this?'

'Yes of course it is.'

'So why tell me?'

'Two reasons. First of all I want to ask you to cooperate with me and secondly I'm backing my judgment about you. You don't write for tabloids and only a tabloid would pay big money for my story. It doesn't affect your country and most tabloid readers wouldn't know what a Stasi was.'

'Tell me about the cooperation you have in mind.'

Bekker looked rather quizzically at Inman as if weighing up the wisdom of what he was about to do, then shrugged as if the consequences of what he was about to say were somebody else's responsibility.

'Let me go back to square one . . .' he hesitated and frowned. 'No. I'm wrong. Let me answer your question about cooperation.' He sighed. 'I need to indulge in a little lecture.' He was silent for a moment as if he was collecting his thoughts and then he said, 'My esteemed leader, Gorbachev, has taken the cork out of the bottle. He didn't intend to and still doesn't realise what he's done. When he started promoting *glasnost* and *perestroika* he was just showing goodwill and good intentions. It was just dreaming out loud. But in my opinion the dream is on its way to becoming a nightmare.

'In the GDR we have all the constituents for real trouble. When Gorbachev came to East Berlin and said his piece about *glasnost* he was telling the East Germans to open Pandora's box and see the goodies inside. They loved him and they loved what he said . . . freedom can be a dangerous word. For ordinary East Germans he made them look at what they'd got. Poor wages, harassment by politicians, the police, and the Stasis, and living in a neutral prison.

'It wasn't news to them. They knew it already. And they didn't like it. For them Gorbachev was inviting them to change it. All of it.' He paused. 'There has never been such a feeling of resentment against authority and anger at the conditions they live under. As yet they don't know how to change it but it's going to happen. And when it happens it could lead to chaos. Because what happens in the GDR is going to happen in the Soviet Union.' He paused and looked at Inman. 'And if your people do the wrong thing we'll have World War Three on our hands. There's a barrel of dynamite just waiting for somebody to apply the flame or the water. There are people in Moscow, Berlin, Washington and London lined up, all ready to go if somebody makes a wrong move. I'm trying to warn Moscow that they are being badly advised on how to deal with the unrest. What happens in East Berlin and East Germany will be the test-bed for what happens in Moscow.

'I've got a track-record for giving a true picture of the facts on the ground. There are people listening to me but I need help from your side. I need an unbiased, reasoned source of opinion on what's going on in London and Washington. What their reactions will be in response to what is happening now and in the next year.' He paused. 'So I offer a trade. I'll paint Moscow's picture for you if you'll do the same for London.' He paused again. 'And now let me go back to what I was about to say before all this – I've been in the intelligence business for a long, long time and I'm not fooled by the freelance journalist cover. You're SIS and doing much the same as I do – trying to give your people an unbiased view of the situation in the GDR. Whether they say so or not your people will be depending on you for almost the only straight information they get on the situation in the GDR. A few people on your side will have recognised that what happens in the GDR will be just a trial run for what's going to happen in the Soviet Union.' He paused. 'So – what do you say?'

'Let me ask you a few questions – OK?'

'OK.'

'Does *anybody* in the Stasis know that you're KGB and Russian?'

'No. On both counts.'

'What would happen if they found out?'

'At the moment the situation's very tense. The Stasis and the GDR politicians are blaming Gorbachev and the Kremlin in general for the public unrest. They're treating the KGB like enemies and the KGB don't like it.' He paused. 'So. To answer your question, I'd guess that I'd have a very rough time if they found out.'

'But you risk telling me – a man you barely know. Is my co-operation worth the risk?'

Bekker shrugged. 'First of all I've spent a lot of time and effort checking you out so I reckon I know you quite well, and secondly, if I can advise Moscow so that they don't make wrong moves against the West and you can keep your people informed about what is really happening and how Moscow are reacting to various situations, we might make a real contribution.' He paused and sighed. 'Let's not kid ourselves, there are people both in Moscow and Washington who are only waiting for their chance to fight another war. Afghanistan was their trial run.'

'You've obviously thought about all this a long time but for me it's something beyond imagination. We may both be wasting our time or even making things worse. But I see no harm in us seeing if it might work. But we need to establish right from the start that our objective is peace for both sides, not a victory for Moscow or London and Washington. It can mean having the honesty to comment unfavourably on our own people's intentions.'

'I'll talk to you, Max, as if you were a Russian. No holds barred. It would be pointless to try and hide any shortcomings or wrong intentions.'

'You must realise that I don't have access to politicians and ministers as you do. I hear gossip of course but it *is* just gossip.'

'It's attitudes you can help me with. And likely reactions.'

'Like what? Give me an example.'

'If Moscow ordered the GDR to allow free access to West Berlin for all citizens of GDR. No identity checks, no money checks, just free passage to anyone. What would London's attitude be?'

'They'd be delighted.'

'And if the government of the GDR refused the Soviet order? What then?'

'It would depend on what Bonn wanted.'

'And if people started demonstrating and forcing their way through the checkpoints what would London do if Bonn encouraged them?'

'They'd openly praise Gorbachev and Moscow's attitude.'

'What would London do if Bonn stopped the inflow of GDR citizens and sided with the GDR? What then?'

Inman smiled. 'The West Germans would bring down the Bonn government.' He smiled and shook his head. 'Whatever happened it wouldn't be that.'

'Any questions from you?'

'Yes. What's going on in the Kremlin? Who matters and where are they going?'

Bekker laughed. 'I don't think that there's anyone in the Kremlin who could answer that. Not even Gorbachev. Maybe *especially* not Gorbachev.' He paused and sighed. 'Gorbachev has lost his popularity. The people were promised big changes but the only thing that has changed is who's taking the graft. People are building power groups – criminals, police, my people the KGB, the army, the Red Airforce. And ordinary people are the losers, civil servants and all the armed forces haven't been paid for months.'

'How's it going to end?'

'We Russians are used to chaos. We seem to thrive on it. But this time I'm not so sure that we'll survive without some blood-letting. There are a lot of prizes for the winners.'

'Will the Party survive?'

Bekker closed his eyes and rested his head back on the chair. For long moments he was silent and then he opened his eyes and leaned forward to look at Inman.

'I'm just not certain but my instinct is that the Party is already finished but doesn't know it.'

'So what good does our cooperation do?'

'An insurance against sliding from chaos into a war.' He shrugged. 'For me it's Russia that matters. Not the party.' He smiled. 'Let me call Room Service and we can eat up here and talk about ourselves.'

Neither of them was a gourmet food and wine man but they shared a bottle of Pinot Noir to go with the *wiener schnitzl*.

When it got to the crème caramel Inman had learned quite a lot about the KGB man. There were questions that he desperately wanted to ask but it was too soon to be asking leading questions. But there was one question that Inman knew he had to ask.

After he had wiped his mouth with the paper napkin, he said quietly. 'Are you going to tell your people in Moscow about this meeting?'

Bekker didn't hesitate, shaking his head vigorously as he said, 'I shall tell nobody.' He smiled. 'I shall claim all the credit for the foresight that you give me.' Still smiling he said, 'I guess you don't have to keep your job by proving that you're better than the next man.'

'Not the way you have to. Depends on what section you work in.' He paused. 'To save me spending time checking you out — are you married?'

'Yes. But we've been separated for just over two years. I only have contact with her so that I can keep in touch with my young daughter.' He shifted his wine glass, holding it by the stem as if for moral support and looked across at Inman. 'She's five years old, very pretty and I love her more than I can say.' He sighed. 'I don't think she thinks much of me.' He smiled wryly. 'Her mother makes sure of that.'

'I'm sorry. Where does she live, the little girl?'

'In Moscow. In my old official apartment.' He paused. 'To change the subject. I got the embassy to send me a tape of a TV interview with your girl – she's really something that girl. How often do you see her?'

'It works out at about once every two weeks. Sometimes she comes here and sometimes I get to London.'

'Do you miss her?'

'I'm afraid I do. I have nobody I can talk with except her. She's extremely intelligent and perceptive and she's sophisticated in the proper sense of the word.'

'And an interesting family.'

'Yes.' He paused. 'Have you got parents in Moscow?'

'Yes. My father's an academic and my mother is a doctor.' He shrugged. 'Poor as church mice of course.'

'How shall we keep in touch with one another?'

Bekker reached inside his jacket and took out two folded sheets of A4 paper.

'I've worked out some possible suggestions. See what you think. I've got a pair of high-security scrambler phones that only top Moscow KGB could hack into. I've got two portable short-wave transceivers, Panasonics, that we can use with one-time-pads and numbers groups. And I've included some notes on Stasi standard surveillance procedures.'

Inman read the details on the two pages of notes and looked at Bekker. 'Can I keep this copy?'

'It's for you.'

'When I think of what we're doing I can only think that we must be crazy to imagine that we can make any difference to what's going to happen. We aren't that important or influential.'

'Maybe not but if we can stop other people who make the decisions from doing the wrong thing because they don't know the real facts, we've done what we can.'

'Some people would see us as traitors.'

'So be it. For me I'm a patriot. And if I can do something to keep us from war then I'll do it.'

'OK. Let's see how it works out.'

Bekker smiled. 'You're not convinced are you?'

'I think we're probably right to try. But I doubt if we can influence what happens. We're not important enough for people to take notice of what we tell them.'

'There may be a war whatever we do but at least we've done our best. And if we succeed it could save the lives of millions of people. The next war will be so devastating that it'll be the last one. People have had enough already. Why should they suffer again because politicians are either stupid or ill-informed?'

'You sound like my Katya.'

'So ask her what she thinks.'

'I don't even talk about my work with her. I don't want her involved.' He sighed. 'After all, I'm still not sure we're right. We'll see how it turns out.'

'There was an American judge, Max, name of Learned Hand, he said, "The spirit of liberty is the spirit which is not too sure that it is right".'

Max Inman smiled. 'I guess having a Soviet citizen quoting a United States judge to justify what could be called treason makes treason acceptable.'

Bekker laughed. 'Let's agree to meet at least once a week. On Sundays. Even the Stasis don't really function on Sundays.'

'Where shall we meet?'

'It would be safer to meet at your place. Have you got windows that can be seen from the street? And curtains?'

'Yes. On both counts.'

'OK. If for some reason it's not safe you leave the curtains drawn. Midday all right?'

'Fine.'

As they went on talking Inman realised that Bekker already knew where he lived and some of his habits. He wondered what else Bekker knew about him.

Max Inman had already met Katya's mother, Gina, several times before he met her father. Twice he had stayed at their flat for the night and nobody had appeared to find it unacceptable that they shared a bed.

Her mother was a plump, handsome woman who seemed used to the people who congregated in the flat when her husband was around. It was non-stop talk of scripts, lighting men, actors and actresses and a love-hate for Hollywood and its moguls who could pronounce some project dead or alive on the negotiations of an extra half of one per cent in a budget. He thoroughly enjoyed the company but realised that he wasn't one of them. But they took to him because he was a generous listener to sagas of people he had never heard of. He was always aware that her mother kept a friendly eye on him to make sure that he was not neglected.

Katya's father talked to him when it was just the family there as if he were part of it. Talking about scripts and treatments and listening carefully as he answered her father's questions on what was a good theme. He remembered that Katya had mentioned some vague Jewish connections on her father's side and their family's love and affection for one another was typical of what he imagined Jewish family life was like.

After one of his early visits when her father was in London, she'd asked him, when they were back at her place, what he thought of her family. He'd thought for a moment and then said it was like lying in a warm bath reading Palgrave's *Golden Treasury* and listening to Barber's 'Adagio for strings'. She had flung her arms round him, kissed him ardently and then drawn back to look at his face.

'I love you so much, little Max. I feel so safe with you. You don't chatter like we do but you're very perceptive. You're a wonderful observer.' She laughed. 'Can I ring them and tell them what you said? They'll be so pleased.'

When she came back from the hall and phoning her mother she was smiling and obviously happy.

'She says to give you her love.'

Chapter Eleven

They had spent the weekend with Max's parents. They lived in a large, pleasant house in Sanderstead. His mother had stifled her doubts when Max had taken her aside and said that they only needed one room. Katya noticed when they went to bed that first night that his mother had put a bunch of roses from the garden in a crystal vase on the dressing-table as a kind of sign of approval.

She had expected Toby, Max's father, a stockbroker, to be a little pompous or at least rather formal. But he was, in fact, a charmer and knowledgeable about every musical comedy that had ever been written. The only exception was anything by Gilbert and Sullivan. He reckoned that all the Lloyd-Webber music was as good as Puccini. But his favourites were the Viennese musical comedies like *Die Czardas Fürstin*. He could sing along in American-accented German with Katya through all the problems of the handsome Viennese charmers who fell in love so easily with every pretty girl they met. Katya guessed that Toby Inman must have been quite a charmer himself before Mary landed him. And it was quite obvious what the appeal of Mary had been. She was still delightful, with big dark eyes and a smile like sunshine. But when, after dinner, Toby had sat down at the piano and they had sung duets from *The Gypsy Princess* that luscious voice still had the glorious appeal that had undoubtedly entrapped the young Toby Inman more than thirty years ago.

She upbraided Max for his original description of his mother as just a housewife. When he had said that their parents should get together, Katya had said, 'Not on your life, *lieber* Max. My father would run off with your mother. If she'd have him. And my Mama would fall for dear Toby at first sight.'

She had seen him off at Gatwick and as he went through the check-gate he turned and waved to her. And for the first time in her life she felt lonely. As she drove back to London she wondered if she should stay with her parents that night. By the time she got to the Hammersmith flyover she decided against it. But she did decide to stay at Max's place instead of her own, just for that one night, despite the fact that it was smaller and less appealing than hers.

She tidied the living room, the bedroom and the kitchen and made herself an omelette. She ate it watching TV. It was Saturday night. Always a night for trash on TV. She'd tried to persuade him to stay over until Sunday but he said he had a meeting that he had to keep.

It was two years now that he'd been in Berlin and there was no sign that it would change. Maybe she should check around and see what chance there was to be based in Berlin herself instead of London.

She had talked with her mother about it but she was aware that because she couldn't talk about what Max was really doing, the advice was based on a false picture of the facts. Max had told her that he was, in fact, in SIS and that although his journalism was genuine it was being used as a cover for intelligence work. She also knew that he had only told her enough to explain the odd, disjointed life that he lived. She was not anxious to know more. That part of his life was too near politics and politicians for her taste. But — *à chacun son goût*. He tolerated amiably her own disjointed life of sudden departures into apparent limbos.

As Max Inman checked his watch and saw that there was nearly an hour before Bekker was due to arrive he moved to his desk to go through the pile of mail that had come over from London.

His Barclays account, for once, showed a vastly improved position in his finances. His other account, with a small merchant bank, never notified him of its status. But it was an account that he never used for withdrawals, it was his equivalent of money under an old lady's mattress.

Notifications of brokers ready to lend him money without collateral went straight in the bin. Offers of double-glazing and loft conversions went the same way. There were two personal letters from men he had met at embassies and a couple of receipts for small service calls at his London flat.

There was also a cutting from a newspaper pasted onto a piece of light card with several lines of text highlighted. Cooper had sent it. It was from a four-day-old copy of *The Times*. It reported that a Frenchman named Henri Duras had been arrested in a joint Anglo-French police operation against a group of terrorists who had published a list of names on an Internet web-site of prominent people who were to be assassinated. Henri Duras who, when he was arrested, was working as a chef in a restaurant in a small town in Essex, was alleged to be the leader and organiser of an extreme political group. Five other members had been arrested in France and were due to stand trial in Toulon.

Inman was pleasantly surprised to see that at least a minor piece of information he had passed to London had been acted on. His stuff normally disappeared so far as he was concerned into some security black-hole.

He turned to check that the curtains were both open and he wondered what Bekker would come up with this time. He was a strange man, typical Russian from long ago. Unusually well-educated and well aware of what the real world was all about. A strange, exciting mixture of Solzhenitsyn and Nabokov. Lolita and Ivan Denisovich. There would be a flaw somewhere in such a character and he wondered what it was.

The buzzer rang and he walked down the stairs to open the door. Bekker was smiling, amused at Inman's surprise at the formal suit that he was wearing and the walking-stick with a silver handle.

'Hi. I guess I'm early.'

Inman smiled. 'The timing's perfect but you look as if you've just come from a rehearsal of *Cabaret*.'

Bekker laughed. 'I should be so lucky.'

The Russian had accompanied Inman into the kitchen while he was making the coffee. He made himself comfortable and seemed perfectly at ease at the plastic-topped kitchen table.

'You got any news, Otto?'

'Not news. But I've got something I want to talk about.' He paused. 'Have you mentioned our meeting to your controller?'

'No.' Inman shook his head. 'We said we wouldn't do that.' He paused. 'Have you changed your mind?'

'Yes. We did. I just wondered if you'd had second thoughts.'

'Not without telling you. Have you had second thoughts?'

'I've had an idea.'

'Tell me.'

'Before I expand let me ask you another question.' He paused. 'You've just had a week in London. Did you work out how to convince somebody to take notice of what you give them?'

'No. Quite the opposite. I couldn't see how I could make my controller take more notice of what I had to say.' He shrugged. 'Why should he?'

'I came to much the same conclusion and I've worked out what seems a possible solution. D'you want to hear it?'

'Of course.'

'To impress my chap I'd have to provide a piece of information about something quite important at the time it happened but where they never knew what really happened. It had to be authentic and provable and it had to be surprising. When you tell your controller you say it's from an inside source but you don't name me or identify me. I'm just a new source from right inside Moscow.'

'Give me some idea of the kind of information you could give me as a starter.' He paused. 'Have you had time to think about it?'

'How about the real inside story of Khrushchev and the Cuban missiles? Why did he put them there? What did he intend doing with them? What was Khrushchev's real motive? Even today people don't know the real reason he got into the Cuba thing.'

'How could it be authenticated?'

'Remember our ambassador in Washington, Dobrynin. It was he who finally worked out the deal with Robert Kennedy. It would be extracts from an original report on what really went on and why. What do you think was the prize K wanted?'

'He wanted the Americans to remove their nuclear weapons from Turkey.'

Bekker smiled. 'Wrong. But that's what your people in London think and so do their opposite numbers in the Kremlin.' He paused. 'It was something far removed from Cuba. Cuba was just a move that went terribly wrong.'

Inman said quietly. 'Yeah. I could sell that material. How long for you to provide it?'

'I've already assembled it.' He smiled. 'I'll hand it over to you when you can put together an equivalent for me.' He paused. 'How long do you need?'

'I've got something in mind but I'd need at least a week in London to put it together. I'd also need a reason to be going back so soon.'

'Tell them that there are even more signs that the GDR is disintegrating. Have they any plans to react when it happens?'

'Are there more such signs?'

'The Stasis arrested a KGB major last week on Honneker's instructions. The whole country is just falling apart. Thousands of citizens heading over the borders to Hungary and Austria pretending that they're just going for a holiday.' He shook his head. 'They won't be coming back. Your diplomats in Vienna and Budapest can confirm this movement. The Stasis want to take action against these people. KGB Moscow have overruled them. Partly because they feel that thousands of refugees flooding into the West are going to create a lot of problems for West Germany and London and Washington. What are they going to do about it? I can give you highly confidential figures on East Germans heading for freedom.'

'When can I have them?'

'Tomorrow. I could give them to you at Charlie. Early as you like.'

'Let's make it ten-thirty.' He nodded. 'That's a good excuse to go back for a few days.'

'And you'll be back in a week?'

'I should think so.'

And that's how it had been left. Inman had caught the afternoon flight to Gatwick from Tegel.

He spent the evening with Katya who was giving a talk at Imperial College. The audience was mainly undergraduates and graduates but there was a sprinkling of journalists and a camera team from BBC 2.

There was a lot of applause as she walked onto the platform. But as she moved to the speaker's lectern and arranged her notes he thought she looked rather lonely. When the applause died down she looked up and smiled, acknowledging the welcome.

Her talk was, as always, of the evils of war and its terrible aftermath. The lights had been dimmed so that her pictures could be projected onto a white screen behind her to her left. They were pictures from her time in Ethiopia and Somalia, Cuba and South America. She had talked for about half an hour on the practical difficulties of photography in war areas. The permits, the 'minders', travel itself, food and accommodation. A press-photographer's identity badge was useless and so was a passport.

Then Katya looked across at her audience for long moments without speaking before she said, 'I want to take you all with me on a journey.'

She held up a battered camera.

'This, my friends, was once my pride and joy. It's a Leica camera, a IIIb.' She paused. 'Value before it was smashed about five hundred pounds.' She paused. 'There are people who say that war is glamorised by photographers and I think that there is some truth in that. Let me show you pictures that possibly do glamorise war.' She clicked the control to bring up the next picture.

'This is a photograph taken by Yevgeny Khalday of Russian soldiers raising the Russian flag on the roof of the Reichstag. We are looking down from the roof at the bombed buildings in the street below and in the distance the smoke from burning buildings. We can all understand the feelings of these Russian soldiers who have taken Berlin and virtually brought the war to an end.'

She clicked the control again.

'Here we have a similar picture. Four war-worn US Marines hoisting the Stars and Stripes to celebrate the recapture of Iwo Jima from the Japanese. A kind of memorial to thousands of dead men. Americans and Japanese.' She clicked the control again. 'And here we have that wonderful picture by Alfred Eisenstaedt, recognised all over the world, of the sailor of Fifth Avenue kissing the girl on VJ Day.' She smiled. 'Who wouldn't be a sailor or a soldier on VJ Day.' Then she said quietly, 'We hadn't been shown the aerial photographs of Hiroshima by then.

'There's a thing that always worries me about how the media report the terrible tragedies of war. The tens of thousands slaughtered like cattle in Africa. Slaughtered by fellow Africans. It creates a feeling in people's minds that those people are used to being slaughtered. It's part of the African life-style. A pity, but what can we do about it? The slaughter of young children in Colombia. Murdered by the police. Just for being alive. There's too many of them. It's very difficult to bring home to ordinary people what it's really like to be a victim.'

Katya paused and held up the battered Leica camera. 'Exhibit number one.' She clicked on the next picture. A head-shot of a quite handsome man in his thirties. Dark penetrating eyes and a black moustache. 'Now he's the leading man. Handsome in his own way, if you like that kind of guy. For me those eyes are a bit of a give-away. But let's move on.' She clicked again and it was a shot of a naked girl lying on her back on the muddy side of a road. 'So here we have a picture of a dead girl. Her eyes wide open looking up at the sky.' She paused. 'Look well, my friends. Look well.' She waited for several moments and then said, 'She isn't dead, my friends. She's just paralysed. She was raped by a gang of Serbian soldiers. No gallantry there, my friends. No glamour of bold deeds well done. Just one young girl who now lives in the cellars of a mental hospital in Sarajevo. The man whose face I showed you was the leader of the gang who raped the girl. There were fifteen of them. They all had their turn. How did they know she was a Croat? They knew because they had known her for years. They all came from the same cluster of villages. She had worked as a waitress in a café in the main village.' She held up the battered Leica again. 'And the smashed-up Leica. That was courtesy of the man in the photo. He smashed it out of my hands with his rifle butt. Fortunately I was able to save most of the film. Equally fortunately a Sky TV camera team arrived and I joined them temporarily.

'There are two more pictures I want to show you. Neither of

them are mine but I shall never be able to wipe them out of my mind.' She paused. 'Thank you for listening to me so patiently.' She clicked the control one last time. The two pictures came up together, side by side. The one on the left was Nick Ut's photograph of the young Vietnamese girl running naked towards the camera, her body on fire from napalm. Her mouth wide open, screaming with pain and fear. The picture on the right was Eddie Adams's photograph of the Saigon Police Chief holding his gun to the head of a Vietcong suspect seconds before killing him. After what seemed a long time the lights in the auditorium had gone up and Inman saw that Katya had already left the stage. There was a little sporadic clapping but the room was strangely silent. People were leaving quietly and there was little talking as they filed towards the main doors. It was something that Inman had seen before after one of Katya's talks. As if the audience had been stunned or cast under some sort of spell.

She was waiting for him in the lecturers' refectory and after a few rather stilted goodbyes they had left together and gone to her place for the night.

She had made them coffee and they sat together at the kitchen table. They had not talked much themselves until she said, 'I'm not doing any good with these talks, am I?'

'In what way?'

'I'm just telling people what they already know if they've got eyes to see.' She shrugged. 'But I'm not suggesting what they should do to stop it.' She frowned. 'I've become just a moaner, a whinger.' She paused. 'Those people tonight. Graduates, lecturers, people who are well-informed. I just frightened them off.'

'Dealing with it is was what the United Nations was set up for.'

She looked at him for long moments and then, shaking her head, she said, 'You must be joking. There is more lying, corruption, hypocrisy, deceit and self-serving concentrated in that building in New York than anywhere else on God's earth.' She paused. 'All of them. It's the world's most expensive pig-trough and one day it's going to collapse because nobody can afford the entrance fee to the dance any more.'

'Maybe you're in the wrong race, sweetie.'

'What's that mean?'

'Your photo-journalism is sprinting but protesters have to be marathon runners.' He smiled. 'And hurdlers as well.' He paused. 'You're a born sprinter.'

She laughed. 'Maybe you're right.' She paused. 'Why are you back in London so soon?'

'Something unexpected cropped up.'

'How much of what you do these days is journalism and how much is the other stuff?'

He smiled. 'Just recently the other stuff as you call it has begun to take over.'

'I really can't see you as a spy.'

He laughed. 'I'm not. There's no such things as spies these days.'

'So what are you?'

'I just gather up information that might be of some use to our government.'

'And stop the other lot doing it to us?'

'No. That's the responsibility of the security services, MI5.'

'I went to a sort of cocktail party at the Soviet Embassy yesterday. It was to meet the new prima ballerina at the Bolshoi and interview her about her impression of our training at the Royal Ballet compared with theirs. There was a chap who was hanging around her all the time and Dimitrov told me he was from MI5 pretending to be a journalist.'

'What was his name?'

'I've no idea. A bit of a wimp.'

'How about we go to bed?'

She smiled. 'I thought you'd never ask.'

Chapter Twelve

It had taken two days for Inman to trace what he was looking for. It was years since he had first seen it. Just two pages of hand-written notes in a file that the registry showed had not been referred to in the last five years. Despite its signatory and its contents it was filed with no special security grading in a folder identifying itself as 'Maclean D'. The security was so lax that he was tempted to take the originals but decided in the end that that would be going too far.

He had contacted Bekker the day he got back to Berlin and the Russian already had his material for Inman to examine. But they waited two days and merely kept to their Sunday meeting at Inman's place.

As they did so often when they met, they sat at the kitchen table and exchanged their packages as if they were birthday presents. Inman's was just a standard foolscap envelope but Bekker's was in a taped A4 brown jiffy bag. They agreed to meet again the next day after they had both read the information offered to them.

Chapter Thirteen

Declaration by Major Tanya Androva KGB

Cuba–Berlin crisis August–Oktober 1962

I was at this time confidential secretary to Ambassador Anatoly Dobrynin at the Soviet Embassy in Washington. He was not at any time aware that I was an officer of KGB. My orders were to keep Moscow informed of situations in Washington and to ensure that the Cuba/Berlin relationship was well served by Dobrynin although he was not aware of the connection with Berlin.

My briefing in Moscow was to the effect that an incident would be created in Cuba which would threaten the USA. This was to be used as a bargaining point for Americans and Britain and France to evacuate Berlin and hand over control of all Germany to the Soviet Union. In return the Soviet Union would withdraw the threat of the Cuba missiles. After the crisis was resolved it was the considered opinion of others that Khrushchev had seriously misjudged the situation to the detriment of the Soviet Union. Particularly criticised was the unnecessary build-up of missiles in Cuba.

In fact the following was the inventory:-

36 SS-4 medium range ballistic missiles.

24 SS-5 intermediate ballistic missiles.

Warheads for above were delivered by Soviet freighter
on Oktober 4.

All above warheads could hit Washington DC.

They had no use for defensive purposes.

Ambassador Dobrynin had secret one-to-one talks with Robert
Kennedy and reported to Moscow that President Kennedy was
being pressured to take military action. President Kennedy
was also angry that Khrushchev had lied to him that the Cuban
weapons were solely for defence.

The final Kremlin conclusion was that the whole exercise was
a failure of judgment by K. It hardened US attitudes to staying
in Berlin where the US and the others were totally outnumbered
by Soviet forces. The weapons in Cuba were too big a threat for
the US to accept. The Soviet Union was publicly humiliated by
having to back down and all we got were a few warheads dis-
mantled on US missiles in Turkey.

At no time was Ambassador Dobrynin given the full facts and
he knew nothing of the basic plans concerning the take-over of
Berlin. I write this solely because Ambassador Dobrynin has been
falsely blamed for the failure of this operation. The blame lies in
the Kremlin.

Signed: Tanya Androva (Major KGB)
24 Oktober 1970

Inman read it through twice and then put the pages back inside
the jiffy bag. He hadn't been around in the days of the Cuban
missile crisis but he knew that it had been the possible start of a
third world war. Commentators had often posed the question

as to why the Soviets and Khrushchev in particular were prepared to take such a risk for the benefit of Cuba. If they knew that it was really about Berlin it would explain a lot. Shapiro would be very interested.

Chapter Fourteen

Bekker looked briefly at the pages. Three were in scrawling hand-writing and one was single-spaced typing. The typed page seemed to be merely a typed version of the handwritten pages. At least it was legible.

A note for the record book and all those shits in SIS and the KGB who lied to the very last.

> **Moscow.**
> **Sunday night.**

My name is Donald Maclean, ex-diplomat, ex-scholar, ex-patriot. I'm pissed but I always am. And now they tell me that I've only got ten days to live.

This is to put on record the facts about Philby finally defecting to Moscow. Kim Philby never came to Moscow. The man who was supposed to be Philby was a chap named Gavin Powell. Nobody in Moscow had ever met Philby in person and SIS sent Powell to Beirut pretending that he was Philby. That's why it was that 'Philby' spent those years in Beirut before the 'defection to Moscow'.

Those bastards in London told us (me and Burgess) that if we went along with the deception when Powell arrived in

Moscow that they would do a deal to exchange us for KGB men they had arrested. We went along with it and for two years we asked them to do the deal and get us released. When I contacted them two weeks ago the bastards said they'd never heard of such a deal.

They kept the real Philby in a remote castle in the Scottish highlands, until he died. He's buried in a churchyard in Crowborough, Sussex. No headstone. They tell me he went mad long before he died.

So much for democracy. So much for 'team-spirit'. And yesterday my KGB 'minder' told me that they had always thought we were all double-agents.

I've had enough. May you all rot in hell.

Very sincerely,

Donald M (agent Homer)

File note: Graphologist and others confirm that the handwriting is definitely that of Maclean. The paper is also poor quality. Moscow manufactured material used in most govt. offices.

Chapter Fifteen

Bekker had called Inman by 10 a.m. the next day. They arranged to meet at Inman's place in two hours' time.

For once they stayed in the sitting-room and for once they didn't go straight to the coffee. They both seemed unsure of how to exchange their views on what they had been given. But finally Bekker had said, 'What you gave me is exactly what I needed. How about what I gave you?'

Inman smiled. 'Sit down for God's sake. We need to talk.' He paused. 'Your material was fine. I realised that by chance we'd both picked on something from the past.'

As Bekker made himself comfortable, Inman took the armchair facing the Russian.

'The other thing we have done is bring up something that people still argue about. In your case – why was Khrushchev prepared to enrage the Americans for no useful reason? In my piece for you it explains something that nobody has ever understood. When Philby was thrown out and went to the Lebanon he stayed there for years before he fled to Moscow. Why didn't he go straight to Moscow? I've heard people arguing about it to this day.' He paused. 'Do you think your people in Moscow will be interested?'

'I'm sure they will. They still argue about Philby being a double-agent or even a triple-agent.'

'When shall we hand the stuff over?'

'As soon as possible for me.'

'I think we'd better establish again what we're both aiming to do. My protocol is that both the West and the Soviets constantly misunderstand one another's motives and actions through an almost complete lack of information as to what's really going on on the other side of that Wall. If I can establish in my people's minds that I know what is really going on it could prevent some idiot from starting the next war because the Kremlin or the Pentagon had misinterpreted some apparently aggressive move.'

'That suits me too. Just one more question. If one of us discovers something that puts the other's country in a bad position because they've misinterpreted the facts, what do we do?'

'We don't have any choice, Otto. We tell each other how it is as we see it. No toning down, no phoney explanations, just the truth. If it's really serious we both discuss it and both decide what to do about it. No censorship.'

'And what if they ignore our stuff?'

'We keep trying.' Inman smiled. 'You know, we'd both better come down to earth. We're beginning to believe that we can influence the fate of the world. In fact we're just two guys trying to plug a few holes in the bucket.' He sighed as he stood up. 'We'd better remember that.'

'So now you'll offer me some of that lovely coffee of yours.'

When Inman brought back the coffee and set it on the low table between them, he said, 'Tell me about your family.'

'My mother's a doctor. A surgeon. Lives and works in Moscow. Earns rather less than she could as a street-cleaner. My father is an historian. At the moment he's researching a book on "The influence of women in Soviet politics".' Bekker smiled. 'It's going to be a very slim volume if he keeps to the truth.'

'And you're separated but not divorced?'

'Yes.' He shrugged. 'It didn't work. I've got a girl-friend here in Berlin. German. Beautiful but not educated.' He shrugged. 'Suits me fine.' He paused. 'And your parents?'

Inman painted a vague but pleasant picture of his mother and father and when he'd finished Bekker said, 'What on earth made you interested in Communism?'

'I'm not. It's Russians that interest me.' He paused. 'When are you going to hand over the material to your controller?'

Bekker shrugged. 'I've booked a flight to Moscow for tomorrow morning.'

'One last question, Otto. Do we agree that no matter what pressures they put on us we never reveal who our source is?'

When Bekker was silent for long moments, Inman said, 'What's the problem?'

'If you refused to tell your people and they turned nasty about it, what would they do?'

'They'd throw me out and I'd find it difficult to get any sort of job after that.'

'If my people turned nasty they'd beat the shit out of me and if I still didn't talk I'd be sent to a labour camp for life. Or death more like.'

There was a long silence before Inman said, 'OK. We'll leave it that you do your best. Even if you identify me there's little they can do.'

'Don't be too sure of that, Max. The top boys in the Lubyanka would classify you as a counter-revolutionary or some such creature and they're not used to being thwarted. There ain't no rules for the game we're playing.'

Inman looked at Bekker. 'You're running far more risks than I do.' He paused. 'Do you want to call it off?'

Bekker smiled. 'For God's sake. It was my idea in the first place. I've no intention of chickening out.'

'Let's see what happens this first time and then decide whether we go on or not.'

'That's fine by me. It'll be interesting to see how they react.'

They agreed that they would have to wait until they were both back in Berlin before they could meet again.

Chapter Sixteen

Katya was sitting on the swinging garden seat and her mother
was sitting on a cane armchair just out of the sun. As she leaned
forward for her orange juice from the low table beside her she
heard the phone ringing. As she stood up she said, 'Probably your
father wanting a lift from the airport.'

She was back a few minutes later. 'It's for you, Katyinska.
Max. Just to let you know he's back here again at your place.' As
she made herself comfortable in the chair again she said, 'How's
he liking his job these days?'

'He doesn't talk about it much.' She shrugged. 'He seems OK.
Dreaming his dreams of putting the world to rights.'

Her mother smiled. 'That makes two of you. Is that what
appeals to you about him?'

'No. And I've long ago abandoned any thoughts of putting
the world to rights. I just show what a stinking world it is.'

'So what is the appeal?'

Katya shrugged. 'I just love him, Mama. I've never done a
balance sheet.'

'Tell me something. Why no thoughts of getting married?
Your father says it's because . . .'

'Give me a single reason why either of us or both of us would be happier if we had a piece of paper saying that we were married. Just one single reason.'

Her mother looked at her fondly. 'I guess that's as good an answer as there is, my love.' She laughed softly. 'I always had visions of you when you were just a little girl of what you'd be like when you grew up. Most of it has already come true. You're beautiful and talented but you spend so much time alone. Don't you miss him? And doesn't he miss you?'

'He's always with me and I'm always with him. Remember what the poet said, "*My true love hath my heart and I have his, by just exchange one for the other given; I hold his dear and mine he cannot miss. There never was a better bargain driven*".'

'It sounds like Shakespeare, is it?'

'No. It's Sir Philip Sidney. Way back in the sixteenth century.'

'You're such a clever girl, you really are. How do you remember all these things?' She paused. 'When are you off to Somalia?'

'I've put it on hold. The Americans are being so stupid. They've no idea of how Somalis live. They were talking about building thousands of homes. They can't grasp that Somalis are nomadic. They follow the rains with their cattle and their families. The last time I was there I got one of the Khadi's young sons to recite his family tree – like in the Bible in *Chronicles* – "and Ahab begat Zadok" and so on. All of it to show that the Khadi is a direct descendant of Sheba and Abraham or whoever. The American couldn't understand it and had never heard of Sheba and Abraham.' She laughed. 'But he remembered an uncle who had a golden setter named Sheba. I love those Americans, they mean so well but they can cause real trouble when they're let loose on Africans or Arabs.' She paused. 'Come to think of it they're not too bright even with Europeans.'

'So what are you planning next?'

'Something I'd much rather do.' She paused. 'It's a book. The photo-journal story of a young girl aged about six going on seven. She's from Somalia. Both parents slaughtered. She's being adopted by a family in this country. They live in Birmingham. And my story is going to be about her first year in this country. Seen entirely through her eyes. I want to make this a story to be remembered by the whole world. A magnifying glass and a micro-scope on what we call civilisation.'

'What a wonderful idea. Have you got a publisher?'

'No. Publishing it won't be a problem. If it were I'd publish it myself.' She paused. 'You'd imagine that giving a home to a little girl like that would be welcomed by everyone. But it's not. To adopt a child the Social Services people give you a kind of exam. You wouldn't believe how difficult they make it for people who only want to give a loving home to an orphan child.' She smiled. 'That stuff will take at least two chapters. Bureaucracy and bloody-mindedness at its British worst.'

Bekker sat waiting as Serov read through the papers for the second time and he wondered if maybe he should have gone to one of the old China hands who had been operative in the days of Philby and the others.

Eventually Serov slid the papers back into the translucent plastic file-cover, pushed them to one side, looked towards the windows and then back at Bekker.

'Where did you get this stuff?'

'In Berlin.'

'I mean who was the source?'

'I undertook not to give any details. I agreed because I believe that there will be more information coming my way if I keep to the agreement.'

'Do you know where the source got it?'

Bekker hesitated and then said, 'From SIS archives.'

'Did you see the originals?'

'No. Just those photocopies.'

'What did you give for them?'

'Nothing. The source is a sympathiser.'

'Has anybody else in Berlin seen this material?'

'No.'

'When are you going back?'

'When you've finished with me.'

'Day after tomorrow then. Stay at the hotel or pick up a pager so that I can contact you.'

'What do you think of the documents?'

'I'd say that they're genuine but there are people who can analyse them who were around in those days.' He paused. 'I'm much more interested in your source. Is it male or female?'

'Male.'

'How long established?'

'Six months at a lower level. Just chat and gossip. I've included most of it in my reports to Moscow Centre.'

'You realise that you'll come under suspicion yourself?'

'Why?'

Serov smiled and shrugged. 'First of all because that's the routine and there will be people who say you're just being given disinformation that SIS want to plant on us.' He paused. 'But in my book it's worth knowing what they want to feed to us.' He stood up. 'Any signs that the Stasis in Berlin have you under surveillance?'

'No.'

'Don't kid yourself. They're good at it. Assume that you are being watched. At least randomly, but more likely full-time.' He shrugged. 'Anyway I'll be in touch later today or tomorrow. You may have to meet a couple of other people. We'll see.'

Back at his hotel Bekker phoned his father to arrange for both his parents to have dinner with him that evening. He called room-service for a coffee and cakes and settled down to watch a TV programme of behind-the-scenes at the Bolshoi. But his mind was

on Serov. He was in his forties, from Tiblis and an early recruit
to the KGB while he was still at Moscow University. He wasn't
Bekker's normal contact at KGB HQ but Serov was responsible
for overseeing special intelligence contacts in Germany, France
and Britain. There were maybe a dozen men like Serov at the top
of the KGB. Men whose politics were realistic. Men who already
knew that if they made their rivalry with the Americans into a
fighting war they would lose. They knew too that the Soviet
Union had lost the arms war already through lack of money and
resources. But they were determined to avoid actions that would
mean that Russia would be destroyed in the struggle. The US had
made the finance stakes so high that Russia was no longer in the
poker game but their opposite numbers in Washington knew that
an open, public defeat of the Soviet Union would cause as many
serious problems for the Americans as for the Russians. But Serov
and his fellows were thin on the ground and elderly generals with
their chests plastered with medals were determined not to allow
any diminution of their powers and aggressive postures. What
Bekker needed to find out from Inman was whether his people in
London were aware of the real situation, and in its way Berlin and
his deal with Inman was going to be a kind of litmus paper
indicating a will to peace or for publicly humiliating the Soviet
Union. When the Red Army had fought its way into Berlin it had
seemed like the end of the story but once again Berlin was going
to be a touchstone. It was obvious that Inman knew that things
were in turmoil in East Berlin and the GDR but he didn't know
that the whole edifice was crumbling to pieces day after day.

His dinner with his parents had been cut short by a telephone
call from Serov. He wanted to see him right away. When he
learned that Bekker's parents were with him, he suggested that
he would come to the hotel in two hours' time. He would not be
alone.

✳   ✳   ✳

Serov introduced the other man as Abramov. Yevgeny Abramov. He was older than Serov but smartly dressed and obviously sure of himself.

Serov waved his arm. 'Yevgeny, it's all yours.'

Abramov looked at Bekker. 'I looked the documents over myself and I got two old hands who are retired now but looked after Philby and his gang after they came to Moscow to look them over as well.' He paused and looked at Bekker. 'I'm rather worried, my friend. Both I and the old boys are quite sure that those documents are genuine.'

'So why does that worry you?'

'Because documents like this can only have come from the archives of SIS or maybe the CIA.' He paused. 'I'd put my kopeks on the SIS archives.'

'So.'

'Whoever you're dealing with is either very senior SIS or got the documents from someone in SIS.'

Bekker shrugged. 'I still don't see what the problem is.'

'The problem, my friend, is why you were given this material. Who gains what?'

'We gain. Our people can go back over the time when these letters were written bearing in mind that whatever Maclean was doing at that time, or the advice he was giving, must be suspect.'

'Everything those three did all the time was suspect.'

'Not by everybody. I read our summaries about them when I was training. They had privileges and treatment that they wouldn't have got if they were officially suspect.'

'So what's your source?'

'I've already told Major Serov that I can't reveal who it was.'

'You're not entitled to make such arrangements without permission from the highest level.'

Bekker shrugged. 'Then I get no more information from that source.'

'Do you expect anything more?'

'Yes. I expect a continuing relationship.'

'More of this past history stuff?'

'No. Current material.'

'Why is this guy going to give you this information?' He paused. 'Is he a Party member?'

'He was when he was young but not these days.'

'So why's he doing this?'

'He thinks that a war between us and the West is more likely if we don't understand what's really going on on the other side of the fence.'

Abramov looked at Serov. 'What do you think?'

Serov shrugged. 'Our friend here is not asking for our approval. I think we let him carry on and see what happens.'

Bekker knew that that was the nearest he'd get to even the slightest sign of approval from above and it was enough. In his worst scenario he'd envisaged being slung in a cell in the Lubyanka. What he had got was all he wanted. He didn't need their involvement or their cooperation. If what he got from Inman was real inside stuff then Serov would get the kudos and that was a kind of insurance policy.

Chapter Seventeen

Cooper had taken the precaution of showing Inman's material to Shapiro who read it carefully and then looked across at Cooper.

'Where did he get this?'

Cooper explained the situation as far as he knew it.

'What do you think of it?'

'It solves a lot of old doubts and it shows how easily a piece of minor stupidity could end up getting us to the brink of war.' He paused. 'What worries me is the fact that this material could only have come from the KGB's archives either at Moscow Centre or the archives kept by FCD, the Foreign Chief Directorate. Both of them are highly secure and the drill for even just looking at this sort of document is very elaborate. To be able to copy it means that somebody took a considerable risk of being caught or alternatively it's being planted on us as disinformation.'

Cooper shrugged. 'Disinformation on something that far back – what's the purpose?'

'I agree. I'd say it's genuine.' He paused. 'And very useful.' He paused again. 'And I gather he won't give us any clues as to his source.'

'No. But it's obviously somebody who's got access to almost anything in their archives. I get the impression that if I really pressured him this material would be the last we get.'

'Does he indicate more to come?'

'Yes. Seems very confident.'

'It's a tricky game he's getting into. Are you sure about him himself?'

'As sure as one can be in these situations. If you feel that what he's given us is important I'm planning to support him.'

'I'd go along with that. We're looking at the KGB archives.' He smiled and shrugged. 'You can't ask for more than that.'

Cooper stood up. 'Why is it that whenever something interesting happens it always worries me?'

Shapiro laughed. 'It's called experience, my friend.'

As Inman listened to Cooper's comments he knew that despite the words of caution Cooper was pleased with what he had been given. The emphasis was on not getting involved emotionally with his source. They still needed to discover why he was doing it. Inman felt that after that warning it was best not to mention that Katya was a special guest at the Soviet Embassy that evening and that he would be accompanying her.

'Do I have to wear a suit?'

'Not for His Excellency. Just for me or I'll feel overdressed in my little black dress.'

'What's HE like?'

'Quite a charmer when he wants to be. His wife's a concert-class pianist and his mistress was in the Bolshoi junior ballet. Pretty and a gorgeous backside.'

'What are they celebrating tonight?'

'The Czech ambassador's birthday.'

'What's his name?'

'Prochazka. Jan Prochazka. A hard-liner and Moscow want

to make sure that the Czechs realise which side their bread is buttered.'

'Do we take flowers or something?'

'Yes. I'm taking a copy of a book in Czech by a guy named Hrabal – it's called *A close watch on the trains*. Full of swear words but somebody, not Daddy, made a film of it that was a great success in Europe.' She smiled. 'Go down and get us a taxi.'

It had been a pleasant evening and it had been turned into a celebration of Katya's piece on the Russians who had fled to Brighton Beach and Coney Island. As so often he was aware that she seemed not to notice the effect that her beauty had on other people. Women as well as men. He too had received a lot of attention. A Brit who could speak Russian fluently and with a vocabulary that could argue from the semantics of the language itself to using the roughest cadences of Moscow cab-drivers, was a rarity to be treasured.

They took a taxi from the embassy to Soho and the small Italian restaurant that had always been their regular eating place. She had tried to persuade him to stay in London another day but he was anxious to get back to Berlin to hear what had happened to Bekker. She drove him to Gatwick mid-morning and wondered why he was so tense. In turn he wondered if she wasn't just a little too much at home in the Soviet Embassy. All the senior Russians seemed to know her so well.

Paul Rimmer noted their names and the date as he read through the standard surveillance report on the Soviet Embassy.

Chapter Eighteen

Int. Memo

From: J. Shapiro

To: F. Cooper

I wondered if it was possible that the material you showed me came from the KGB archives at their embassy.

I can now confirm that this could not have been the case. It seems that for security reasons KGB Rezidents abroad are not allowed to keep copies or originals from Moscow Centre. Incoming signals are kept for not longer than three or four weeks. Correspondence from the Centre is in the form of developed 35mm. film sent via diplomatic bag but destroyed after two or three months.

My specialist informs me that there would be no archives kept at the KGB detachment in East Berlin.

This leaves only two possible archive sources. Important key papers are duplicated and stored in a bunker in the vicinity of Omsk, Western Siberia. The other source is the Archive Department at Moscow Centre itself. It is felt that this latter facility is the most likely source of this material. This in turn indicates that whoever is the provider of this material is almost certainly a senior member of the KGB. Bearing this in mind I feel that we should encourage and support this activity.

Chapter Nineteen

They had taken a break for a cup of tea and sorted out the next two records. Then it was back to the recording.

'And what's your next record?'

'It's Judy Garland and 'Somewhere over the Rainbow'.

'Why that?'

'Oh for several reasons. It reminds me very much of my time at Cambridge. It was one of my mother's favourites and she gave me a copy to take with me to college.

'The words kind of represented the thoughts that young people had in those days. It had been around for ages and it went against the grain of those times. Despite what was going on in the world we were sure that our lives were going to be different – not rain but "rainbows, and bluebirds will sing". We weren't a cynical lot. We believed that things were going to be good.'

Sue Lawley said quietly, 'Were you all so naive?'

'No. On the contrary. It wasn't being naive. Maybe we were innocent but we believed what we believed.' Katya paused. 'University was a real milestone for many of us. It certainly was for me.'

'In what way?'

'Well, because of my rather disjointed life, I guess I was more aware of the world than most youngsters of my age. I was pretty bright and I took it for granted that I was brighter than most people I met. And then college. And surprise, surprise, everyone was brighter than average. As bright as I was, and believe it or not, there were some who were a lot brighter than me. That was a bit of a shock. A very useful shock because it made me aware that there were other kinds of brightness than mine. It was then that I realised that I was an observer. The others were analysts or philosophers.'

'What's the difference between analysts and philosophers?'

Katya laughed. 'Analysts are like waiters who ask you if you want your fish off or on the bone, and philosophers don't want facts – just ideas.' She laughed again. 'Over the rainbow types.'

'You said it had to be Judy Garland's version, why?'

'Well, it's her song but apart from that it's the voice. So young, so clear, like a bell, and that little tremor in the delivery that asks you to believe it.' She laughed. 'Like when in *Peter Pan* the audience has to say it believes in fairies.'

'Right. Let's all believe in Judy Garland and her rainbow.'

She was sorting out the books on her shelves and Max Inman was sitting on her bed watching her.

'There ought to be at least one thing wrong,' he said.

She turned to look at him. 'What are you on about?'

'I'm on about you. You're so, so beautiful. But you ought to have some small thing wrong. Big feet or big ears – something.'

She looked at him, smiling, and said softly, 'D'you want to love me again? Is that it? You just want to see my appendix scar again.'

He laughed and put his arms around her as she settled on the bed beside him.

It was nearly midnight when he walked back to his own room in the dark. They'd had an omelette and a coffee at the café they used regularly and the subject for discussion had been posed like an exam question — 'What is the difference between loving and being in love? Discuss.' They both agreed that loving was rare and it meant loving the loved-one more than you loved yourself.

Back in Berlin Inman tried Bekker's number for two or three days but there was no response. He wondered if Bekker was in trouble or was he taking some time off to see his parents and friends in Moscow. There had been vague hints of a girl-friend who sang in a night-club at one of the big hotels.

He had been commissioned by an American press agency to do a piece on the comparative virtues and vices of East German big industry and its opposite numbers in West Germany. He spent a lot of time at the central library and at the library on the other side of the Wall at Humboldt University. He interviewed trade-union leaders on both sides of the Wall and found that the West Germans were far more militant and disgruntled than the East Germans. It was obvious that the whole East German manu-facturing sector was grossly uneconomic in terms of productivity but with its output taken entirely by its Communist neighbours it had no costs for marketing, selling and distribution. The average hours worked were about half those worked in the West. The West German union leaders openly despised but privately envied their colleagues in the East.

He faxed 2500 words through to the Chicago office and asked if he could place the article in a European magazine or newspaper. They praised the article and agreed to let him have second-use rights provided he passed them 40 per cent of any additional income.

A week later the BBC's World Service who had seen the article interviewed him by phone, and paid him radio rates for the inter-view to be used in the UK and what was called 'The old Commonwealth countries'.

An East German magazine had ignored his copyright and

printed the piece in full. They offered no payment and ignored his invoices.

He had been back for nearly three weeks before Bekker contacted him. He seemed quite perky and suggested a meeting later that day. As usual at Inman's place.

Chapter Twenty

There was just one message on the answerphone. He wasn't sure but he thought the voice was Bekker's. The message was brief. It just gave a telephone number for him to contact. And it was an East Berlin number.

He rang the number three times. The first time the phone at the other end was lifted and hung up. The second time there was no response. But the third time what sounded like Bekker's voice suggested a meeting at his place in an hour. When he agreed the phone was hung up.

It was nearly two hours before Bekker turned up looking slightly embarrassed as he followed Inman into the kitchen.

'I'm sorry about all the rigmarole, Max. But I think somebody's trailing me, and I'm not sure who he's working for.'

'Who do you think it is?'

'My guess is that it's someone from the East Berlin Stasis.' He shrugged. 'It could be East Berlin KGB but they'd need a clearance from Moscow to do that.'

'How did you get on in Moscow?' He poured their usual coffees as Bekker pulled a chair up to the kitchen table.

'About how I expected. They were impressed by getting sight of a document that was obviously top-secret and genuine. It confirmed things for the old boys from Philby's days and they made clear that whoever my contact was they wanted me to keep it alive.'

'Did they press you to identify the contact?'

'Of course. But that's just routine.'

'What did you tell them?'

'Nothing.'

'And they approved of your keeping the contact?'

'Yes.'

'Tell me about the guy who's watching you?'

'Very professional. Looks like a German. In his late forties. But I dropped him whenever I wanted to, so I'd guess he's not Moscow trained. Anyway they'd use at least three bodies if they were doing it.'

'Are you scared?'

'No. Just being extra cautious.' He paused. 'How did you get on?'

'They were definitely impressed. Like your people they pressed me to identify my contact. I told them nothing. Encouraged me to keep up the contact.'

'I think we need to reconsider what we're doing.'

'In what way?'

'First of all, if we concentrate on top-secret documentation we'll get caught sooner or later. Secondly, I'm not sure that that sort of material is significant. Interesting but short-term.' Bekker paused. 'I've got a small item that your people could find useful but I had to hang around for five days before I could get access to the files that matter. The real value from that time spent was what I learned about Moscow's thinking on current affairs. That's what we should be concentrating on. What's going to happen, not what has already happened for better or worse.'

Inman was silent for long moments and then looked across at Bekker. 'You're absolutely right, Otto. Absolutely right. Let's talk about it.' He paused. 'I guess there are two categories of information that we need to look at. What's the significance of something that London or Moscow are doing at the moment and secondly what's the official reaction likely to be in both places. Yes?'

'Absolutely. So let's talk about those things.'

'I feel we should both think about it for a few days and find out a major problem area or what looks like that to us.' Inman smiled. 'I think we both already know an area that we could usefully discuss and compare notes.'

'What's that?'

'Maybe I've been in Berlin too long but I've grown to feel that this is where everything is going to happen. Very soon.' He paused. 'You've told me a little of the rivalries in East Berlin and other quite well-informed people have told me the same. If I'm right and something *is* going to happen it's going to happen right here in Berlin.' Inman shrugged. 'You can fill in most of the gaps.'

'And in return you give your views on how people will respond this side of the Wall?'

'Yeah. Of course.'

'This would need a lot of discussion. Days not hours. We might need to check on something we don't know enough about. Any ideas?'

'I agree that we have to take good time for discussion and maybe the checking could mean several days' work or travel.' Inman paused. 'How busy are you on your normal duties at the moment?'

'Flexible. I'm independent. I can fit in.'

'OK. Three days' thinking and then we meet all day next Monday and Tuesday. You can sleep here overnight.'

'Suits me, Max.'

They sat talking for some time as Inman kept the coffee going and it was while they were talking that Inman realised that they were very similar to one another in as much as neither had any close friends. So far as he was concerned it was the first time he'd had anyone, apart from Katya, to talk to openly since he'd been recruited to SIS.

'Do you see much of your parents, Otto?'

'No. They are both deeply involved in their work.' He sighed. 'They don't see much of each other in fact. But they get by. They're not political but they grew up in times of turmoil and they are just glad to be alive with a roof over their heads and food to eat.'

'Have they met your girl-friend?'

'No. They both lost many relatives in the war and, like most Russians, they won't ever forgive or forget what the Germans did to our people.' He sighed. 'And she's too young to understand what all the fuss is about.'

'Does she have a job?'

'She works in a bar. How about your parents?'

'Like you I don't see them very often. I'm only in London for a day or two at a time. We get on very well and they are very fond of my Katya.'

'How does she feel about your job?'

'So far as she is concerned I'm a full-time journalist. We never discuss the other work.'

'But she must guess that you're more than a journalist.'

'Why should she?'

Bekker laughed. 'You look, and you see, but you don't join in. You're a loner. Same as me.'

'And your girl. What does she think you do?'

'She's very naive. She's rather proud of me being a Stasi.' He laughed. 'That was until the Stasis tried to persuade her to inform on me. She couldn't believe they spied on one another.' He paused. 'She told them she'd report them to the proper police and was angry that they were so amused.'

'What do you do in your spare time?'

'Listen to jazz.' He waved towards Inman's hi-fi. 'And you listen to concertos and symphonies.'

Inman smiled. 'Yes, but only the nice, easy, romantic stuff.'

'There are a lot of Russians among your CDs. Tchaikovsky, Rachmaninov, Glazunov, Prokofiev and even Shostakovich.'

Inman smiled. 'Only Shostakovich's Second Piano Concerto and the second movement.'

'But you are a bit of a romantic, aren't you?'

'Am I? I would have said I was a realist.' Inman smiled. 'Changing the subject, what are you going to do about the guy you think is tailing you?'

Bekker laughed. 'I shall report it to Moscow.'

'And if he stops tailing you you'll know he was theirs?'

'No way. They're too smart for that. If they called him off I'd know he was theirs. They'll pass the word to the Stasis and have him arrested. Something like that. And they'll charge him with some routine offence and know that I'll know about it.'

'I know you're independent but what was your actual remit?'

Bekker shrugged. 'Officially to keep an eye on the Stasi and act as liaison between the Stasis and the KGB at Normannenallee.'

'Do the KGB in Berlin use you for liaison?'

'No. They'd see me in hell before contacting me officially.' He smiled. 'But they keep in touch off the record.'

'How often do you come across here?'

Bekker smiled. 'About twice a week but I don't come through any of the Checkpoints.'

'Are those visits for the Stasis or for the KGB?'

'They're for Moscow.'

'What are they interested in?'

Bekker shrugged. 'Your people. The SIS section at the Olympiad and the West German intelligence people, the BND.'

*　　*　　*

After Bekker had left, Inman was conscious that he and the Russian had more in common with each other than they had with their colleagues who would see their plans as either pathetic or arrogant. And in a way their colleagues were right. But the fact that they felt it was worth doing was a measure of their awareness that despite espionage, diplomacy and all the organisations responsible for providing information that would help politicians make calm, sensible decisions, each side knew too little of what motivated the other side. It seemed incredible, but they knew that it was fact and that was what gave their plans a kind of authenticity. For some odd reason his thoughts went to Frank Cooper. He remembered him saying at the end of a refresher seminar on terrorist groups, 'Gentlemen. Just one last word. You've all heard that wonderful phrase from World War One – "making our country a land fit for heroes to live in" – well I want to tell you that it's our duty to make this country a "land fit for cowards to live in". Thank you, gentlemen.' It was typical of the man that despite the fact that three of the academics were women he still addressed the assembly as 'gentlemen'. He wasn't a supporter of having women in the SIS, the Royal Navy or the Army. And was impervious to the rules of 'political correctness'.

Gina Felinska had done them each a *Wiener schnitzl*, Jan's favourite dish. When he had finished he put down his knife and fork and looked across at his wife.

'Now give me the bad news.'

Looking amazed she said, 'Why should there be bad news?'

'You always do *schnitzl* when you've got some problem. What's today's problem?'

She sighed and stood up reaching out her hand to him. 'Let's have some wine in my room. It's cosier.'

Jan had opened a bottle of Margaux and had poured them each a glass before he sat down.

'*Na zdrovye*,' he said lifting his glass.

'*Na zdrovye*,' she said and sipped the wine before putting down her glass.

She leaned back in the cane armchair. 'Katya came over yesterday and we went out for a meal.' She paused. 'She seemed to have lost all her enthusiasm for her work and I asked her if there was anything the matter. We talked all evening and she stayed here for the night. She didn't ask for my advice but she obviously needed to talk, so we talked.'

'Don't tell me there's another man.'

'No. Quite the opposite.' She paused and then went on. 'You know everybody sees her as a very tough creature. Seeing ghastly things, photographing them and writing about them. There was a piece about her in one of the women's magazines a couple of weeks ago. The headline was "A tough cookie". It was quite sympathetic and as usual it concentrated on what a beauty she was. And mentioned briefly that she didn't believe in marriage despite having the same man for years.' She paused again. 'She asked me if that was how you and I saw her. As a tough cookie.' She shrugged. 'I said that was only half the story, the superficial bit. She asked me what the other half was.' She looked at her husband. 'What would you have said?'

Jan Felinski was silent for several long moments before he looked back at his wife. 'You need to look first at the "tough cookie" picture. Our girl was never a tough cookie. You've only got to recall that advice she gave to beginning photographers in some programme – "Wear your heart on your sleeve and go out and take pictures" or words to that effect. Tough cookies don't have hearts – on their sleeves or anywhere else. What gives that false impression of her is that she realised that angry as she may be about victims of war or disasters there was nothing she herself could do about it. All she could do was to make sure that hundreds of thousands of people could see what was being done to their fellow creatures.' He paused. 'My old father used to say to me – "if you want to stop somebody from drowning you don't jump in the river with them, you reach out and haul them out to safety".' He paused. 'And our girl's bright enough, intelligent enough, to be a realist. It suits her job, her calling, to apparently accept the "tough cookie" label but it's totally wrong.' He paused. 'How did this all come up?'

'It's hard to explain, Jan. To a man. Even to you. But she's depressed about her relationship with Max. Feels that it's become sort of routine. I don't know how to put it.'

'What's made her feel this?'

'I think that despite all her trips and work she's actually very lonely. They don't see very much of one another.'

'But I can remember them outlining how it was going to be. Both with interesting jobs. Independent but at the same time dependent. I can remember asking them what they were going to be dependent on. They just looked at one another – very affectionately – smiling at the old man who didn't understand.'

'Are you saying "she made her bed and she must lie on it"?'

'No way.' He paused. 'Did you suggest she talked it over with Max?'

'I didn't suggest it but we discussed it. But a woman can't do that, Jan.'

'You know what this means, don't you?'

'Maybe. You tell me.'

'You can't make somebody love you the way you want. Maybe they love you in their own way but if it doesn't work like love for you, you either have to call it a day or you make the best of it. All this talk about rational behaviour is rubbish when the chips are on the table.'

'So what do you think she should do?'

'I know what she'll do. She'll carry on.' He paused. 'Who knows, something might change it all as time goes by. And it's no good blaming Max Inman. I'd say he has genuine affection for her and he's loyal and dependable within his limits.'

'It seems such a waste, Jan. She's so beautiful and so intelligent.'

'Intelligence is not one of the constituents of love, my dear.' He paused. 'Did she ask you to do anything?'

'No. In fact she wasn't complaining, just sad that she felt so lonely.'

'If she actually wants help, tell her I'll help any way I can. She's not lonely in the ordinary sense. I've seen her at receptions and embassy parties. The men are all over her but she smiles them away.' He sighed. 'You're right. It's a great shame but it's got to take its course. Us interfering could easily destroy the little she has.'

'You don't feel that she's being short-changed?'

Felinski was silent for a long time before he replied. 'Maybe she just has more to give than the fellow has to give.'

He stood up and Gina knew that although she wasn't satisfied with the outcome it was all she was going to get for the time being. He was right of course in a way. A man's way.

Chapter Twenty-One

The meeting had not taken as much time as they had expected. The likely wrong moves seemed to be mainly on the Soviet side and the West's mistakes were likely to be wrong counter-moves to actions by Moscow.

By the end of the first day Inman knew enough to feel that he could impress Cooper with what he had to report. It confirmed some of London's thinking but it indicated that there could be many opportunities for London to make mistakes based on ignorance that the report could prevent.

The separate information and photographs that Bekker gave him would be useful to the people who were trying to assemble the pieces of what caused the air disasters. But they were no longer much more than a sign of Bekker's good faith and co-operation.

Inman had phoned Cooper at his home that evening and they had agreed to meet the next day. Cooper had offered to come to Berlin but Inman had suggested that Cooper would almost certainly want to discuss his report with others. Particularly Shapiro. He phoned Katya too but there was no answer and no answering-machine.

☆   ☆   ☆

As they settled down at the conference table in Cooper's office, Frank Cooper said, 'You sounded a bit tense on the phone. Has something gone wrong?'

Inman shook his head. 'No. If I sounded tense it's because I feel that what I'm reporting is vitally important.'

'So why the tension?'

'Because I'm worried that some people won't see how important it is.' He passed a brown envelope across the table to Cooper. 'How about I come back in an hour when you've had time to consider it?'

Cooper opened the envelope and took out two sheets of paper and a couple of photographs.

He looked at Inman. 'Just these two sheets, Max?'

'Yes.'

'Just bear with me then while I read it.'

As Inman waited he felt he understood the impulse smokers had to make time pass.

Cooper read the two pages carefully and then re-read them before looking at Inman.

'There are a number of people who will want to see this, Max. Especially Joe Shapiro. Is that a problem?'

'No. So long as they realise two things. Firstly that under no circumstances will I identify the source except in very general terms. And secondly that much of this material is way above top-secret in Soviet terms and a man has possibly risked his life in providing it. None of this is conjectural or surmise. It's fact.'

Cooper nodded. 'I understand, Max. How long can you stay?'

'As long as you want.'

'I'll arrange a meeting for tomorrow when the people concerned have had a chance to read and digest your report. I'll phone you at your place and give you a time and place. Probably at Gower Street. OK?'

Inman stood up. 'Fine.' He hesitated for a moment and then said, 'What's your first impression?'

Cooper hesitated for a moment and then said, 'It's just what we need, Max. But some will cast doubts.'

'What matters is that somebody at the top knows what's going on and what's going to happen.'

Cooper smiled. 'They will, Max. They will. I recognise what it's taken to put this together. It isn't just SIS material. It's at least Foreign Secretary and maybe the PM himself.'

When Max Inman had left, Cooper re-read the report and started making a list of names on his pad. Before calling any of them he read Inman's report once again. It was so clear, so logical, and so frightening.

Nov 5 1988

Report on current situation in Soviet Union and German Democratic Republic and future prospects.

Present Situation

In East Berlin there is considerable public unrest about living conditions. Information indicates that this applies throughout the GDR. President Gorbachev's announcement about *perestroika* and *glasnost* has unintentionally added fuel to the flames. Those statements are blamed by the government of the GDR for the unrest. Especially by General Secretary Honeker. Hard-liners are in touch with Soviet hard-liners who are anti-Gorbachev.

The KGB situation is mixed. In Moscow KGB policy is to appear to be neutral but the top brass are almost certainly looking for a chance to oust Gorbachev. They have had secret talks with senior commanders in the Red Army who appear to be ready to cooperate. In Berlin the KGB blame the government of the GDR, and in particular Honeker, for allowing the situation to get out of hand. Their relationship with the Stasis is almost non-existent as the local KGB also see the Stasi support of the present regime as highly dangerous. There is considerable tension between KGB Moscow and local KGB because of conflicting orders from Dzerdhinski Square.

In the HQ of the GDR political organisation there is a small number of senior politicians who would like to get rid of Honeker.

Forecast

We have positive evidence that Gorbachev is planning to announce a cut-back in Soviet armed forces. In a matter of weeks. There is talk in the Kremlin that indicate secret talks with the Bush camp in USA for a meeting to be held in some neutral venue if Bush is elected president. The talks have gone far enough for it to be rumoured that the meeting would be about fundamentals and the venue Malta on a Soviet warship the *Salva*.

There have also been unpublished contacts between President Gorbachev and Chancellor Kohl. The subject of those contacts is not known but considerable tensions have arisen in East Berlin, Moscow and Bonn by the rumour that the subject discussed concerned an eventual amalgamation of the two Germanys.

Note: Could I have indications as to particular areas I have covered which are of special interest to London. In addition I would welcome comments on other areas that would be useful.

Subsidiary report

Photographs marked A and B.

Photograph A is of the detonator used in the bombing of TWA Flight 204.

Photograph B shows the detonator carried by two Libyan agents arrested in Dakar, Senegal in February of this year.

It will be seen that the two detonators are identical. My source indicates that a similar detonator was taken into the Congo in the Libyan diplomatic pouch and delivered to three (3)

Libyan-trained Congolese terrorists by an official of the Libyan embassy in Brazzaville and was used in the bombing of French UTA Flight 772 in September this year.

These photographs are *not* for distribution or reproducing, internally or otherwise.

Chapter Twenty-Two

It took two days for Frank Cooper to assemble the people for his meeting and he had arranged for it to take place at the safe-house in Gower Street.

There was the usual cast of Shapiro, Rimmer and Potter with Waring representing SIS Admin. The new boys were Purdey from the Foreign Office and Maclean from the Cabinet Office. They had all read the Janus report under strict security conditions and they had all asked that Inman himself should be at the discussion to answer questions that had already been framed. It was also agreed that they should use Inman's name at the meeting not his code-name.

Coffee and tea were available and when they were finally settled around the conference table Cooper had introduced Inman and given a short resume of the activities he undertook as the Janus operation.

As Cooper finalised his piece, Joe Shapiro raised his hand. 'Maybe it's worth me mentioning that I was listening to the early news on Radio Moscow as I was having breakfast this morning. The main item was a statement from Gorbachev that there were to be substantial reductions in all Soviet armed forces except the navy.' He nodded to Inman. 'Nobody in SIS or GCHQ had indicated that this was about to happen. I don't know whether the Foreign Office had any warning of reductions.'

Purdey shook his head but said nothing.

Maclean said, 'We had heard nothing about this. Not even rumours.'

Cooper nodded. 'Has the PM seen the report?'

'No. But she was told all the details.'

'Have the rest of the cabinet been told?'

'No. Like we agreed. It's PM and Foreign Secretary only.'

Cooper looked at Joe Shapiro. 'Any other comments, Joe?'

'Yes. I think our friend here is to be congratulated. It warns us of likely problems in the next few months and gives us time to sort out how we ought to react to various situations.' He paused. 'Bearing in mind the location of most of their problems, I wonder if we ought to improve our liaison with the West Germans. Especially the BND.'

'Not revealing what we know.'

'Of course not. Just a small fishing expedition.'

Cooper looked at Rimmer. 'Paul. Any comments?'

Rimmer shrugged. 'It seems such a mess that I'm inclined to thinking that it's all true. It indicates a lot of confusion both in Moscow and Berlin about Gorbachev and *perestroika* and *glasnost*. It looks as if it isn't working at home but is working in the satellites.' He paused. 'I've got some reservations of course.'

'Like what?'

'As you know. I've never favoured this operation but this report puts it in a new dimension. What worries me is that the informant is obviously high-up in the KGB. What's he getting back in exchange?' He paused. 'This chap would be in real trouble if they suspected him. It could easily have been no more than the KGB in Moscow playing games. Disinformation planted very carefully to lead us astray. But I think that the very nature of the information we've been given tends to destroy that theory. If it was planted it wouldn't be so self-critical of the situation.' He smiled. 'It would mean that they'd moved from disinformation to treason. I think our friend Inman has given us a genuine inside picture. But I must warn him that he and his contact are walking around on some very thin ice.'

Cooper looked at Inman who said, 'We're being very careful and a lot of my contact's information comes not from documents but conversations with the top people concerned. He eliminates anything that he feels is biased.'

Purdey said, 'Purdey, Foreign Office. Would it be possible for us to give you a small number of questions to which we'd very much like to know the answers?'

'What sort of questions?'

'What's going to happen to Honeker? Will they leave him to his fate or what?'

Maclean chipped in. 'Cabinet Office. The PM is anxious to know more about the prospective meeting with Bush. It's our guess that he'll be elected. Any ideas of what Gorbachev wants to discuss with the White House?'

Cooper intervened. 'I imagine that everybody here has a question he'd like answered. Can I suggest that you let me have a note of them later today and Joe Shapiro, Inman and I will sort them out.' He smiled. 'We don't want to go too far.' He paused. 'Does anyone feel that this contact, and this arrangement, should be stopped?'

There were no critics and Cooper closed the meeting. Joe Shapiro stayed behind with Inman and Cooper.

Shapiro said quietly, 'It's taken a long time and a lot of work to get this far, Frank, but it looks like Operation Janus is paying off.' He looked at Inman. 'Is there anything I can do to help you?'

'Yes. I'd like to know what our reactions are likely to be if the various things turn out like the report says.' He paused. 'They'd have to be the truth.'

Shapiro looked at Cooper. 'How about you and I spend the rest of the day and maybe tomorrow doing some checking?'

'That suits me, Joe.'

Inman stood up tentatively. 'Have you finished with me for today?'

'Yes. But keep in touch. Carry your pager.'

After Inman had left Cooper turned to Shapiro. 'Are you satisfied, Joe?'

'Yeah, but I've got my fingers crossed.' He smiled. 'And now we've got to play games and decide how we would react if we were the government faced with these various situations. At least if these forecasts turn out to be true our politicians won't have to react on spur-of-the-moment thinking.'

'Let's make a list of our own questions and a list of the people we need to talk to.'

It took them an hour and Cooper contacted the head of SIS's German desk on current West German thinking and their relationship with the German Intelligence, the BND.

Joe Shapiro got the name of a contact from Purdey at the Foreign Office. The West German junior minister who was responsible for liaising with the East Germans on relationships between the two Germanys.

The day of the Gower Street meeting was publication day for Katya's new book. *Aftermath* was a collection of her black-and-white photographs of the devastation left behind after a war. And the text emphasised that wars were no longer about tanks and artillery. Not even about soldiers. But about psychopaths who slaughtered defenceless civilians. Old people, women and children. People who died not even knowing why they died. Young girls and children whose big eyes stared in fear towards a camera moments before they were hacked to death by machetes and *pangas* wielded in the name of some cult or ethnic roots that had long ago lost their significance.

She had reluctantly agreed to book-signing sessions at half a dozen bookshops and when those were over she and Max had gone to a small drinks party at Amnesty International. In that company she was a different person. She was among like-minded people. People who cared. People who would spend hours of hard work to save just one abused person in some filthy prison. Writing hundreds of polite letters to ruthless dictators as if they were unaware of the atrocities committed in their names. Like Katya their efforts were mainly on behalf of individuals and not concerned with routine politics or religion. Max wondered if perhaps Katya and the others were not more effective than he was.

Max had checked with Cooper and it seemed that he wouldn't be needed for a couple of days and he'd taken Katya to Paris. They'd stayed at a small hotel in Rue des Capucines. She had contacted a Magnum photographer she knew and they'd had a meal together with him and his wife. By the time they were drinking their coffee the conversation had inevitably turned to their work. André specialised in photographing out-of-the-way places and their people but was more interested in Katya's work.

'Is there anything you wouldn't photograph because it was too revolting?'

She was silent for long moments and then she said, 'I took a photograph in Bosnia last year. There was something about it that sickened me so I've never offered it or shown it to anyone.'

'Tell us about it.'

She shook her head. 'It would upset me to talk about it.' She paused. 'It wasn't physical cruelty. Just something obscene that I've never been able to understand.' She put her hand on Max Inman's hand. 'This man would understand but nobody else would.' Max Inman smiled affectionately but was aware that Katya had not been very complimentary to their guests. He waved to the waiter and signalled that he wanted the bill. He took them all for a last drink at La Closerie des Lilas and half an hour of Ivan Meyer at the piano. At least half a dozen people had recognised

Katya and had come across to chat with her and André. Les Lilas was home to Paris's beautiful people.

The day they got back to London Inman had had a long meeting with Cooper. It seemed that he would be able to go back to Berlin the next day.

That evening they had booked a table at Il Cappuccino and as they sipped a glass of house white wine she had delved into her large handbag and brought out a small parcel. As she pushed it across the table to him she smiled. 'Happy Anniversary.' He reached in his jacket pocket and took out a small square packet. 'Happy Anniversary to you too.' She looked at his face in disbelief. 'You remembered. I can't believe it.'

He laughed. 'At least open your present.'

As the wrapping was peeled off it revealed a small square jewel box and when she opened it she sat in silence. It was a gold ring with a large opal in a claw setting. She looked at his face and he saw the tears at the edges of her eyes. 'I'm ashamed. I didn't think for a moment you'd remember.' She stood up and leaned across the table, crockery tinkling as she kissed him on the mouth.

When she sat down he opened his package, it was a leatherbound edition of *The Rubaiyyat* of Omar Khayaam.

She said softly, 'It's the Fitzgerald translation.'

'Thanks, my love.' He smiled at her. 'What made you choose this? It's so right for me.'

'That day all those years ago when we sat on the corner by the Clare bridge, you said that when you were rich you wanted a copy.' She paused. 'And how did you choose the ring?'

'It reminded me of you. The smooth pale stone with all that fire glowing inside.'

'You never cease to surprise me, my love.'

'About what?'

'About you yourself. So calm, so reserved, so occupied in

putting the world to rights. And yet you remembered the anniversary of the day we first met.'

'Why not? It was the most important day in my life.'

'Why, Max, why? Why am I important to you?'

'Because I trust you and I don't trust anyone else.'

'Trust me about what?'

'Your feelings, your judgment. I know I'm safe with you.' He paused. 'Nobody else matters to me.'

She smiled. 'Except all those down-trodden Russians.'

He shrugged and said quietly, 'Twenty million Russians died fighting the Nazis. It has to count for something.'

'You're right. It was a silly remark. I take it back.'

They had walked back along the Embankment and stopped to lean against the stone parapet to look through the mist over the river to the lights on the other side. As they looked Max Inman said, 'This is Pasternak weather.'

'Why Pasternak?'

'He called his poem "White Night" and there was a verse –

> *There, far off in the misty distance*
> *Of this night of Spring-like whiteness,*
> *The nightingales with glorious thunder*
> *Announced the frontiers of summer.'*

She said softly, 'We'd better cherish the nightingales while there are still a few left.'

Later she was sitting on the bed watching him brush his teeth and wondering if she should tell him about the picture, and almost without deciding she said, 'Can I tell you about that picture?'

Washing his toothbrush under the running water from the tap he said, 'Will it help?'

'Yes. I think so. It was so strange and I've never been able to understand it and the effect it had on me.'

'Tell me then.'

'There were the dead bodies of three people. A woman in her early thirties, a child about six or seven, a boy. And a young girl about eleven or twelve. They'd all been killed and stabbed. You could still see that the young girl had been very pretty.' She hesitated and took a deep breath. 'She had worn her long hair in a ponytail tied with a ribbon and they'd cut off her ponytail and stuffed it in her mouth.' She leaned up at his face. 'Why, Max? What motivates a man to do something like that? It's not physical cruelty but what is it? I don't understand. It's so . . . so . . . so irrelevant.'

He sat down beside her on the bed, his arms around her, aware that there was no way you could expunge images like that from anyone's mind. No words to comfort with. No words even to explain. Because there was no explanation.

Chapter Twenty-Three

In the end it had taken four days before Cooper and Shapiro had checked on what the government's likely reaction would be to the various events that had been indicated in Inman's report. They had warned him that they had consulted the people likely to make those decisions but without being able to indicate that they were talking about the real thing rather than hypothetical situations.

He contacted Bekker as soon as he got back to Berlin and arranged a meeting for the next day. Bekker had sounded tense on the phone.

Inman had brought back American cigarettes for Bekker and a small bottle of Chanel No.5 for Bekker's girl-friend.

'You sounded a bit up-tight on the phone. Are you?'

'No. Just realising that this meeting is going to mark a decisive stage in our little scheme.'

'There are no problems on my side, Otto. Have you prepared your questions?'

'Of course.'

'OK. Let's get started. I told my people that under no circumstances would I identify or give away clues as to who my informant was. They didn't like that but they went along with it. There's no doubt that they were impressed by what we had put together and they treated it seriously so that a lot of people were consulted who would actually make the decisions if things went as we forecast. But they were given the impression that it was just an exercise rather than the real thing. Believe me, it was treated very seriously.' Inman paused and smiled. 'Your turn now.'

'If there was some kind of uprising in East Germany like we said was a possibility, what would your people's reaction be?'

'Strict neutrality. No help to the rioters and no public approval.'

'And the West Germans?'

'No public support from Bonn for the uprising, but no criticism either. Our analysis of what they said was that they probably would officially be neutral but behind the scenes press for the East Germans to get rid of Honeker.'

'And what about our thinking that the rioters might fight their way into West Berlin?'

'They were convinced it couldn't happen.'

'And what if Moscow openly approved the riots?'

'Our people would refuse any comment, on the grounds that it was a Communist internal problem.'

'And criticism of Moscow's failure to control the East Germans.'

'No. No criticism. Just no comment, official or unofficial.'

'Why not?'

'Because my people are not in the mood to criticise Gorbachev. They think he's shown courage with *perestroika* and *glasnost* but is not handling the present situation too well. But they blame the Kremlin for that, not Gorbachev.'

'And what were their views on the in-fighting in Moscow?'

Inman shrugged and smiled. 'They said that that was normal. The only difference this time was that the army and the KGB were cooperating. But they think that they'll go on until they can oust

Gorbachev. They reckon he's there for about two years.' He paused. 'They said they could do a better forecast if they knew who was running the various groups.'

Bekker nodded. 'I'll see what I can dig out. Have you got anything for me?'

'A little. Our ambassador in Washington is keeping close contact with Bush and his people. Our people too think he'll win the election. They think that Bush is genuinely interested in meeting Gorbachev but not until Bush has settled in. Washington are pro-Gorby and we've put our word in too. And that brings up another point. My lot, and Washington, want to know who Gorby listens to. Who influences his thinking. Particularly on foreign policy.' He paused. 'Any more for you?'

'Do you have good contacts in Bonn?'

'Yes. But mainly politicians.'

'I'd like to know what they're making of the East German situation. Everybody in Moscow thinks that they will give secret support to the dissidents.'

Inman shook his head. 'That's not the picture I get.'

'Tell me.'

'There are several influential people in Bonn and London who think that Moscow is behind all the unrest. Hoping that Bonn might involve itself in the riots if the Stasis can't cope and it gets out of hand, so that the West Germans are dragged into it on behalf of their fellow Germans.'

'That's not what I was getting but I'll root around and see if they've changed. It sounds like journalists' chatter and they're always wrong. Kohl's too shrewd a politician to get involved in being seen as helping rioters. They've got enough of their own trouble-makers.'

Bekker paused. 'Do your people at the SIS detachment know about you and what you do?'

'No. I meet them at odd functions but so far as they are concerned I'm a journalist.'

'I've grabbed the guy who was doing surveillance on me.'

'Who was he?'

'Gives his name as Werner Laufer. I've got him in a Stasi interrogation house and I'm going over him very carefully. I've no doubt that he's a professional. Probably a freelance but I want to know who hired him and why they're interested in me.' He paused. 'He's not talking at the moment but he will. They always do.'

'Should be interesting.'

'Did you have a good time with that beautiful girl of yours?'

'Yes. We managed a couple of days in the country but she had to go off to do an assignment in Turkey.'

'Don't you get jealous knowing every man is staring at her?' Bekker paused. 'I saw a bit of a surveillance film that had been taken at a reception at our London embassy and she was in it and you could see that men just couldn't keep their eyes off her.'

Max Inman laughed. 'I sometimes feel a twinge of something but she's used to all that and knows exactly how to deal with it. For me it's like having a beautiful boat, or a handsome race-horse or a Rolls Royce Silver Shadow. All rolled into one. We kind of grew up together at Cambridge and we knew from the start that we'd both need to be independent to do our jobs well.'

'D'you miss her when you're not with her?'

'Yes. Of course. But that's part of the price we pay for our independence. I think of her every day.' He paused. 'I've brought you some Yankee cigarettes and some perfume for your girl. What's her name by the way?'

'Toni at the club. Maria at home. She's very pretty but not quite beautiful. Long legs, big boobs and the greatest smile I've ever seen.'

'D'you love her?'

Bekker frowned. 'A big word, love.' Inman tried to remember who he had last heard saying that. 'Let's say I care about her. Quite a lot. She's a wonderful contrast to the rest of my existence.

Simple, uncomplicated . . .' he smiled '. . . and quite pleased with her Stasi man.' He paused. 'Makes a nice change to be liked.'

Otto Bekker was doing a second check on Werner Laufer's two rooms in an old building in Pankow. There was nothing to give any clues to the personality of its tenant. No pictures on the walls. No books, no telephone, no radio and no personal belongings apart from two pairs of slacks, a couple of woollen sweaters and a well-used pair of Nike trainers. There was little in the small refrigerator and only basic crockery and utensils on the draining-board of the sink. It was a place for short-term transients. He looked around for about an hour but knew by instinct that he would find nothing. There was nothing to find.

Back at the Stasi safe-house he looked through the few things that had been found on Laufer when he had been picked up. A wallet with 300 Ostmarks and 30 D.Marks, a standard ID card with a genuine stamp, keys to his rooms and what looked like a car key. There was a small pack of tissues and two cough-sweets. The wrist-watch was digital but the electronics people said it had not been modified and was on sale both sides of the Wall. About 25 Marks of either currency.

The guards had said that Laufer had only got off the bed to go under escort to the toilet and had eaten very little of the food that had been offered him. He had been interrogated by two different Stasi men but had refused to answer any questions.

Bekker looked through the observation port with its wide-angle lens that showed the whole of the small room. Laufer was lying on the bed, his arms across his chest and one leg bent up casually. His eyes were closed but Bekker was sure that he wasn't asleep.

The guard unlocked the door for him and he went in, pulling up the wooden chair to the side of the bed.

'It's time to talk, Laufer. Maybe we've made a mistake and you aren't the man we're looking for.' He paused. 'Just help us get it straightened out.'

Laufer didn't respond and Bekker went on. 'Have you ever been to Moscow, Werner?'

Laufer sat up slowly, stretching his arms as he turned to look at Bekker.

'You're wasting your time little man.'

'I've got all the time in the world and you'll talk in the end, my friend. But it's more comfortable for you if we do it now. The longer it takes the worse it is. You know that as well as I do.'

Laufer lay back on the bed but still watched Bekker's face.

Bekker said, 'We've got special interrogation teams, Herr Laufer. They'll take you over later today.' He stood up. 'The guard can contact me if you change your mind.' He looked at his watch. 'You've got about two hours before the experts take you over. It's up to you. They won't take long.'

It was 2 a.m. when Bekker got the call and drove back to the safe-house. He listened to the tape. It wasn't long. Ten minutes to get Laufer going and then an hour answering questions before he passed out. Bekker breathed a sigh of relief that the interrogators had no idea of what it was all about. He signed for the tape and drove back to his office and locked it in the safe. He drove to the club and picked up Toni, trying to take his mind off what was on the tape. It was a long time since Otto Bekker had been scared but he was scared now. At first he'd thought it was a pack of lies but as the interrogation went on Werner Laufer was way beyond the stage when you could control what you were saying. He knew things he couldn't have known if it wasn't the truth. And Otto Bekker for once had no idea what he should do about what he had learned.

Chapter Twenty-Four

It was eight years since Katya had been in Havana and she was pleasantly surprised by the changes. She remembered having to walk miles to get even a drink of water the last time she was there. But now there were little coffee and pizza stands everywhere in Havana, and peddlers with pushcarts with everything from lemon ices to hot rolls. But for her the attraction was the beautiful ruins of the city's collapsing mansions and ruined apartment blocks.

Her favourite place was the Cathedral Plaza of Old Havana. Tourism was beginning to be a major source of foreign currency again and the Plaza though small was one of the main attractions. Refurbished, cleaned and freshly painted it was almost too pretty to be true. The tourists were mainly Italians, Mexicans, Canadians and Germans. The light was perfect for Kodachrome 25s and she had shot forty cassettes before she turned her camera on the people. And that was a different story. You can't refurbish and repaint people who have to get on with their daily lives. The nuclear plant that was supposed to free Cuba from its dependence on foreign aid had been abandoned only two-thirds finished. Hospitals discharged patients who were still only partly out of anaesthesia. Leaving them with neither pain-killers nor even the means to go home as they lay on stretchers outside the hospital. It took time for her to realise that all Cubans were poor. Even those she had met who had influence lived in apartments where there was water only every other day.

What saddened her most were the pretty, smiling, under-aged prostitutes who paraded the Plaza at night like hungry doves and pigeons.

The constant subject of all conversation was how to get hold of a few US dollars or spares for a broken-down Lada. It was like the aftermath of a war that was only just over and the survivors were waiting to see what was to happen next.

The first Secretary at the British Embassy was doing his best to be helpful but Katya Felinska was posing her usual problem of being stunningly beautiful and implacable at the same time. All she wanted was a US visa clearance to fly direct to Miami. She made no attempt to disguise the fact that her visit was to meet and report on Cuban refugees in Florida.

Tom Holroyd was an amiable man but she was trying his patience to the limit.

'But what reason do they give for refusing?'

'They don't have to give a reason. But the reason is obviously that they don't want Cuban refugees or even Cubans in Cuba to be featured in the media.'

'But they don't know what I'm going to say. I don't even know myself until I've talked with them.' She shrugged. 'I might be writing good things about the US attitudes to Cuba.'

He smiled. 'I think they gave up any hope of that years ago. Why don't you go back to the UK and then go separately to Miami?' He paused. 'But remember that your current Cuban visa could be a problem. Maybe your father could help in Washington.'

She said indignantly. 'My father doesn't have anything to do with my work. He doesn't even know that I'm here in Cuba.'

Tom Holroyd stood up slowly and she knew that her time was up. As he walked her to his office door he said, 'I suspect that you'll find your own way to Miami, Miss Felinska.'

'And American politicians still wonder why people find them arrogant and dictatorial.'

Holroyd laughed softly. 'I remember reading your piece entitled – "*Politicians and Psychopaths*". Beautifully argued but ignoring real life.'

For a moment she stood still and opened her mouth to speak. Then she laughed and shook her head as she left.

Back at her hotel she cancelled her flight to Miami and booked herself back on the CU444 flight to London.

She had been back for nearly a week when her agent phoned. 'What happened in Cuba, honey?'

'Nothing special. Why are you asking? I'm just going through my notes. The Americans wouldn't give me a visa to fly direct to Miami. I'll go from here direct.'

'I had a call from my New York agent. The *Washington Post* have backed out. They'll pay the agreed fee and expenses so far and give you a release on whatever you've done already.'

'Why are they backing out at this stage?'

'Officially they say that they now feel that the subject's been overdone.'

'And unofficially somebody's got at them. Who? And why?'

'My little bird hinted that somebody had checked on your contacts in Havana. Thought they were trouble-makers.'

'That's crazy. I had no contacts. I just interviewed people I happened to meet.' She paused. 'Can you place my piece with somebody else?'

'Yeah. No problem, but I suspect you'll have difficulty getting into the States.'

'Don't worry. I'll get in. The bastards.'

'Be very careful, my dear. Washington seem very touchy about Cuba these days.' She paused. 'How are things with you anyway?'

'I'm OK. I'm going to have a look at Poland. My father says there's a lot going on there at the moment. They've got a new political slogan – *solidarnosc*.'

'What's the angle?'

'That ordinary working-people can beat the professional politicians providing they stick together.'

There was a laugh at the other end of the line.

'You really are the limit. Come and see me soon.'

Katya Felinska had made her way down to Miami via the Canadian border and a tourist trip to Niagara Falls. She had stayed a week and had covered what she wanted. She flew home on a holiday charter with spare seats. Nobody bothered too much about checking passports for tourist flights, and she still had her original US visa which was valid for another month.

The piece she wrote and some of the photographs appeared as a six-page spread in *Der Spiegel* and in *Paris Match*. Both of which were far superior to the *Washington Post* in her opinion. She guessed that most likely it was the CIA who had put their two-pennorth in with the *Post*. Hoping that the world had forgotten their abortive games in the Bay of Pigs operation. And the recently revealed crazy plans to poison Fidel Castro. She had touched on these points but her main theme had been about the cruelty of big nations who put sanctions on dictators in the name of justice but left the dictator in his luxury and the ordinary people starving and desperate. Her piece wasn't even-handed but at least all the facts were true.

Chapter Twenty-Five

'And that was Charles Trenet singing in that sexy voice of his '*La chanson des rues*'. You've got one more record to take to the desert island but before that a couple more questions.' Sue Lawley paused and said quietly. 'What would you want to be if you weren't a photo-journalist?'

'Nothing,' she said quickly. 'For me it's like saying who would I rather be than myself. I'm one of those lucky people who knew right from the start what I wanted to be. I've no qualifications for doing anything else.' She laughed. 'I guess I've no qualifications for doing what I do either. It's just how I was born.'

'Ah well. Thank heaven you don't have to make such a choice.' She paused. 'Not tempted by filming?'

Katya laughed. 'I'd better be careful what I say in case my father hears it. But no. For me filming is artificial. Directors and cameramen decide what's going to happen. It's contrived, not real.' She paused. 'I'm not explaining myself very well but when I take photographs I've given no directions nor arranged anything. Certainly not posed people. I just record what my eye sees of what's there.'

'Does it depress you that so much of what you see is so terrible?'

'It angers me rather than depresses me.'

'What are you most trying to put over?'

'I don't feel "put over" is the right description. What I want to do is make people think of what's in the picture. Not just the girl holding her long-dead baby but what she does after I've gone and nobody's looking at her. Where can she go? Will she find something to eat? Will they kill her or just rape her before she dies of starvation?'

Sue Lawley said quietly, 'Are you religious at all?'

'No. Not really. But I treasure that wonderful piece from St Matthew – "Blessed are the meek for they shall inherit the earth – blessed are the peacemakers for they shall be called the children of God – blessed are those that mourn, for they shall be comforted."' She paused. 'Nobody has laid out the virtues so well and so memorably.'

'And God?'

She paused. 'I couldn't believe in a God after what I've seen. I'm afraid I go along with Mary McCarthy who said, "If that's what God's all about I wouldn't ask him to tea."'

Lawley said, 'For the benefit of our listeners I must say my guest is smiling.' She pauses. 'And now your last record.'

'It's an old Viennese song called "*Sag beim abschied*". It says you don't have to say goodbye as if it were for ever. Just say "*abschied*" and we'll meet again. Same time, same place.'

As the music came up Sue Lawley smiled across at her guest and waited for the couple of minutes for the music to fade.

'"*Sag beim abschied*"? And now a luxury. Nothing useful. What shall it be?'

'An open airline ticket, first-class or at least business class, to fly to anywhere I choose to go to after I'm rescued.'

'And one book apart from the bible and Shakespeare which are already there.'

'I'd choose one of my mother's books. One she wrote for me for my fifth birthday. It's called – *The two white doves*.'

'*The two white doves* by Gina Felinska. So – Katya Felinska, thank you for talking to us and choosing your favourite records.'

'Thanks for having me.'

Chapter Twenty-Six

Dealing with the wretched man Laufer meant that Bekker had to fly to Moscow to see what Serov wanted to do about it.

As Bekker related the facts that came from the interrogation of Laufer, Serov could hardly believe what he was hearing.

'You mean that Kuznetsov, the head of the KGB in Berlin, actually gave permission for this man Laufer to carry out surveillance on you?'

'I think he not only gave permission but actually initiated the operation.'

'What's Laufer's background?'

'He was German intelligence. The BND. Just did leg-work and routine checking. Thrown out for taking bribes and minor blackmail scams.'

'Who did he send his reports about you to?'

'Nothing in writing. He reported verbally to Kuznetsov.'

'But Laufer didn't follow you when you went into West Berlin?'

'No. I don't think he could. I think there's a warrant still outstanding on him.'

'So what did he cover?'

'Just reported on where I went. Nothing of any use to anyone.

I think Kuznetsov was not best pleased with what he got.'

'Where's Laufer now?'

'At the safe-house under close arrest.'

'Did Kuznetsov give Laufer any hints about what he was looking for?'

'No. Just routine surveillance.'

'Did he sign receipts for his payment?'

'No, it was all cash and Kuznetsov paid Laufer himself.'

'Right. I'll deal with Kuznetsov, the cheeky bastard, and I'll send a guard escort to take charge of Laufer.'

'What'll you do with him?'

Serov smiled. 'He can help with the cleaning-up around Chernobyl. A couple of years will do him good.'

'And Kuznetsov?'

'We're starting a two-man KGB detachment on the Mongolian border. Just a little device to show the Chinese we still care about the frontier. The nearest village is about two hundred kilometres away. A great place for contemplation.' He paused. 'Have you told your contact about all this?'

'Not yet. I told him I was being watched in case it was his people playing games.'

'What was his reaction?'

Bekker laughed. 'He said it was probably Moscow checking on me.'

Serov smiled a bored smile. 'D'you think that there's any chance that Laufer has seen you with our contact?'

'No. Definitely not. We meet the other side of the Wall and not in public.'

When, a couple of months later, Max Inman casually asked about the man who'd been watching Bekker, Bekker had shrugged and said he'd passed him over to the Stasis and left it to them to decide what to do with him.

Bekker realised that his operation with the Brit must be

high-priority in Dzerdzhinski Square for Serov to be acting so decisively. Heads of KGB organisations in foreign countries were top men and peremptorily removing one was an unusual step.

It was after one of their regular meetings at Inman's place that they had sat around talking in general as Inman arranged the pieces on the chess-board. Bekker was a good average player but Inman always won. And he did it so casually. No long intervals of indecision, he seemed to know exactly how a game would go. Even when he gave Bekker a rook to even things up.

Inman had just mated Bekker's king for the second time when Bekker leaned back in his chair and looked at Inman.

'Who taught you how to play chess?'

Inman shrugged. 'Nobody really. I read a few books and learned the basics and I just started playing. I don't think I've improved much from when I started.' He paused. 'Can I ask you a personal question?'

'Sure. But I might not answer it. Go ahead.'

'What's your real name, Otto? Your Russian name.'

For a few moments Bekker looked away towards the window and then back to Inman's face.

'Chebrikov. Alexander.'

'Any relationship to the famous Mikhailovich Chebrikov?'

'My uncle, but I've never met him. My father dislikes him and KGB in general. So when Mikki became head of the KGB that ended all contact. My mother gets on with his family quite well. She treated the youngest daughter for meningitis.' He paused. 'The KGB doesn't encourage you to have friends so you end up with a strange bunch of characters. Like it or not you're a loner. Even my parents I keep at a distance. It's safer for them and easier for me. But I'm not a natural loner.'

'I guess it's just part of our jobs. Just one of those things, like the song says. And there are benefits.'

'Like what?'

'We live pretty independent lives. We've got an insider's view of what's going on in the world. Our jobs aren't routine – and brains not physical work.'

'Frankly I don't give a damn about what's going on in the world – why should I care – there's nothing I can do about it.'

'You're doing something about it right now. Trying to stop your idiots and my idiots from starting a war because of some stupid misinterpretation of the facts.'

Bekker smiled. 'You should either be in a university as a professor or a cabinet minister in your government.'

Max Inman laughed. 'I thought you were a friend, Otto.'

'D'you still think they take notice of what we tell them?'

'I know they do. Like you, I'm surprised. but they do. It's discussed by top people. Not just SIS, but the Foreign Office, the military and the Prime Minister.'

'I think my stuff acts more like a drip-feed. Your people want to know the facts, my lot just want to prove that they're right in their prejudices.'

Inman smiled. 'I have to recommend St Matthew to you again. He said, "A prophet is not without honour, save in his own country and in his own house."' He paused. 'Have you got a translation of the New Testament?'

'No.'

'I'll get you one. It's worth a read.'

Bekker smiled. 'How the Holy Bible saved the Soviet Union from collapse.'

'You've used the word "collapse" several times recently, is that a hint for me?'

'It's the facts as I see them, Max. Maybe "collapse" is the wrong word. It ought to be disintegration.'

'You mean it's imminent?'

'It's already started. Once Gorbachev opened that box of Pandora with *glasnost* and *perestroika* it was like the starter's gun.

We're heading for the end of the Soviet Union. All the states want independence. Georgia, Belorus, Ukraine. You name it. We'll still have Soviet Russia but there won't be a Soviet Union this time next year. Every Soviet state is making plans for independence.'

'And Moscow will go along with this?'

'Eventually, yes. They've got no choice. And they've got no time. It's that or civil wars.'

'Can I pass this onto my people as current Kremlin thinking?'

'Sure. But they must know.'

'I don't think they do. It's not easy to recognise. At least not as certainly as you indicate.'

Bekker shrugged. 'That's how it is. Maybe nobody says it out loud in case they get stuck in the wrong scenario. Anyway, Gorbachev is preaching "freedom" for all, so who's to complain?'

'Why hasn't somebody thrown out Gorbachev?'

'Because he's a tough politician. He knows all the moves and they'd need the Red Army to get rid of him. And right now there are at least three competing groups in the army. The first group to make a move has got the other two against them.'

Max Inman realised that Cooper and Shapiro would want to hear what he was being told as soon as possible.

'Why haven't you mentioned all this before, Otto?'

Bekker shrugged. 'I thought you and your people must know already. Your embassy people in Moscow should have told you.'

'They would probably put it down as just gossip or wishful thinking. Not worth reporting.'

Bekker smiled. 'I've heard they're not very bright.'

'Diplomats never are, or they wouldn't be diplomats.'

'If I need to contact you in the next two or three days will you be around?'

'I'll see that I am.'

*　　*　　*

Cooper was obviously asleep when Inman phoned him but he agreed immediately to come over the next day. He said he might bring Shapiro with him if he was free.

Inman met them in at Tegel and suggested that they talked in the coffee shop before going to his place.

They both listened intently as he told them of what he had learned from his contact. There was a long silence and then it was Joe Shapiro who spoke.

'Did he give you any names, Max, of the instigators of the groups?'

'No. I wouldn't have known who they were anyway.'

'I know there have been meetings in and around the Kremlin but I've not had anything as positive and serious as what you've told us.' He paused. 'Could you possibly ask him to name names? Politicians, military or whoever. People he is sure are planning to make substantial changes.'

'I can ask him.' He paused. 'How long can you stay in Berlin?'

'How long do you need?'

'Two, maybe three, days.'

Shapiro looked at Cooper. 'How about you, Frank? I'll stay as long as it takes but I know you've got meetings and things.'

'If you don't need me positively I'd like to go back today.'

Shapiro looked at Max Inman. 'I'll hang on for a bit to talk to Frank. How about you book me in for a week at Kempinski's and contact me there later today?'

'That's fine.' Inman turned to Cooper. 'Thanks for coming so quickly. I thought it was important.'

Shapiro interrupted. 'If it's even half true it's the most important piece of intelligence we've had in years.'

Bekker had given Max Inman several names but needed another day to check on the latest information.

Inman phoned Joe Shapiro at 8 p.m. and arrived an hour later at Shapiro's hotel room where Shapiro had ordered a meal for the two of them. Inman read out the names from a page of a note-book.

'The first name is a minister in the present cabinet. Named Shevardnadze. Eduard Shevardnadze.' Inman looked at Shapiro. 'He's planning to be head of state when Georgia goes independent.

'The next one is Aliev. Gaidat Aliev. He wants to take over Azerbaidzhan when it goes independent. Doing some big oil deal. Among the military men there's Major General Igor Giorgadze. Then there's a General Lebed aiming for the independence of Moldova. Talks of joining it to Romania in some sort of deal.

'A KGB man named Korzhakov was made bodyguard for a Politburo member named . . .' he glanced at his notes '. . . Yeltsin. Boris Yeltsin. Represents Sverdlovsk where he's got a reputation for running a very tight ship. A bit rough and ready and a bit of a boozer.'

Inman looked at Shapiro. 'Have you ever heard of any of them?'

'Yeah. All of them. But I've heard nothing about those games they're playing.'

'Do the names help?'

'They certainly do. Your man puts together a surprising picture. But totally credible.'

'There was one other thing. My guy says that the military think that the first fighting will be in a place called Chechnia.'

'Any more to come if I hang on for another day?'

'He's going to give me a picture of what the KGB are up to. Sounds pretty rough. I'll have his stuff midday tomorrow. He'd got some checking to do.'

It was midnight as Joe Shapiro went down with him in the elevator to the ground floor. They stopped by the double doors to the bar talking about some recent reshuffling at Century House.

As Shapiro's eyes wandered over the gorgeous hookers sitting at the tables, Inman said, 'They're all Russians. Everybody says they're special.'

'And so they are but the cream of the cream are the Hungarian girls at the Bleibtreu Club.' He patted Inman's arm. 'It's beginning to rain, you'd better get going.'

The phone was ringing when he got back to his rooms. It was Bekker. He was at a café near the cathedral and he wouldn't be able to get back through Charlie that night. He had some new information to pass on that was urgent. Inman told him to come round and stay the night.

Bekker's clothes were soaking wet and Inman gave him a bathrobe and a coffee.

Bekker said, 'I came a couple of hours ago but you were out and I thought I ought to pass on the news as soon as possible.'

'Tell me your news.'

'The third week in November Gorbachev is making an official visit to Italy, and he's been invited to meet the Pope. An official audience. All this is still confidential. But it's probably just a cover for what's really going to happen. There's more and this part is absolutely top-secret. A meeting has been arranged between Bush and Gorbachev to discuss the whole of American-Soviet relations under the new regime. Only six people on each side know what's going to happen. The scenario is that Gorbachev wants to see around Rome and Milan. Privately. Just him and his wife. In fact he will fly to Malta and the actual meetings will take place on a Soviet battleship, the *Slava*. There will be several rounds of talks and the agenda covers everything. Economics, politics, defence and spheres of interest. Some of the sessions will be one to one – just the two presidents and one interpreter.'

Inman was silent for a few moments and then he said, 'I need to make a call so why don't you settle down in the spare bedroom.'

Bekker said, 'If it leaks they'll not rest until they've got the leaker.'

'I'll see to that, Otto. Thanks for what you've done.'

As Inman dialled the Kempinski's number and then asked for Joe Shapiro's room, it passed through his mind that Joe may not be too pleased with a middle of the night call. His gaze had lingered long on the girls in the bar. There was no reply from Joe's room and Inman asked for him to be paged. It was nearly ten minutes before Joe came on the line.

'Shapiro. Who is that?'

'It's me, Joe. I've got some important information but I can't speak freely at the moment.'

'Speak Russian.'

'It wouldn't help.'

'OK. You'd better come back here. I'll be in my room.'

Joe drank a whisky as Max Inman retailed his news. When he was finished Shapiro said, 'This is your usual source, yes?'

'Yes.'

'How does he know this if it's such high security?'

'He didn't want to go into details but I understand that he has a friend, a woman, who is Head of Protocol at the Soviet Embassy in Rome. Way back my man saved her son from going to a labour camp on false charges.'

Shapiro said, 'I can't deal with this here but you need to wait around for that information on the KGB situation in Moscow.' He stood up. 'I'll get an RAF plane back and I'll be back here in a couple of days.' He sighed. 'It looks like the Americans are playing games again.' He shook his head. 'They never learn. They seek allies but are always ready to go it alone if it suits them.' He looked at Inman, slowly shaking his head. 'We're watching the end of a world power and the wrong moves could be disastrous. This is why we trained you and used you, to make sure that we knew what was really going on. However carefully we go we're in for ten years on a roller-coaster and we might as well get used to the idea.' He shrugged and smiled not very amiably. 'See you in a couple of days. God willing.'

A team of six did the checking in London. The *Slava* was a medium-sized cruiser but wasn't in Malta. The only Soviet navy boat in Malta was the *Maxim Gorky*. And she was tied up in the harbour. Test bookings were made in half a dozen hotels and there was plenty of accommodation available from now to New Year.

A member of the Pope's Swiss Guard had told a pretty 'tourist' that there were no official or unofficial state visits to the Vatican until the New Year.

The Maltese President was due to be visiting relations in Chicago in December and the Prime Minister and his 'companion' were booked into Claridges in London for the first three weeks in December.

No special security arrangements had been made at Fiumicino Airport, for the Maltese President's visit. And there were no official appointments apart from a possible visit to Mother Teresa.

Shapiro, Cooper and Rimmer talked for hours but ended up convinced that the apparent absence of any arrangements for a visit to Malta by Gorbachev only gave credence to Inman's information. But why Malta? Malta hadn't been a venue for international conferences since World War Two. And why should they meet on a warship? Maybe, because it would be outside Malta's territorial waters, it could be considered as a neutral venue. Whatever the answers were they would act as if it were going to happen. There was work to be done by the ambassador and his personal team in Washington which might puzzle him because he would have no idea why Whitehall should suddenly want to cuddle up with the White House.

In the last week in November, the *Slava* anchored four miles out from Valletta harbour, and President Gorbachev and his wife, Raisa, flew in on an Aeroflot Ilyushin 62. The *USS Belknap* had weighed anchor a mile from the Soviet warship.

The *Maxim Gorky* was already tied up in Valletta harbour to serve as a hotel and base for the Soviet President's entourage. In the event the only change to the proceedings was that the sea was too rough to take the two statesmen and their parties to the *Slava* and they had agreed to hold the meetings on the *Maxim Gorky* in Valletta harbour.

Apart from a certain resentment and irritation with the White House playing a solo game with the Soviet Union there was nothing to alarm the Brits in the information they had received or in the events themselves. What really did matter was the positive proof that Inman's source was the real thing. They had been accurately informed, in advance, of names and meetings that were intended to be top-secret. It was decided that Operation Janus and its flow of information, no matter whether it was routine or vital, would now be routinely made available to the Prime Minister and the Foreign Secretary. Operation Janus didn't, even unofficially, exist beyond the small control group in SIS, the PM, and the Foreign Secretary. But the importance of Max Inman's work was recognised by upgrading him to the same grade as Cooper and Shapiro. It made little difference to their relationships but it meant that Inman no longer had to 'sell' his information to the others. His judgment of what was worth passing on was enough.

Chapter Twenty-Seven

Katya had been asked to give a talk to the Students' Union at Cambridge and Max had gone with her. They got there a day early so that they could see their old rooms. But this time they'd taken a double-room at the Garden House Hotel.

After lunch they had gone back to sit on the bank of the river where they had first realised that they were going to be more than just friends. He had been thoughtful enough to buy a half-bottle of champagne but not thoughtful enough to bring at least one glass for them to drink from. She had laughed as they took turns drinking their champagne from the bottle. She saw it as typical of the man. Thoughtful enough to buy the champagne to celebrate but finding the niceties of how you drink it as totally irrelevant.

As she drank the last drop and laid the bottle on the grass she said, 'What sort of social life do you have in Berlin?'

He shrugged. 'Intentionally, none. Sometimes I have to go to some do because of a story but otherwise I keep away from the so-called social stuff. I find it totally boring.'

'Isn't that a bit arrogant? Surely they aren't all bores.'

'You could be right. But half the time I don't understand what they're talking about, and if I do understand I wish I didn't.'

'What do they talk about?'

'The same as social idiots talk about over here. TV soaps, game shows with big prizes, the weather, the rise or fall of the D.Mark and the problem of getting reliable servants.' He paused. 'They genuinely don't know what's going on in Europe and the Soviet Union. They hear that there's a lot of turmoil in East Germany but that's the East Germans' worry not theirs. They shouldn't have voted Communist.'

She looked at his face and said softly, 'Has the other work got in the way of the journalism?'

He shrugged. 'Maybe. But I still do a few pieces.'

'Just enough to keep your cover?'

He smiled. 'Am I getting to be a bore myself?'

She shook her head. 'No, my love, you'll never be a bore. Not for me anyway. But one has to be careful not to let an interest become an obsession.'

He sighed. 'You're right of course. But we're living in sensational times and I'm amazed that most people don't seem to have the foggiest idea of where we are heading.' He paused. 'Most people take it that life will just go on as it always has. A touch on the tiller here and there, and tomorrow will be much like today.'

'And where do you think we're heading?'

'It's crazy but I could tell you more surely what is going to happen in Moscow than I can tell you about us and the Americans.'

'And what's going to happen in Moscow?'

'It's not just Moscow, it's the Soviet Union itself. It's collapsing and if we make a wrong move the West could be involved in it.'

'What about all that Gorbachev magic?'

'He won't last. They're all fighting for power and he doesn't really matter any longer. He's a first-class diplomat and a shrewd politician but he's not equipped for the tough guys who are just waiting for the right moment to get rid of him. He's made all the right moves but the timing's all wrong. It's greed and power that matter now.' He shrugged. 'The first time in decades that they've had a real reformer and they see him as a fool.'

'What are our people going to do?'

'God knows. They're only just beginning to realise that what I warned them was about to happen is actually happening. All they can usefully do right now is sit on the side-lines and resist the temptation to stir things up.' He shrugged. 'The East Germans will be the first. The Austrian and West German embassies behind the Iron Curtain have hundreds of East German refugees camping out in their gardens and the embassy buildings are virtual refugee camps. Something's going to give – and soon.'

'Is there anything to be done to stop it?'

'Nobody wants to stop it and it's now like a tidal wave. Nobody could stop it even if they wanted to.' He shook his head. 'All I can do is try to keep our people informed. There's so much happening that there's no time to analyse it.'

'You sound like you need a break, my love.'

'And what would that do? Just stop the flow of information.'

'You could go back to being an observer not a participant.' She smiled. 'You've got to learn not to inhale.'

He laughed. 'Hark who's talking. The cool, calm photographer who shows us all how it is and only sheds tears at home because there's nothing else she can do.' He looked at his watch. 'We'd better get going or they'll be scared you've forgotten about the talk.' He smiled. 'What's the title of the talk?'

'"Where to go for your holiday".' She stood up, smiling. 'Where would you choose?'

'God knows.'

She laughed. 'I suspect he needs a holiday too.'

He watched her as she stood up from her seat and walked across to where the chairman of the Students' Union had introduced her. Even very distinguished academics and celebrities from the arts usually didn't get more than a reasonable hand-clap but Katya was a favourite and much loved. She smiled and bowed at the standing ovation. When it died down she raised the microphone on its stand.

'My friends, you said I could choose my own subject and some of you who know me well will have been surprised – and even disappointed at my choice.' She smiled. 'Have no fear. I have, like so many alumni of this wonderful place who come back later, abused your generosity in the name of a virtue.' She paused. 'Let me explain. My subject's title is "Where do I recommend you go for a holiday". A simple enough title. A normal domestic problem. But only normal if you ignore the facts of life.' She paused. 'The title arose because two friends of mine were discussing their summer holiday. The girl said she would like to try Turkey. A nice sandy beach on the coast. But the guy was horrified and claimed that he couldn't enjoy a holiday spent in a country that imprisoned and tortured its own people without trial. A country that is trying to destroy the Turkish Human Rights Association, the HRA.' Katya paused. 'My girl-friend conceded the point and then quite innocently threw a bomb into the discussion by saying, "So. Where shall we go that's OK? You tell me." Her boy-friend turned to me and said, "You decide. You know where it's OK to go".' Katya paused. 'I understand from my own man that in the game of cricket there's a way of bowling the ball as if it's going to do one thing but in fact does something else very nasty and gets you out. My guy tells me it's called a "googly". But if you're a photo-journalist who operates from time to time among psychopaths in ragged uniforms, a googly is par for the course. So I took a deep breath while I pondered the answer. I have to tell you that a deep breath wasn't enough. Ten thousand deep breaths aren't enough. Let me prove it. Let's forget me giving a talk. Let's combine forces, you and me, and see if we can find an answer to the real question – Where in the world can I have a holiday without ignoring what's happened to my fellow human beings?' She looked eagerly towards the audience. 'Suggestions please.'

A young man stood up. 'What about a safari? Just you and me and the lions?'

'Are you or have you ever been, to coin a phrase, a member of a students' union?'

The young man half stood. 'Of course.'

'Well, you'd have a real bad time. The Kenya government has expelled all Students' Union people from Moi University. And I'm sure you saw the newsreel shots of Richard Leakey's bare back with deep welts from a leather whip. He spoke during the elections against the corruption of the government.' She paused. 'You could of course have a real adventure holiday in Uganda, where they don't torture enemies of the state. They just kill them outright. We supply their army and police with tear-gas. It says "Made in Britain" on the canisters. Tear-gas first and then beatings until there's nothing left to beat.' She smiled. 'Next please.'

When nobody offered a new name, she said, 'Not Mexico where the police treat killing children as a kind of birth control. Not Myanman where you too could be a beautiful girl in prison or house arrest just for saying it might be a good idea to try democracy. Rwanda you can't bear thinking about where half a million unarmed civilians were slaughtered because they spoke the wrong dialect. Stick to Swahili my friends. Bosnia – forget it. We all know what happened there and is still happening.' She paused. 'Sadly there is no place I can recommend for a guilt-free holiday. Half the world population are refugees or wish they were. And for what? For some religion, some tribal incident before Christ, Mahomet or the Buddha were born. Dollars, oil, diamonds, gold, water, drugs – and power. The psychos will kill you and laugh while you scream for mercy for a baby, for a child, for your wife or for yourself.' She took a deep breath. 'I'll have to stop, but I'll answer one more question so long as it's not – what can we do about it?' She paused. 'Because I don't know the answer.' She waited for a question but no question came. She said, 'Thanks for being so patient with me.' She looked around briefly and then hurried back to where he was standing. She was crying as his arms went round her, her head on his shoulders, shaking it in despair. The silence in the room was a kind of applause. The applause of despair.

They ate alone at the hotel and then he took her for a walk along the river until they found the Clare bridge again. When they got back to the hotel there were a dozen or so young people waiting to buy her a drink. She was touched and obviously cheered by their friendliness.

It was just beginning to get light when she got out of bed and slid into a silk dressing-gown. She looked at her watch as she stood by the big windows that overlooked the river. It was 3.15 a.m. and already the sun was gilding the roofs of the buildings on the other side of the river.

She half-turned to look at Max Inman who lay with his face towards the windows, one hand cradling his cheek. There was a book on the bed-side table. It was Solzhenitsyn's *The First Circle* in the original Russian and only recently published. She smiled to herself. She was more impressed by Pasternak and *Doctor Zhivago*. Pasternak didn't just question Stalin but the very legitimacy of the Revolution. Sometimes when he talked in his sleep Max Inman spoke in Russian but that night he had been muttering '*To be or not to be*' in German. *Sein oder nicht sein, das ist doch die Frage.* He didn't sound agitated. But Max was never agitated; always calm and uninvolved. But the picture he had painted of things in the Soviet Union had obviously disturbed him. It was strange that they were both caring people but they cared in such different ways. Max cared for humanity *en masse* but for her the cataclysms of wars and warfare left her merely angry and disgusted. What she cared about was individuals. As somebody had once said of her, 'only one dead baby at a time'.

She moved across to sit at the coffee table where she had left her gadget bag. The Velcro partition spacers needed to be adjusted and she used a camel-hair artist's brush to dust the camera body and the three lenses. The 24–200 zoom was big and heavy. Heavier than the camera body itself but it produced such sharp pictures that it had become almost a permanent fixture on the F90X Nikon. There were two other lenses, a 50 mm. and a smaller zoom. An SB22 flash in a neat leather case was pushed in with a dozen films already unpacked from their boxes. She still carried the small manual for the camera and three sealed batteries. Handling photographic equipment was always a pleasure. She never went anywhere without a camera even if it was only the small compact Contax T2. The compact had certainly earned its keep in some awkward situations where brandishing a Nikon or a Leica could make you an object of suspicion for half-crazed drunken soldiers looking for another victim to add to the day's score.

She slept for two hours before the maid brought them their breakfast trays. He had left for Berlin on the evening plane.

Chapter Twenty-Eight

Bekker's report to Inman on the turmoil in the KGB Moscow was as confused and vague as the actual situation.

'Any idea of who's running the rival groups?'

'No. My guy Serov is controlled by Abramov. Yevgeny Abramov. But there will be people above Abramov involved. The man who the gossip says is leading the other faction is a man named Ustinov. Viktor Ustinov. He's the top man for internal operations.'

'What kind of internal operations?'

'Operations against suspected subversives. Individuals and groups. He covers the whole scene of internal security including politicians, the military, the KGB itself and military intelligence, the GRU. He's anti-Gorbachev and has been right from the start. He's got all the influence and power he needs to do whatever he wants.'

'And who's above Abramov?'

Bekker shrugged. 'I'm only guessing but I'd say it's either Krasnov or Grechko.'

'Are they pro-Gorbachev?'

'No. Nobody's pro-Gorbachev. But they all realise that it's gone too far to put the cork back in the bottle. They're just staking out the battleground.'

'To do what?'

'To take over.'

'Could they do it?'

'They could destroy what's there but it's no good taking over a crumbling machine when you don't have any idea of how to put it together again. The thugs and the criminals will move in from day one. At least they know how to make things go the way they want.'

'And where does this leave the Party and socialism?'

'They're going to be just a chapter in the history books, Max.' He paused. 'You and I are probably wasting our time.'

'That's for others to decide. Who knows what's going to happen? All this intrigue could be no more than wishful thinking. Chaos is one thing, war's another. That's what we cooperated for – to avoid a war because of sheer ignorance of the real situation.' He smiled. 'I'll take care of you, Otto. No matter what happens.'

Chapter Twenty-Nine

Ustinov was a big, powerfully-built man who dominated any meeting. Self-confident and impatient, he was not a man to argue with even if you were right. He had arranged for them to meet at his *dacha* in Peredelkino. The others there were Sokolov whose official brief was surveillance of all members of the Politburo and their associates, Sverdlov who was the KGB's top administrator including all budgets, and Yazov who covered surveillance of the military and was responsible for the internal surveillance of all KGB officers above the rank of major. Between them they controlled the intentions of at least half the wielders of influence in the Soviet Union.

They had spent the morning comparing notes on the backing they had achieved from their contacts and supporters. The last item on the agenda was the question of Serov and his informant. It was Ustinov himself who answered the problem.

'Abramov won't even admit that Serov has a special source but it's obvious that the Kremlin see it as a major asset. And they're keeping it inside their little circle.'

'What's the position in Berlin now?'

'I ordered Kuznetsov to put an unofficial surveillance on Serov's man in Berlin. I reckon he's the contact with the other side. It turns out he was limited in what he could do with the

Kraut they appointed. It turned out that he couldn't even risk going into West Berlin because they had warrants out for him from the BND, the German intelligence people.

'Eventually Serov, who's a very experienced operator, realised what was going on and had him put under surveillance. He used his status with the Stasis and eventually had him arrested. They gave him the treatment and of course the bastard talked. Told them he was hired, paid for by Kuznetsov, and reported solely to him. Kuznetsov denied it all of course but Serov got Abramov to move Kuznetsov to some clapped-out detachment on the Chinese border. I stopped the move but Serov doesn't know that. I've put Kuznetsov on hold for the moment.' He smiled. 'And I've got the Kraut stashed away in a labour camp.' He paused. 'He's not going to be a problem. The problem's Serov and his fellow. Calls himself Bekker. Otto Bekker, but in fact his name's Chebrikov, Alexander Chebrikov . . .' he smiled at the others, Chebrikov was the overall boss of the KGB, '. . . yeah. The old man is his uncle but they're not on speaking terms. Some problem with the old man's brother, our chap's father.' He sighed. 'I've had it on good grounds that Serov doesn't know the contact's name or anything about him.' He paused. 'But he's the one we've got to squeeze — Bekker.' He looked around at the others. 'Any ideas?'

It was Yazov who spoke. 'How far are you prepared to go, Viktor?'

'We don't have any choice, comrade. Serov and his stooge have got more influence in the Kremlin right now than Gorbachev himself. And it's going straight to the top. No filtering on the way. They tell me that those close to Gorbachev say that it's as good as having a direct line into what the Brits and the Americans are thinking. What their reactions will be to every contingency from getting rid of Gorbachev to pressing the button for the final showdown.'

It was Yazov who spoke again and even in that tense

environment his words were barely audible. 'There won't ever be a final showdown, Viktor. You know that.' He waved his arm at the others. 'We all know it. We've already lost the arms race to the Yanks, the banks are without real money and the people and the military wouldn't cooperate. I can tell you that right now.'

'And we just sit on our arses while Serov and his stooge pass the word back to London and Washington. Yes?' He paused. 'How long have we got?'

'Two months, maybe three.'

'So we take out Serov and his Bekker guy and squeeze the bastards until they tell us who this Brit is.'

'And then?'

'We take him too.'

'And when he goes back?'

'He won't go back – ever. Not unless he goes along with us. Meantime things here in Moscow will be calmer. They'll know where they all stand.'

'And where will they stand?'

'Back to the old days. No frigging *perestroika* and no frigging *glasnost*. Back to being a power, my friend, not a bloody spectator.'

'Do they know who Bekker is?'

'I don't know. I doubt it. It's been very high security. None of our people know even the cover name of the Brit who's working with Serov's man.'

'When are you going to pick up Serov and Bekker?'

'As soon as a chance comes to do it discreetly.'

'Who's going to do it?'

Ustinov smiled. 'I've put together a little team. All experienced at playing games.'

'Where will you hold them?'

'I shan't touch Serov until I'm sure we need him. But the Bekker fellow will go into one of the Berlin safe-houses that

Kuznetsov's got.' He shrugged his heavy shoulders. 'I'll deal with all that, don't worry.'

Ustinov stayed at the *dacha* and the others drove back to Moscow. It was beginning to snow.

It was Yazov on the back-seat of the car who eventually asked the question. 'Do you think our friend, Ustinov, knows what he's doing?'

Sverdlov said quietly, 'We'll soon find out, my friends. He's not a planner, our Viktor, but he's pretty good at getting what he wants.'

And that was how they left it. There were too many other things going on to spend much time on one little episode. Especially when the only reward success could bring was stopping the flow of background information between some people in Moscow and London. But Ustinov was a man who needed action and they might as well humour him. If things worked out the way they were going, Ustinov wouldn't matter when they had taken over.

Two of Ustinov's 'team' picked up Bekker a couple of nights later when he was on his way to the club to pick up his girl-friend. It was smoothly done and he was in the back seat of the black Mercedes before he realised what was happening. The hand clamped over his mouth and nose was pressing the pad soaked with old-fashioned chloroform and the last thing he saw was the lights of Alexanderplatz tilting and turning as he lost consciousness.

Fifteen minutes later the Merc turned into a narrow court-yard alongside a double garage whose living space for a chauffeur was an apartment with steel bars on the windows and no access apart from the courtyard. All the rooms inside were heavily sound-proofed but the apartment itself was well-decorated, brightly painted and spotlessly clean. The most noticeable oddity was the very large bathroom that was ceramic-tiled all over, floor, walls and ceiling. Men seemed unaware or unconcerned at the apartment's rather strange atmosphere. One of its temporary inhabitants had dismissed its strangeness sweepingly by assessing it as 'just a place to change your shirt before you went back into the real world'. Not even a hard-pressed East Berlin woman would have described it as home.

The team made no move on Bekker's apartment because his girl-friend lived there too. They could check it over when she was at work at the club. She wouldn't be alarmed that he didn't come home for he was frequently away in Moscow and other places. For her he was safe because he was a Stasi officer.

The man in the blue sweater sat watching Bekker as he lay on the bed, stirring fitfully as the effect of the anaesthetic gradually wore off. It was a ritual the watcher was used to. First the stirring, then the vomiting and finally the eyes opening, staring at the ceiling as they tried to remember what had happened. Then the slow realisation that they were in trouble.

Bekker groaned as he opened his eyes and struggled in vain to sit up. He turned his face to look at the man and said slowly and indistinctly, 'Where am I? What happened?' It was the standard dialogue from every cops and robbers film ever made.

The man in the blue sweater didn't answer. It was pointless anyway. It would be another hour before Bekker could talk coherently. Another man brought him a ham sandwich and a mug of coffee. Real coffee. The team always lived well. Keeping up the standards was good for discipline. Like the weapons instructors always said, 'a man should be like his gun — clean, bright and slightly oiled'. They'd go through the standard routine and then, if he wasn't giving them what they wanted, they'd take the girl and his parents. It was just a question of time and Ustinov had briefed them thoroughly. There was no real rush but a couple of months was the outside.

✳   ✳   ✳

Max Inman sat in his armchair with his feet up on a chair from the kitchen. He looked at his watch. It was far beyond Bekker's usual time and he had never missed a Sunday meeting before unless it had been arranged beforehand.

He turned back to his reading. It was a thin volume of Russian poetry. Mandelstamm or somebody had once said, 'Russia is the only place where poetry is really important. They'll kill people for it here.' Maybe he could end his days translating poetry and try and explain that translations could never be as good as a good original. They had to fight it out on the page – the original that was too good to be filleted with a translation that didn't do it justice. Or a translation that was so good that the translator was the real poet and the original just a vague prod of a memory. But English and Russian lent themselves well to translation. Yevtushenko had once said, 'Poetry translation is like a woman. If it's beautiful, it's not faithful, and if it's faithful, it's not beautiful.' Max smiled. Maybe they'd let him have a *dacha* just outside Moscow. Peredelkino would do. And he's spend his days translating Russian and English poetry just as now he tried to translate their thinking and their philosophies. Maybe Pasternak's wonderful translations of Shakespeare were the exceptions that proved the rule. But people who loved Yeats, Eliot, Pound and Auden would find their like with Akhmatova, Pasternak and Mandelstamm.

Inman phoned Katya's number but there was no answer. Not even the machine.

Chapter Thirty

It was four hours before Bekker came to and as he struggled to sit up he realised that his hands were shackled to the metal frame of the bed. As he lay back he could just see the man sitting on the chair watching him. He was shocked when the man spoke to him in Russian. Not Moscow Russian but fluent with an accent that could have been from one of the occupied countries. Latvia maybe, or Estonia. The man asked him his name and for a few moments Bekker wondered if he should pretend that he couldn't understand Russian. As a compromise he said nothing.

The man said quietly, 'We need to talk, Comrade Chebrikov.' He paused. 'You know the rules of the game as well as I do, comrade. And you'll know that they always do talk. It's just how long it takes. The longer it takes, the more painful the process. If that's how you want to play it, it's all the same to me. I've got all the time in the world.'

Bekker hesitated for a few moments and then said, 'Who are you?' And he said it in Russian.

The man in the blue sweater stood up slowly. He was tall and well-built and he had deep brown eyes. The kind of eyes that were supposed to be indications of a gentle, loving nature. He stood at the side of the bed looking down at Bekker.

'Who's your contact man with the English?'

Bekker shook his head slowly. 'I don't know what you mean.'

The big man grabbed a handful of Bekker's shirt, lifting him up before slamming his head against the wall. The big man knew from long experience that you mustn't break the jaws or damage the throats of men who you wanted to talk. It was easily done and caused a lot of pain but it hindered the talking.

Bekker vomited but the big man knew that that was just an after-effect from the chloroform. Grabbing Bekker's hair he twisted his face around to look up at him.

'Don't be stupid man. Just answer the questions.'

But Otto Bekker was well-trained and tougher than he looked, and two hours later, despite the bruised face and the broken fingers, he still hadn't talked. But he'd screamed a lot and the big man knew that that was at least a beginning.

Four days later the big man had phoned Ustinov on the secure line but they had both been cautious about what they said.

'Who do you want first, the male or the female?'

'Both at the same time. And I'll need the tapes.'

'What about the girl-friend?'

'We'll deal with her. She's no problem.'

Max Inman had a weekly mandatory phone call to Cooper. A standard routine to establish that everything was as expected. No matter what was happening or that there was nothing to report, a mandatory call was just that — mandatory. Bekker had not turned up for the second Sunday meeting, Inman had mentioned it to Cooper who pointed out that their friend could have the 'flu or be on a trip somewhere else. No names or places were ever mentioned and Cooper didn't seem concerned. They both knew that the only contact they had with Bekker was the telephone number and that was currently just ringing until the auto-control cut the call off. Cooper had had the number checked-out way back in the hope that they could get at least an idea of the exchange that the number used. But nothing had come of it. Official records said that there was no such number. That meant that it was almost certainly KGB controlled.

The big man in the blue sweater had been careful not to damage Bekker's face. They might need at some time to have him in public looking normal even if he had broken ribs under his clothes and bruises all over his body with open wounds from modest blows with a leather strap. The four men never used their names and referred to themselves by the colour of their sweaters. One of them, the one in the red sweater, had taken no part in the beatings. For several days he was Bekker's guard and the only member of the team who had any contact with him.

Bekker had been in the room for over three weeks and his early defiance had gone. Beaten out of him. As he lay on the bed with his eyes closed the man in the red sweater said quietly. 'You know they've got your parents and the girl.' Bekker turned his head slowly to look at the man.

'What do you mean?'

'They've been arrested and they're being questioned.'

'Questioned about what?'

'Don't go back to those old games, comrade. You are in custody as an enemy of the State. Guilty of treason. They are accomplices of yours.'

'For God's sake. They know nothing about any of my work. My mother's a neuro-surgeon and my father's an academic. And the girl is just an ordinary girl who acts as a hostess in a night-club. If I was a traitor are those the kind of people I'd have as my collaborators? For God's sake. You people must be mad.'

'They will say anything we want them to say. I've got tapes you should hear of their latest interrogation sessions.' He paused. 'Do you want to hear them?'

'No.'

The man smiled. 'I think you should.'

He stood up and walked over to the table where there were several pieces of electronic equipment and a pair of small speakers. Bekker saw him making some adjustments to what looked like a piece of hi-fi equipment but without the knobs and buttons. There was just one large knob and a pair of up-down switches. The man turned briefly to Bekker and nodded.

'Tell me if it's too loud.'

Turning back to look at Bekker the man in the red sweater pressed just one of the switches.

At first Bekker couldn't make out what was going on and then he recognised his mother's voice and a man questioning her roughly. Who was her son's English contact? What were they doing? His mother saying that her son was a KGB officer and she knew nothing about his work. She didn't even know where he was. There was a few moments of blank tape and then his mother's voice, screaming, begging them to stop. The sound of blows on flesh and his mother's hysterical voice, crying as she pleaded with them to stop. The man switched off the recorder and turned to look at Bekker, dragging a chair over to the side of the bed.

'They've got your mother and your father. They're having a bad time because they're not helping us. We can stop questioning them if you talk with us.' He shrugged. 'Why not save them any further trouble? Just talk.' He paused again. 'We've traced your girl-friend but we haven't picked her up yet.'

Bekker looked at the man's face. 'Who's in charge of you people?'

'D'you want to talk?'

Bekker didn't answer and the man left the room. Bekker heard the heavy key turn in the lock in the heavy metal door.

A few minutes later the man in the red sweater came into the room. Standing, looking at Bekker's bruised body before he sat down on the chair beside the bed.

'Are you ready to talk?'

'Tell me who you people are?' He paused. 'You do know that I'm a KGB officer, don't you?'

The man smiled. 'You were, comrade. Right now you're just a man who's guilty of treason. An enemy of the State.'

'Do you know Serov? Major Serov?'

'Forget Serov and forget Abramov. They can't help you. You're on your own now. And you're no longer KGB.'

'Are you KGB?'

'We're just here to talk to you about your contacts with the English.'

'Why don't you ask Moscow? Or are you so illegal you daren't contact them?'

'Your parents have both asked us to tell you that they'll be sent to labour camps if you don't talk.'

'You must be under orders from Kuznetsov.'

The man smiled. 'You must be joking.' He paused. 'Just think about your position. And your parents and the girl. Forget the old loyalties. They don't exist any longer.' He stood up and looked down at Bekker. 'We'll talk again tomorrow.'

'What about my parents – and the girl?'

'I'll arrange for them to have a couple of days without interrogation.'

After he had left, the blue sweater man came in with a plastic jug of warm milk mixed with some powdered food substitute. He spooned it slowly into Bekker's mouth until Bekker turned his head away. Bekker lay back, his ribs and his arms inflamed and swollen.

He lay back with his eyes closed, desperately trying to sort out some clue from what he had learned. They must be insiders because they not only knew Serov's name but Abramov too. That made Serov and Abramov either their allies or their enemies. From the way they spoke he reckoned that they were enemies. But how did he come into it? Serov had told him the last time they met that Gorbachev himself had said that the information from Serov's operation was of real assistance in making decisions that could affect relations with the West. The freedom of action that Moscow had given him was an indication in itself of its importance.

He remembered that way back he had been on a course for field-operators who ran intelligence networks. There had been a talk on how to cope with being caught and interrogated by the enemy. The instructor had said that they should resist any pressures including torture and say nothing for forty-eight hours so that the other members of the network could be warned. He remembered too that it sounded phoney to him. Forty-eight hours from when? Not from the time of arrest, for how the hell would they know that you'd been picked up. Most agents were in custody for at least a week before it was known that they were out of the game.

But through all that crazy thinking he couldn't wipe out the sounds of his mother's voice pleading with them. Begging them to leave her alone. Maybe they had done what they sometimes did and faked the voice and the screams. He was beginning to sweat from the pain in his chest. He didn't even know their names. Their only identification was the colour of their sweaters. They even referred themselves just to the 'guy in the blue sweater' or some other colour. He was sure by now that they weren't ethnic Russians but from one of the occupied Baltic countries. Their accents and their crude speech made them foreigners despite their fluency. Who would hire such people when, if he was a problem, they could just have posted him 'somewhere else' or given him a different job.

Viktor Ustinov was a man of action and sometimes such men mistook mere movement for action. When he had decided to intervene in Serov's operation he was undecided as to whether it was better to go for Serov or his boss, Abramov. He decided on Serov.

They had picked up Serov as he left his office. There was no rough stuff apart from bundling him into the back of the big Zil. He'd asked what it was all about and they'd just smiled. Serov saw that they were heading out of Moscow and going west. It was beginning to get light when they pulled up at a farmhouse with its lights blazing.

He had been out of circulation for nearly two weeks before Abramov realised that he wasn't around. They had chosen a time when Abramov was stuck in days of meetings about the re-organisation of the KGB and its possible absorption of military intelligence, the GRU. He told his people to find out what was happening. He even vaguely wondered if Serov had decided to call it a day and go over to the other side.

By the end of the second day he knew by instinct that Ustinov was behind whatever was going on. Seething with suppressed anger he planned what he should do. And Abramov had been one of the KGB's toughest operators. But he knew instinctively that a wrong move could lose him his undoubted support way above Ustinov's level. He wanted Ustinov arrested and accused of treason, and for the sabotage of a high-security operation. An operation approved by the men who advised Gorbachev himself. This meant a meeting with Yakovlev, the head of the First Chief Directorate. The FCD was responsible for all foreign intelligence. He had heard rumours that Yakovlev was neutral about the present leadership, happy to wait and see how things developed. But he was too shrewd to tolerate private ventures like Ustinov's. Unless of course Yakovlev was party to the action himself. That was a risk he'd have to take. He had no choice. It was shit or bust.

Yakovlev had been head of the First Chief Directorate for seven years and seemed to have no immediate rival. He was in his fifties, a Georgian, not unlike in appearance his fellow Georgian, Joseph Vissarionovich Djugashvili, who the world knew as Stalin. A man of black hair, heavy eyebrows and an old-fashioned moustache. But it was the bright, penetrating brown eyes that people remembered.

He pointed to the chair in front of his desk and leaned back unbuttoning the top two buttons of his uniform jacket. When he had lit the inevitable cigarette he raised his eyebrows and looked across at Abramov.

'What's the problem?'

Abramov went over the history of Serov's operation in Berlin and then related what he knew of Serov's abduction. For a few moments Yakovlev was silent, moving the open packet of Benson and Hedges in front of him.

'Where is Serov now?'

'I don't know.'

'You mean to tell me that you reckon Ustinov has arranged to remove a senior officer from another department?'

'Yes, comrade.'

'And nobody senior to Ustinov has given any kind of approval to this action?'

'Not that I can discover.'

'Any idea of why he's done this?'

'From the gossip that I've heard Ustinov and his supporters think that the Serov operation is having an unfavourable effect in the Kremlin on their ambitions to take over control themselves.'

'Has the President been told about all this? The abduction.'

'No. I thought it was best that you informed him yourself if you thought it necessary.'

Yakovlev smiled and reached for the phone.

'Get me General Rykov. Here. Right now.'

As he hung up the phone, he looked at Abramov.

'I'll keep in touch. Don't leave Moscow. And don't talk to anyone else about it.'

Yakovlev walked with Abramov to the door and patted his back as he turned to leave. Abramov was relieved. Yakovlev was not one for the social graces and the pat on the back signified Yakovlev's approval. He passed Rykov in the corridor as he headed for his own office. Gen. Rykov was head of the Federal Security Services.

As Yakovlev related the situation to Gen. Rykov he was well aware that the general's surprise and indignation were a little exaggerated. He suspected that the news was not news to the general. When Yakovlev told Rykov to deal with the matter personally and as a matter of urgency, Rykov knew that he was, himself, suspect.

The general packed an overnight bag and said goodbye to his wife. He would be away for two or maybe three days. She could contact him through the office wherever he might be. Back at his office he drew cash and phoned his mistress who had just joined the Bolshoi stage company, thanks to his influence. It was a short journey and he could have driven himself but decided it may be necessary to have some physical force at his disposal on the return journey.

They drove under the tunnel into Volokolamskoye Chaussée and then turned left to Petrovo-Dalniye Chaussée. The park overlooking the Moskva River is one of the most pleasant spots near Moscow. The conglomerates of pavilions, museums and a theatre stand apart from a couple of medium-sized houses which are used as rest-places and sometimes to confine senior officials who need to have their views on budgets and policies changed but without a lot of physical pressure.

There were lights on all over the larger of the two houses and as Rykov walked up the steps he was recognised and saluted by the Red Army sergeant guarding the big oak door. As he walked into the main hallway he shielded his eyes from the bright lights of a dozen candelabra. The hallway was empty but there was music from one of the rooms. As Rykov pushed open the door to the room he saw Ustinov and several others playing cards at a low coffee table. It pleased him to see the fear on Ustinov's face as he was recognised.

Ustinov half-rose but Rykov pushed him roughly down again. 'Where is he?'

'I don't understand, comrade general. Where is who?'

The smack of Rykov's leather-gloved hand on Ustinov's face seemed to echo through the room.

'Cut out the bullshit, Ustinov. You're in trouble enough already. Where's Serov?'

'Oh, Serov. He's upstairs. He'll be asleep I expect.'

'Go get him. Now.'

It was ten minutes before Ustinov came back with an exhausted-looking Serov. Meanwhile Rykov had checked the identities of the other men who had been playing cards. He told them that they were now under house-arrest.

He took Serov into a smaller room and looked him over. Apart from being deathly pale and trembling he seemed OK.

'Any damage, Serov?'

'Just some bruises on my back and ribs.'

'At least you'll know what it's like in future when you send your chaps out on dodgy missions.'

Serov sighed but didn't respond.

It was Ustinov's turn next, and the usual exuberance wasn't there any longer.

'So. Ustinov. What else has been going on?'

Ustinov hesitated for a moment and then shrugged and opted for a shortened version of the truth. When he finished, Rykov said, 'How do you contact these people?'

'There's a scrambled telephone line at the safe-house.'

'What's the address of the safe-house?'

Rykov had had a word on the telephone to Yakovlev who had decided that Serov's man should be kept until further orders. Rykov guessed that Yakovlev was going to take over that situation himself. Yakovlev had also left Bekker's parents in the jail at KGB HQ in Dzerdzhinski Square. Just being in the Lubyanka had its own depressing effect on prisoners. It wasn't all that inspiring for those who worked there.

Rykov walked out of the house to find the army guard who saluted him and stood to attention as he was spoken to.

'How many guards are there?'

'Fourteen, comrade general.'

'Who's in command?'

'Major Levin.'

'Give him my compliments and tell him I want to see him.'

'Yes, comrade general.'

Major Levin was in his fifties and had made his way up to field rank by doing what he was told and doing it conscientiously. A faithful retainer.

Rykov told him that the men in the house were to be put under house-arrest. He would get further orders the following day. He was to tell them that the charges were very serious and concerned the security of the State.

Ten minutes later the general stood impassively as the elderly major gave the bad news to Ustinov and his co-conspirators. Then he walked into the room where Serov had been given the traditional revival – chicken soup.

'Tell me about what went on.'

'They wanted the identity of the English contact.'

'Did you give it to them?'

'No. I don't even know it. Only my man in Berlin knows who it is. That was part of the deal. And the English in London were not given the identity of our man.'

'How much did we pay for the information?'

'Nothing. There was no money involved on either side.'

Serov was aware that Rykov was not impressed by the amateurish operation. But if Yakovlev approved it that was all that mattered. It was not until the next day that they discovered the Ustinov had also taken Serov's man in Berlin and that he was in a bad way. It was Vlasov who Yakovlev chose to sort out the mess in Berlin.

Vlasov was in his late thirties and was a desk man not involved in active intelligence. But he was highly intelligent and well-educated, responsible for assessing the value of information gleaned by field agents. Yakovlev ordered Abramov to brief Vlasov and authorise him to sort out the situation. The prime purpose was to ensure that the original operation was reinstated at almost any cost. Unlimited resources of high-security information and unlimited powers to order any action he deemed necessary. He was told of the kind of information that the two men had exchanged. He recognised immediately how vital some of that information had been in the moulding of Kremlin thinking. He was given a written authorisation addressed to 'all who may be concerned' to carry out whatever instructions he gave them.

His plane landed in Berlin at noon and he went to the Interhotel in Alexanderplatz to sign in. Moscow had booked him a suite that was equipped with a scrambled phone-line to Moscow and an assistant who was also KGB and would give him whatever help he needed. There was also a car and a driver available for him anytime he wanted them.

For nearly an hour he sat in his room and read the background notes on Serov, the man whose cover name was Bekker, and the four men who had been hired by Ustinov to abduct Bekker. He assumed from their names that they were all Bulgarians. The team-leader was an ex-Special Forces man named Zakov. Ustinov had not been in touch with them for three days and they had been told that their calls to his number in Moscow had been logged and would be dealt with as soon as possible. Rykov had phoned them and told them to expect Vlasov and to carry out his orders immediately.

Vlasov's orders were specific. The contact between Bekker and the Brit must go on. That meant that he couldn't just release Serov and take him back to Moscow to be posted to some other area. But from what he could make out the contact had not been active for at least three, or maybe four, weeks. The Brit would be highly suspicious and some routine tale of illness or personal problems wouldn't wash.

Nabokov himself opened the door to the apartment for Vlasov. Vlasov realised after talking to him in the small office that although Nabokov looked like the usual thug that the KGB used for such enterprises he was, in fact, quite intelligent. Perhaps shrewd was a more appropriate description.

Vlasov told him that he wanted to see Bekker before he discussed what he intended to do.

He insisted on seeing Bekker alone and was shocked to see the state he was in, his body covered in bruises and swellings, barely capable of talking.

He pulled up a chair and sat beside the bed.

'I'm going to use your real name, comrade. Let's forget our friend Otto Bekker for the moment. So, Alexander Chebrikov, I've been sent from Moscow to sort out the mess that certain people have created.' He paused and said quietly. 'Are you able to talk?'

'Yes.' It was a croak rather than speech but he went on, 'My throat hurts.'

'I'm going to get a doctor to look at you. You may have to spend a few hours in a hospital so that you can be scanned.'

'They'll just give me an injection to kill me.'

'No they won't. I'll be with you all the time. By the way, my name's Vlasov. Josef Vlasov.'

'Who is Ustinov? What's this all about?'

'We'll talk when you're better. Try and sleep until I get you into hospital.'

He was deep asleep, sitting on the chair in the doctor's office, when Dr Falin came in to talk to him. He shook Vlasov awake and pulled up a chair to face him. As Vlasov came to, Dr Falin said, 'Do you speak German?'

'Yeah. More or less.'

'I don't speak Russian so it'll have to be German.' He paused. 'This man you brought in for me to check up has been beaten up. And whoever beat him were professionals. They wanted to bring pain rather than just fear. And they've done a very thorough job.' He paused. 'If you hadn't made me sign that document I have to tell you frankly that I'd have had you put in jail right now.' He paused again. 'But you know all about that, my friend.' He sighed. 'There are multi-fractures in his ribs but they will heal if we strap them for a few days to get some adhesion. What really matters is what you people have done to his mind. He won't ever get normal speech back because of his raw throat being grossly infected. But apart from that the man's suffering from serious trauma. The damage to his brain has also meant that he has lost the sight in his left eye.'

'What's the brain damage?'

'Too early to say precisely. We'll need to put in more surgery before we know what actual damage has been done.' He paused. 'But crudely and simply that man will never be able to think straight again. The physical stuff will heal inside a few weeks. But the wound to his mind ain't curable, my friend.' He shrugged. 'Maybe that doesn't matter to you people.'

Vlasov's face flushed with anger as he glared at the doctor.

'If we were people like that, Doctor Falin, you'd be in a black van by now on your way to the city jail.' He stood up. 'Do whatever needs to be done. A private room. There'll be a guard on the door permanently. I'll be here every day and I'll want a written opinion on the man's condition every day too. Goodnight.'

Vlasov phoned the Berlin KGB and arranged for guards to be posted. Moscow had already warned Berlin KGB that they would be required to supply services to Vlasov. They hadn't been told what it was all about – and they hadn't asked. When the voice at the other end is the KGB's Director General you don't ask questions.

Back at the hotel, Vlasov made notes of the questions he needed to put to Nabokov the next day.

'What did you get out of Bekker about his British contact?'

'Nothing. Absolutely nothing. He just clamped his jaws together and took what we gave him.'

'I want to hear the tapes you played to him of the interrogation of his parents. Were they actors or real?'

'Real.'

'Where are his parents now?'

'I've no idea.'

'How much were you paid?'

'I get two thousand dollars a day and the others get a thousand.'

'And a big bonus if you got the Brit's identity, yes?'

'Yes.'

'How much?'

'A hundred thousand.'

'Did he ever give any reason why he wouldn't identify his contact?'

Nabokov shrugged. 'He just said he had given his word and he wasn't going to break his promise.'

'Did you try anything other than the rough stuff?'

'Like what?'

'Discussing it with him.'

'I don't know enough to discuss anything and I wasn't authorised to make deals. Just the identity was all they wanted.'

'What was Ustinov going to do if you got the Brit's identity?'

'I've no idea.' He shrugged. 'We just did as we were told.'

'Did he order you to beat up Bekker?'

'Not specifically. He just said go as far as you have to, but keep him alive.'

'Are you KGB?'

'No. We're freelance.'

On the third day in hospital Bekker was fit to talk and slowly Vlasov built up a picture of what had happened. He had probed very cautiously at the identity of the Brit contact but Bekker had almost imperceptibly shaken his head.

'I won't identify him, no matter what they do to me.'

'So the operation of information exchange wasn't really all that important.'

'Moscow found it important.' The faint tone of indignation made Vlasov realise that he had touched a tender spot. Bekker must have wondered many times when they were beating him up if it had all been worthwhile. It had obviously been only the desire to protect the Brit that had motivated Bekker's resistance.

'Did you and the Englishman share the same views on Soviet politics?'

Bekker lifted one hand and let it fall.

'We weren't interested in politics. He cared about the Russian people. Spoke fluent Russian and we both wanted to help stop any chance of a war because one side or the other was misinterpreting what the other lot were doing or thinking of doing.' He paused. 'Only Moscow and London can tell you if we were wasting our time.'

'Moscow sent me down here solely to protect you and to try and preserve the arrangements with your Brit friend. My impression was that a lot of influential and important people set great store on what you have been doing.'

'How long have I been out of circulation?'

'Just over three weeks as far as I can tell.'

'What day is it today?'

'Sunday.'

'That means I've missed four meetings including today's meeting.'

'Would it be a problem to revive the meetings?'

'Who knows. He may not trust me anymore.'

'Would you trust me to contact him and explain what has happened?'

'No. No way.'

'Tell me why not.'

'Because that's our deal. His people have no idea who I am and nobody on our side knows who he is.'

'Not Serov or Abramov?'

'No. Neither or them.'

'So. Where do we go from here – any suggestions?'

'No.'

Max Inman's concern about what was happening to the operation became more than mere concern as the third missed rendezvous went by. Cooper had made things worse by suggesting that it had been poor planning not to know how to contact Bekker on his home ground. After all, Bekker knew exactly where Inman lived. Why should the other side not be equally forthcoming?

At first it seemed to Inman that Cooper and the others were prepared to let the operation fade out but when the third meeting had been missed Inman detected a faint annoyance that he had not succeeded in making contact with Bekker. Shapiro had heard rumours from other sources that the public turmoil in East Germany now involved the government itself and that Honeker was about to be overthrown. What had he heard?

Abramov hated travel and even more he hated Germans but Vlasov insisted that if there was to be a meeting it had to be in Berlin. Such tentative goodwill as he had established with Bekker was too delicate to withstand him being away. He was having to try and fulfil the conflicting roles of guardian, friend and adviser.

He had learned a lot in their chats about Bekker's background and motivation but he was making no progress in reviving the connection with the Brit.

The meeting with Abramov was in the middle of the night while Bekker was sleeping but Abramov listened intently to what Vlasov was telling him. When he had finished Abramov was silent for long moments and then he said, 'We need to get it going again. There are problems coming up where we need to know what the Brits' reactions will be.'

'Like what?'

'Like what their reaction will be to what amounts to civil war here in East Germany.'

'Forgetting his mental attitude Bekker isn't capable of going anywhere except in a wheelchair.'

'You say his contact's very sympathetic to the Russian people, yes?'

'Yes.'

'How about we appeal to that sympathy?'

'Tell me how.'

Abramov shrugged. 'Tell Bekker how important his operation

is. People in the Kremlin depending on him. That sort of stuff. Promotion, a decoration. Recognition.'

Vlasov was silent for a few moments and then he said, 'OK. Let's say he agrees, how does he meet his contact in a wheelchair?'

'You said he's got a phone number for the Brit?'

'Yes.'

'So make contact by phone. Explain he's been in an accident in hospital. Desperate to keep operation going, can the Brit meet him this side of the Wall?'

Vlasov smiled wryly. 'D'you want to have a go at talking him into it?'

'Don't be a smart-arse, Vlasov. This is serious.'

Vlasov sighed. 'OK. I'll see what I can do. You'd better meet him and tell him how important his operation is. The Kremlin watching his efforts and all that sort of stuff.'

As Abramov talked to Bekker, Vlasov realised that he was doing a good job. Bekker was obviously impressed by what Abramov said. Vlasov almost believed the sincerity himself. And Bekker obviously recognised that with a man as high up in the KGB as Abramov coming from Moscow just to talk to him meant that the operation was being treated seriously in the Kremlin. There had been times in the past when he had wondered whether it wasn't just a little side-show. Two amateurs passing on gossip as if it were the considered policy of their governments.

Abramov realised that he was connecting when Bekker asked about his parents and Abramov had been able to say that they had been released and appropriate apologies made. But Bekker knew all too well that the KGB didn't go in for apologies no matter what blunders they made. Bekker also asked about his girl-friend and Vlasov was able to tell him that the thugs had not contacted her.

✻   ✻   ✻

Inman reached for the telephone as it rang and then hesitated. Only Bekker and Cooper knew his second number and Cooper was in Washington for meetings.

He picked up the phone slowly and listened. There was a silence for a moment and then a voice said, in Russian, 'I'm speaking for Herr Bekker. He has been in hospital and is anxious to make contact with you again.'

'Who are you? What's your name?'

'He said we were not to use names.'

'Why is he in hospital?'

'He was quite severely hurt in a car accident. He's making good progress but he is obviously distressed about not having been able to contact you.' The speaker paused. 'He still needs to use crutches and he can't go far.'

'How long before he can get about?'

'He wants to see you as soon as possible.'

'Why does he want to see me?'

'I think you know very well why he wants to see you.'

'So who are you?'

'Just a friend of his.'

'Which hospital is he in?'

'I could arrange for a car to pick you up at the Checkpoint and take you there. Just me driving.'

'When?'

'What about this evening? Say 7 p.m. at Checkpoint Charlie?'

'OK. But no silly games.'

'It will be a black Mercedes with diplomatic plates.'

'OK.'

There seemed to be a lot of people on the streets around the Checkpoint as they drove away. The hospital was not far from

the centre of the city and at the hospital there had been no problems. Whoever his escort was he was obviously important.

The guard on Bekker's room had been removed for the
evening and Inman's escort gave him a pager.

'Just press the red button when you've finished. Take as long
as you want.'

Inman knew as soon as he saw Bekker sitting in the wheelchair
that Bekker's bruises and cuts hadn't come from a car accident.
And as he sat down opposite Bekker in a cane chair, Bekker
pointed at the light-fitting in the ceiling and put his finger to his
lips.

'How are you?'

Bekker winced as he shrugged. 'I'm OK.'

'Can you talk?'

'I'll do my best.'

There was a knock on the door and the escort came in and
walked over to the TV set and switched it on. As he was leaving
he said, 'You'd better watch this,' and closed the door, obviously
agitated.

It was the last few minutes of a press conference in the HQ
of the East German Communist Party and the spokesman was
waving a piece of paper in the air. Then he read from the paper,
announcing that from then on there would be no travel restric-
tions on any East German citizens. There were no more frontiers,
and citizens were free to cross into West Berlin as they wished
with a guarantee that they could return. There would be no more
checkpoints and no more checking.

The film was looped again and again to show the same scene
and then a TV camera was looking down on thousands of people
forcing their way past the confused guards. The scene moved to
another official crossing-point where people were smiling and

waving as they streamed past what had been another checkpoint. It was November 9, 1989.

Inman and Bekker watched in silence and then Bekker said, 'I can't believe it.'

Inman said quietly, 'You said yourself way back that there was going to be trouble with your Germans.'

'I can't take it in. It seems unreal. A dream. What now? What's going to happen? What will the West Germans do?'

'And what will Moscow do?'

'They'll wash their hands of our Germans. They warned Honeker and his idiots what would happen if they ignored what the people want.'

They had talked for over an hour but Inman had pointedly asked no questions about Bekker's condition or what had happened to him.

All the time they were talking the TV cameras were on the Wall, showing people with sledge-hammers and cold-chisels hacking at the massive structure with its sad graffiti.

The grainy black-and-white shots of Inman approaching the car at the checkpoint, leaving the car at the hospital entrance and at several places on the way to Bekker's private room had been sent down the wire to Moscow. They were captioned for the urgent attention of Abramov and Yakovlev.

The phone call to Vlasov came through an hour later. Abramov told him that Yakovlev was already on his way to Berlin and would be with him in about two hours. The Brit was to be kept at the hospital until Yakovlev took him over. Held by force if necessary but every effort should be made to keep things civilised.

*   *   *

The turmoil at the Wall had been excuse enough to suggest that the Brit should wait until the streets were calmer.

As Vlasov took Yakovlev up to Bekker's private room he sensed that something had happened or was happening, that he didn't understand. At the door of Bekker's room Yakovlev told him to wait outside. Yakovlev went into Bekker's room without knocking. Inside the room Yakovlev walked over and sat on the edge of Bekker's bed. He was full of praise and reassurance. It was several long minutes before Yakovlev turned and still sitting, looked at Inman, raising one eyebrow quizzically as he seemed to smile.

Part Two

Chapter Thirty-One

Cooper waited as Sir Brian finished talking on the phone, and thanked God that the Director-General of SIS was one of the old China hands and not one of the military types that the Foreign Office sometimes appointed in the vain hope of calming the wilder elements of MI6. Cooper wondered how politicians thought SIS provided the information that they used so eagerly.

Sir Brian was already in dinner-jacket and black tie for his dinner engagement with a couple of members of the Joint Intelligence Committee to argue the case for an increased budget for their operations in the Soviet Union. When Sir Brian hung up the phone he loosened his jacket buttons and leaned forward.

'You sounded on the phone like you're bringing me bad news. Am I right?'

'Not necessarily bad news but disturbing news.' Cooper paused. 'It's about Janus. He has missed the mandatory contact for three weeks running.'

'Where is he?'

'That's part of the problem.' Cooper shrugged. 'I don't know where he is, and I can't use our detachment in Berlin for security reasons.'

'Who else knows about Janus besides you and me?'

'Just a very small group of us.' He paused. 'The only other person who probably knows something is his lady-friend.'

'The photographer woman?'

'Yeah.'

'Have you tried her out?'

'No. But the arrangement we have with Janus is that when he's operational they can use me as a link. I thought I might risk it and see what she knows, if anything.'

'How close are they?'

'Very close. But it's an odd set-up. They've been a couple for years since they first met at Cambridge, but they still have their own pads.'

'Why aren't they married?'

'From what I've gathered they don't see any point in it. They've both got jobs they are totally involved in. As you know, she's not just a photographer. She's more a photo-journalist. And she's got a world-wide reputation. And, of course, Janus's standard cover is as a foreign correspondent.'

'Do you trust her?'

Cooper shrugged. 'You know me better than to expect me to answer that. But I'd say she's as concerned about him as any wife would be. More than most, and very influential with him.'

'What's your instinct say?'

'To try her out and make it look like a routine contact. But she's nobody's fool and she's as well-connected and informed as we are. She's helped Janus with advice and contacts on several occasions. Probably without realising what it was all about.'

'So why are we talking about it?'

'For two reasons. Firstly because I don't want to start a hare running if there's no need to and secondly there's only you who I can discuss it with fully.'

'So go ahead. I'd back your instincts any day.' He smiled as he stood up. 'And you? How are you making out?'

Cooper looked as if it surprised him that anyone should ask how he was.

'I'm OK.' He paused. 'By the way the lady's being interviewed on BBC 2 on Friday. A programme about Amnesty International. You might like to watch it or tape it. She's very interesting.' He smiled. 'And very beautiful too.'

Sir Brian smiled. 'It beats me how you people always end up with pretty women. They can't be all that smart to put up with the lives you people lead. Always flying off at an hour's notice and not sure when you'll be back.'

Cooper laughed as he headed for the door. 'Must be the old adage – "absence makes the heart grow fonder".'

As Sir Brian buttoned up his jacket he wondered if Cooper had ever considered that other old adage – 'out of sight, out of mind'. If the number of divorces that the Legal Secretary was having to supervise was anything to go by the latter was nearer the truth.

Chapter Thirty-Two

He left a message on her pager. Just the codeword she had chosen – Fuji – and asked that she phone him. He had a number that could get him twenty-four hours a day no matter where he was. It worked even when he was out of the country. She called back an hour later and they fixed to meet in an hour at Il Cappuccino, a café they both knew in Frith Street. She had always said that he chose there because it was of maximum inconvenience to both of them.

He was glancing at the Stop Press on the back page of the *Evening Standard* when she came in and he watched her chatting to Giorgio *il padrone*, who was kissing her hand and generally bowing and scraping. She glanced in Cooper's direction and waved a hand before a last word with Giorgio. They all loved her. Not only because she was beautiful but because she spoke fluent Italian with a slightly snobby Roman accent. She was wearing a well-cut dark purple trouser-suit with a tailored collar, her long black hair shining as she passed through the sun and shade from the Venetian blinds at the street windows. She smiled as he helped her into the cane chair, taking her heavy handbag and placing it beside her on the window shelf.

She looked at his face. 'You look worried. Is there a problem?'

'Do you fancy a pastry with your coffee?'

'Yeah. Black coffee and a chocolate eclair. OK?'

'Fine.'

Cooper signalled a waiter and gave him their order. A cappuccino for himself. He turned back to look at her.

'I don't know if there's a problem or not, but I wondered when you last heard from our friend.'

She reached into her handbag and took out a leather-bound notebook, turning back the pages slowly. Then she stopped and said without looking up. 'Nearly three weeks ago. He phoned me late at night.'

'Did he say where he was?'

'Yes. He said he was in Dresden covering an engineering exhibition. A trade fair. Said he would be leaving the next day for Berlin. We talked about the possibility of going to the wedding of friends of ours but he wasn't sure of his movements.'

'Did he seem OK?'

'So far as I could tell. But you know what he's like.'

'We have a fixed arrangement for him to contact us at a pre-arranged time on the same day every week. It's what we call a mandatory call. You have to make the call even if you've nothing to say. There's a word you can use, a safety check, if you're in trouble or talking under duress. He's missed three weeks' calls so I'm a bit concerned.'

'Has he ever missed before?'

'No.'

'Can you not contact him even if he can't contact you?'

'No. It's a one-way thing. I've no idea where he is or even where he might be.'

'Can't your people in Berlin do anything to try and trace him?'

'They probably don't even know him. They certainly don't have any idea that he's SIS. That's to give him maximum security. They've no need to know. His operation is highly confidential. Only one other person in SIS knows the full story.'

'And who's that?'

He hesitated and then said, 'Sir Brian. Sir Brian Slater, our Director-General.'

'Tall guy, grey hair, very blue eyes. Quite handsome. Salmon fishing in Scotland and all that sort of thing?'

'That's him. How do you know him?'

She smiled. 'He chatted me up way back at a French Embassy press party. He heard me talking French and thought I was important. Speaks not bad French for an Englishman.' She paused and the smile had gone. 'What are we going to do about Max?'

'I've sent one of my top chaps out to Berlin to ferret around. But I daren't put him too much in the picture for the sake of security.'

'When's he going?'

'He left for Berlin last night. I've had to tell him that Max is SIS as well as being a foreign correspondent so that he realises that it's important and urgent that we contact him.'

'Who do you think might do something to him – the Russians or the Germans? The East Germans?'

'Could be either but it would end up being a Russian thing.'

'I always had the impression that part of Max's role was to keep in with the Russians.'

'Yes it is. And he gets on well with them too. They've always seemed to like him as a possible ally. A favourable piece about Soviet medicine or space stuff. He understood them and was vaguely sympathetic. Genuinely sympathetic. Now we've got glasnost and perestroika there should be even fewer problems.'

'What was he doing for SIS?'

'I can't talk about it. I'm sorry.'

'How serious for the other side?'

'Serious enough. Let's leave it at that.' He smiled. 'Another coffee or eclair?'

'No thanks. Will you keep in touch? Every day?'

'Yes. Of course.'

'Remember that I too have connections. Including the Russians and including the KGB.'

'Where?'

'Here in London at the embassy and in Moscow too.'

'Would you be willing to use the connections if it helped?'

'Of course.'

'Don't ever discuss his role with us with anybody.'

As she stood up he pulled back her chair and walked with her into the street. He had already paid Giorgio and left a tip for the waiter.

The sun was still shining but she felt a sense of foreboding as Cooper waved down a taxi for her.

There were three messages on the answering-machine. The usual one from her mother. One from a man in LA who fancied her and offered to pay for a trip to Carmel for the weekend. The last was from her father who was also in LA reading scripts and hunting for studio backing for a film about war-criminals. She saved the messages but did nothing about them. She'd given Cooper her private 'private' number.

Chapter Thirty-Three

Bennet was the head of the SIS detachment in Berlin. They were responsible for covering not only both East and West Berlin but the whole of East Germany. When London told him to give every assistance to Parker he attached no particular importance to it. Anybody who was sent over from London was supposed to be given 'every assistance'. He usually gave them ten minutes of his own time, listening to their version of some cock-up in London that involved a visit to Berlin, and then passed them to one of his underlings depending on what was involved. But Parker was high up enough on the totem pole to really require his personal attention. They had met several times before and had got on well together, but Bennet was suspicious of the rather vague description he was getting from Parker about what the actual problem was.

'Let me just go over this again, Tony. You've got an agent working both sides of the Wall who you haven't informed me about before. He's missed three mandatory contacts. You want to contact him but you've no idea where he is. You'd like my people's help but for security reasons you can't tell me who this guy is. Am I missing some vital point that makes sense out of this?'

'I wish you were.'

'You say he's working under cover. What's his cover?'

'A journalist. A foreign correspondent. Freelance.'

'How long has he been out here?'

'Several years.'

'For Christ's sake and you've never had the courtesy to put me in the picture?'

'There were good reasons for that.'

'Like what?'

'Like his mission. It wasn't hard-edged. Very loose and informal.'

'Sounds like he was playing footsie with the other side, am I right?'

'That's one way of describing it.'

'And the fact that it's you who's been sent over here it almost certainly means that he was being controlled by Cooper.'

When Parker didn't reply, Bennet shook his head. He pointed at the red phone. 'It's a double scrambler. Call Cooper and tell him I can't help without I'm given a proper briefing.'

He stood up, pushing back his chair as Parker reached for the phone and then closing his office door behind him he walked down to the computer room. He asked for a print-out of all free-lance journalists on their data-bank as covering both East and West Germany. He drank a cup of coffee as he waited for the print-out and then walked back with it to his own office.

Parker had finished his call and looked a little more relaxed. 'I talked with Cooper. He's suggested a compromise.'

Bennet sat down. 'Tell me.'

'That if you agree I put you completely in the picture and it's up to you how far you go in briefing your people.'

Bennet smiled. Not an amiable smile. 'And then when you find this poor bastard in one of the canals it's down to me, not London. Yes?'

'That's not fair. You know that.'

'Too bloody true it's not fair but it's what it's all about my friend.' He paused. 'So fill me in.'

Bennet sat listening attentively as Parker outlined the facts but deliberately omitted what Max Inman's actual mission was apart from passing back information on the general political situation in East Germany. His by-line was his real name, Max Inman, and he wrote as a freelance for a number of magazines and newspapers on both sides of the Wall.

'Where are you staying?'

'At the Remtor.'

'I'll phone you there. If I've got anything I'll come over.'

Bennet sat in the only armchair in Parker's hotel room and Parker read the report carefully.

INTMEM
010895

Re: specified subject. Prelim.

Subject is known to us and has always been friendly but has refused to assist us in any way. Operates as freelance and supplies features and political pieces to newspapers and magazines in both the GDR and the Federal Republic, the United States and Italy. Not member of NUJ or any other union. His registered office is at the address of a firm of solicitors in Chelsea. No report as yet from Inland Revenue. (We have no valid authorisation.)

At Dresden trade fair he spent time on several stands, both British and Russian, and was entertained by a Soviet electronics company on the first evening. A check at the hotel where he had booked-in indicated that he had stayed there only one night.

Subject appears to move freely between East and West Berlin. Passport issued from Peterborough a year ago.

A negative aspect is that we should normally expect that the hotel room of a foreign journalist would have been visited by either police or Stasi.

As requested will report daily.

Capt. Shaw I.C.

Parker looked at Bennet. 'What d'you think?'

'Here's a guy who's a foreigner. They'll have kept tabs on him constantly on all his visits to East Berlin and the GDR. They don't let foreigners disappear and do nothing about it.' He paused. 'Yeah, I'd say they've got him. Could be some admin mistake but say what you will the Stasis are highly efficient.'

'What contacts do you have with the Berlin Stasis?'

'Some. Nothing solid but we can try a little fishing expedition. But I'd guess we'll only get vibes rather than facts.'

'Have your people carried out surveillance on him?'

'We did when he first appeared on the scene but there was nothing suspicious. Journalists are always a problem but his pieces were printed in important magazines and papers. His cover was first-class because it was more or less true.' He paused. 'I'll drive you back and you can use our secure phones to contact London.' He looked at Parker. 'Any idea where he lived in West Berlin?'

'No.'

'How was he funded?'

'I got it from Accounts and passed it to a bank account in London. I guess he drew from that.'

'Did it cover all his expenses and living costs as well as salary?'

'Yes.'

'You'd better get your people in London to have a look at that bank account. Is he married?'

'No, but a long-standing relationship.'

'How long has he been with SIS?'

'On one basis or another he came direct from university. It's about fifteen years now.'

'You'd better give me some sort of CV and any photographs you've got.'

'Have you got any of their people in the nick at the moment?'

'Are you thinking of an exchange?'

'Yeah.'

'What could they squeeze out of him if they've got him?'

'A hell of a lot.'

'Political?'

'Basically yes.'

'Who would be embarrassed?'

'Everybody.'

'We've got nobody in the nick at that level.' Bennet paused and looked at Parker. 'If Cooper gave you the nod we could always pick up one of them. Somebody higher up. But it would need to be planned. No cowboys and Indians stuff.'

'I'll see how he reacts. Have you got anyone in mind?'

'Yeah. Two of 'em. But it would be complicated and we'd need to use one of our safe-houses on the other side. We'd never get either of them through a checkpoint.' He paused. 'One thing worries me. They must know that our friend is a Brit. He mixes with them. They know him well and I've got doubts that the Stasis would take him out without KGB approval. And if that's the case we're in a different ball-game.'

When they got back to SIS Berlin's HQ there was an 'eyes only' message from Captain Shaw for Bennet. The message gave him a phone number and a password – Janus.

When Bennet phoned the number the receiver was lifted at the other end but nobody spoke.

Bennet said, 'Janus, Bennet here.'

'Our friend was logged going through Checkpoint Charlie at 19.10 hours on 8 Nov – the night the Wall came down. He was picked up by a black Mercedes with diplomatic plates. That's all I've got.'

And the receiver was put down. Parker had listened on an

extension. He turned to Bennet. 'I'd better let Cooper know.' He stood thinking for a moment before he reached for the double scrambler.

He heard his call being passed from one cell to another until Cooper answered.

'Cooper.'

Parker related what they knew and Cooper asked to speak to Bennet. When he had the phone Bennet said, 'Bennet speaking.'

'Use every connection you've got to find out *why* they've lifted him. It could be some petty infringement, you know what they're like over there and I don't want to start a hare running if it isn't necessary. Also get one of your people to put together all you've got on the Berlin Stasis, names, responsibilities, CVs and any background.'

'Right, sir, do you want Mr Parker again?'

'No. Just put him in the picture. Ask him for any help you need that requires London approval.'

'Right, sir.'

But Cooper had already hung up.

Chapter Thirty-Four

When Cooper's call caught up with her she was at the Park Lane Hilton photographing a very pretty and up-and-coming girl cello player and Cooper had suggested that he came across and that they could meet in the hotel's coffee shop.

She fastened the strap of her camera bag to the spare chair while Cooper got their coffees. As he put the big cup in front of her she looked up at him. 'Good or bad news?'

'A bit of both,' he said as he stirred his coffee slowly. He looked across at her. His frank look. She was far too used to people trying to deceive her to be taken in.

'Give me the bad first.'

'We know now that he was picked up by the Stasis or the KGB. We don't know why.'

'Don't bullshit me, Frank. Stasis don't arrest foreign journalists for a parking offence.'

'We just don't know any more as yet, my dear,' he said quietly.

'So what are you doing to get him freed?'

'We've got to move very discreetly. We don't know why they've picked him up, and we don't want to go in there with all guns blazing or they'll recognise that he's something special. It's got to look like a routine contact and a routine exchange.'

'Exchange for what?'

He shrugged. 'Maybe for one of their people we happen to be holding at the moment.'

'I thought he already had a good relationship with both the East Germans and the KGB in East Berlin.'

'He does, and unless they've uncovered what his real mission is we've no idea why they're holding him.'

'What *is* his so-called mission?'

He shrugged. 'I can't tell you that, Katie. You must know by now that his work is more than top-secret.'

'How long is it going to take before you can make contact to get him freed?'

'We're planning it now. All our resources in Berlin are available but like I said we've got to play it low-key until we know more about the situation.'

'So how long before he's free?'

'You've got to bear with us, Katie. Could be a week at least. You know what they're like.'

'Don't forget that I've got contacts with the Soviets.'

'Tell me.'

'With their embassy here in London. With the GDR political bosses. I did a neutral piece on life in the GDR which they liked.'

'I hope we don't need to go that far but I'll remember those contacts if and when they might help.' Cooper paused. 'What are your movements in the next few days?'

'Tomorrow I'm giving a talk at an Amnesty conference. I was due to go the next day to Nairobi and then Mogadishu. But I'm holding it up until I know more about Max.'

Cooper looked at his watch. 'I'll have to go, Katie. I'll keep in touch. And you've got my number if you need it. Don't worry, we're doing all that can be done at this stage.'

Chapter Thirty-Five

———————◆———————

Bennet pushed a copy of Capt. Shaw's latest report across his desk for Parker to read.

INTMEM
10390

Re: Specified Subject.

With Checkpoint Charlie no longer functioning it has not been easy to trace the identities of the East German guards on duty the night of November 8. The best I can offer is not very clear but I doubt if I can go much further.

It seems that a man answering Janus's description was logged at Charlie about 1900 hours on November 8. He went alone to a black Mercedes which had been waiting there for about 20 minutes. He got in the car which drove off in the direction of the town centre. The car's number plates were diplomatic but not recorded.

A car with the same description was recorded at Tempelhof in the early hours of the following morning. The only passenger on the plane it was waiting for was a Russian. The plane was registered as a KGB plane. The car took the passenger to Saint Teresa's hospital. The car was parked all night in the hospital's senior staff car-park.

Owing to the confusion of the Wall break-through that night it is unlikely that I will be able to pursue this further.
Capt. Shaw. I.C.

Bennet sat waiting for Parker to finish reading the report and when he had finished Bennet said, 'With the Wall down we're into a different ball-game. Half our old informants have gone missing and we've got Stasi men queuing up offering their services.' He paused. 'It's going to take a long time to sort things out.'

'It doesn't make sense what we know about Inman. He seems to have gone over voluntarily and he got into the car without any rough stuff. Why? Why was he over the other side anyway? And why didn't he let us know that he was taking that risk?'

'Maybe there wasn't a risk. He had passes to go into East Berlin and he seems to have gone there fairly regularly.' He paused. 'Do you want me to put Cooper in the picture?'

'No. I'll do it. I expect he'll want me to go back to London.'

The meeting was at the Gower Street safe-house and apart from Shapiro and Rimmer, Cooper had brought in Parker to answer any questions about the Berlin episode.

They had all been kept briefed about what was happening but Cooper went over it all again to bring them up-to-date. When he had finished Joe Shapiro said, 'So what are we here for?'

'Because we've had a contact. From Moscow via their embassy here.' He paused. 'They're willing to release him.'

Paul Rimmer said, 'How did we get the offer?'

'His lady-friend got a message from their embassy where she is well-known and she phoned me about two hours ago.'

'What do they want in exchange?'

'They just want Operation Janus to continue.'

Rimmer said sharply. 'So why have they taken him?'

'I don't know. They just said it had been a mistake. An administrative cock-up.'

'And they just ship him back on the next Aeroflot flight to Heathrow?'

'No. They want our written assurance that Janus will continue.'

'No way,' Rimmer snapped. 'No way. They'll use it to embarrass us some time when it suits them.'

'Could be.' Cooper paused. 'But first of all what are our feelings about Janus? Do *we* want it to carry on?'

'Where is he, Frank?' Shapiro said quietly.

'I'm not sure but reading between the lines I think he's in Moscow.'

'And how long have they had him?'

'Four weeks tomorrow.'

There was a long silence and then Joe Shapiro voiced what each one of them had been thinking.

'We'll have to have a very careful de-briefing after he's back.'

'I agree. But what would we be looking for? All they want is that an operation that has suited us well will carry on.'

Rimmer looked around the table. 'Frank's right. But the whole thing stinks for me.'

'Any particular reason, Paul?'

'Yeah. We were never allowed to know who his contact was. And the deal was that only his contact knew who our guy was. Nobody else. So how did they know who to pick up?'

'Maybe he'll be able to tell us.'

Cooper paused and then said, 'So. Do we go ahead?'

Shapiro shrugged. 'I don't think anyone proposes to leave him there do they?'

Cooper sighed. 'No. And we'd better bear in mind when debriefing him that if he gets the impression that we really don't trust him then Operation Janus is as good as dead. Has anyone got any views on that?'

Shapiro shook his head. 'For my area it's been invaluable. Even today with the Wall down it's allowed us to avoid a number of potential blunders. It would have helped the West Germans too with their new situation.' He paused. 'Let's keep it going.'

There were faint words of agreement and then Shapiro said, 'Where are you going to keep him while he's being de-briefed?'

'I've got a safe-house lined up.'

'Where?'

'Tunbridge Wells.'

'Who will question him?'

'The three of us. Joe, you Paul and me.'

'When's it going to happen?'

'I'd guess tomorrow night's Moscow flight.' He paused. 'I'll meet him in and take him over.'

The cabin staff on the Ilyushin had let him sit with Inman until all the other passengers had left. He had cleared with Customs and Immigration that they could go directly to his car.

Inman looked a little pale and drawn but he'd smiled when Cooper eased himself into the seat beside him and said, 'Long time no see.'

Cooper told him that they'd have to go through the usual debriefing routine and Inman had been long enough in the business to know that it was standard practice if you'd been in the hands of any Soviet authority. Cooper told him that Katya was waiting for him at the house in Tunbridge Wells.

* * *

The three of them had dinner together at the High Rocks Hotel and then Cooper had left.

As they sat together drinking coffee he said, 'I gather that you raised hell with His Excellency at the embassy. Tell me about it.'

She shrugged. 'I just told him I knew that they'd taken you somewhere, probably Moscow, and if they didn't release you I'd publish a piece I'd written about all those zinc coffins coming back from Afghanistan.'

'What was his reaction?'

'He obviously wasn't impressed but he said he'd inform Moscow of what I'd said.'

'Then what?'

'He phoned me the next day for a meeting. Very amiable now. Moscow had informed him that you were being released in a matter of days. But they wanted my assurance that I would not inform the press of what had happened.' She paused. 'I said – no problem and he walked me to the door and said it would be very much to your disadvantage if I didn't just leave it to them to sort out.' She looked at him. 'What the hell was it all about, Max?'

He was silent for a moment, turning away to look towards the window before looking back at her.

'Politics in Moscow at the moment is like a civil war. Let's say I just got stuck in the middle.'

'Why are you stuck in this place? Don't they trust you?'

'It's a kind of routine, Kate. De-briefing. Just going over whatever happened.' He paused. 'And what you said and did if you were under any kind of pressure – physical or mental.'

'Were you under pressure?'

'Not really.'

'You aren't going to tell me what went on, are you?'

He smiled. 'No. How've *you* been getting on?'

'What happens after they've de-briefed you?'

He shrugged. 'Providing they're satisfied that I was a good boy I expect to take up again where it all ground to a standstill.'

'How long will the de-briefing take?'

He shrugged. 'Not long. Maybe a week or ten days.'

'And then you can come back to my place?'

He smiled. 'Yes, if you want me to.'

'Do *you* want to?'

He laughed. 'Of course I do.'

The girl in the black Granada Estate was listening to the World Service on the car radio. When eventually all the lights went out in the house in Broadwater Down she switched off the radio, dictated a note on her small Sony tape-recorder and then drove off towards the centre of Tunbridge Wells. She wondered why they were interested in what time the lights went out in a safe-house.

Chapter Thirty-Six

Shapiro, Rimmer and Cooper had avoided any of the formalities of a normal de-briefing and had just chatted with him about what had happened. And Max Inman stuck more or less to the basic facts of the episode, from the telephone call to his contact and then the weeks that he had spent in Moscow. The doctor's examination confirmed that he had not been physically abused and the laboratory reported no traces of any toxic or unusual material in his blood samples.

Knowing that Rimmer was the sceptic about him, it was Rimmer who posed again some of the questions he had already answered.

'How did you pass the time at the apartment?'

Inman shrugged. 'I read, I listened to music and the radio and I walked around the local streets.'

'Alone?'

'Mostly alone but sometimes one of them came with me.'

'Where was the apartment?'

'On the Arbat over a bookshop.'

'And the Abramov guy – you say he was strongly for the operation continuing?'

'Yes. I think they all were. They said that people who advised Gorbachev wanted it to continue.'

'Did they offer you any inducement?'

Inman shrugged and smiled. 'They made clear that if I wanted money they were happy to provide it.'

'How much of all this have you told to your friend, Katya?'

Inman shrugged dismissively. 'Just enough to play fair. It looks like it was her efforts that straightened things out and so she's due an explanation. But I've never discussed the actual operation outside SIS.'

It was Cooper who said, 'Are you willing to carry on the operation?'

'Yes. If you feel it's useful.'

Two days later he was at Katya's place. She was at a Magnum meeting. She always came back in good humour from Magnum meetings where photographers of real flair and genius quarrelled like polecats over imagined insults from publishers and fellow photographers. Nothing ever got settled or even pursued but she claimed that it was a kind of balm for their insecurities.

She smiled as she saw him. 'Have they decided you were a good boy after all?'

He laughed. 'More or less.'

'When do you go back to Berlin?'

'Tomorrow but I'll be back at the weekend.'

'Do you need a lift to the airport?'

'No thanks. Cooper and Rimmer are seeing me off at Gatwick.'

The Lufthansa flight had been held up for nearly an hour and they had gone to one of the coffee shops to pass the time. When Cooper had asked him if it would seem strange being back in Berlin after what had happened, he shrugged. 'It'll be strange for me anyway. I haven't seen it with the Wall down.'

'How will you feel about your contact?'

Inman shrugged. 'Much the same.'

Rimmer said, 'There's an old SIS saying that you ought to remember. I expect you know it. The three rules for SIS agents.'

'No. Remind me.'

'Firstly, don't believe that everybody who drops you in the shit is your enemy. Secondly – don't believe that everybody who gets you out of the shit is your friend. And last – whenever you're in the shit keep quiet about it.'

Inman smiled. 'That's not just funny. It's quite profound, or at least philosophical.'

Rimmer smiled, shaking his head slowly in disbelief. 'You should be teaching back at Cambridge, my boy. An academic if ever I met one.'

Inman smiled too. 'What should I teach?'

Rimmer screwed up his eyes, thinking. And then he said, 'How about Russian romantic poetry from the nineteenth century onwards?'

Inman was silent for a moment and then, looking at Paul Rimmer, he said quietly, 'You're a very perceptive man, Paul Rimmer.' He smiled as he looked at Cooper. 'You should watch him, Frank. He's dangerous.'

And then the loudspeakers were calling Inman's flight, assembling at Gate 16. For some reason they shook hands with one another, a thing they would never normally do.

It seemed strange to find the flat exactly as he had left it almost five weeks ago. Tidy but dusty, an open book on the floor beside the low bed and dirty crockery in the sink still waiting to be washed. He picked up the book and closed it carefully as he checked the title. It was Bertrand Russell's *History of Modern Philosophy*. He smiled as he placed it alongside a paperback on the bedside table. The paperback was Scott Fitzgerald's *The Great Gatsby*.

He looked at his watch and decided that there was time enough for him to walk over to Friedrichstrasse and have a look at what had happened to the Wall.

There were dozens of people still hacking and hammering at the concrete slabs of the Wall. But people were laughing and shouting to one another as if it were all some sort of activity holiday. The defiance of the graffiti artists had lost its message but the defiance itself had worked.

The wooden guardhouse on the East Berlin end of the checkpoint was still there but it was not manned by frontier guards or police. A British redcap was standing outside the Allied guardhouse and two US Snowdrops were chatting up a group of young girls on a school trip to see history in the making. Or the unmaking.

The whole thing seemed unreal, more a rough surrealistic stage-set for a Bertolt Brecht play. How could grown men have thought that a Wall could keep a whole nation from wanting TVs, Mercedes and more than one orange a month for the kids. But the kind of men in East Berlin and Moscow who had decided to build the Wall were the same the whole world over. Men with no imagination. Maybe no more than a thousand idiots in Moscow who felt entitled to decide how many millions of their fellows should live. No grand gestures to show off Russian writers and musicians, doctors and scientists, or even pretty girls and *babchas* who made chicken broth that would cure anything from a cold to a broken heart.

He walked back slowly to his place thinking about poor Bekker and Vlasov his new 'minder'. He had let Cooper and the other two assume that with the operation continuing it would be the same contact that he'd work with from the other side. But Bekker was never going to be in the intelligence business again.

Back at his place he made the two phone calls and arranged the meeting at the hospital. It seemed strange and unfair that Bekker whose mother was a neuro-surgeon should now be in the care of a neuro-surgeon in Berlin. Moscow had eventually agreed that they would fund the medical and living costs for Bekker for the rest of his life and Bekker's childlike dependence on Max Inman had touched him enough to undertake to look after him, with help, for as long as it made a difference.

Professor Brandt indicated the chairs set around a low coffee table. They had talked in general terms about Bekker for several minutes before Brandt finally got to the point.

'I understand that a neuro-surgeon in Moscow has diagnosed the condition as dementia. And, of course, there were colleagues of mine here who labelled the condition as Alzheimer's.' He sighed. 'In fact my diagnosis is that it's brain trauma. The sort of thing we frequently come across in bad vehicle accidents. There has been significant injury of the brain. White matter pathways have been torn and strained. Damaged blood vessels have haemorrhaged and it is obvious that the patient's head has been subject to gross and deliberate abuse.' He shrugged. 'But that's your business. I gather that your friends want me to act as consultant for as long as the man lasts? Yes?'

'How long will he last?'

'God only knows. Literally. He could go in the next few months. Or with careful nursing and caring he could go on for a couple of years.'

'Would you take him on at your private clinic?'

'Yes. With one proviso.'

'What's that?'

'That you keep in regular touch with him. He's not sure who

you are but you're his one and only link with reality. You're his life-belt in a very strong sea.'

'Yes. I'll see him regularly. As often as I can.'

'How often?'

Inman shrugged. 'Say every other day.'

'Why should you take on this responsibility? Is he related to you?'

For a moment Inman was silent. 'No. We're not related but he got like this because he thought he was protecting me.'

'From the scum in Moscow, yes?'

'No, professor. Just men. It's always just men. Germans, Russians, Japanese, Nazis, Commies are just easy labels.'

'What label would you apply?'

'It's genes and environment – more in your hands than mine.'

Brandt stood up. 'Well. We'll both do our best. Contact me anytime you want. At the clinic or here at the hospital on consulting days or at my home. You've got my card and I've got a pager.'

He held out his hand. 'I'll have him in the clinic by tomorrow night.'

It had been part of the deal that Vlasov would take over Bekker's old role of contact. They got on well together and Vlasov was more aware of what was going on in Moscow. Inman had deliberately not told Cooper and the others of the change. He considered it as his business not theirs. Why should they care who his contact was? They thought it was they who had got him released.

And Frank Cooper had not mentioned to Inman that the SIS detachment in Berlin now knew his identity but not much of what he was doing. They had never heard of Operation Janus.

✻   ✻   ✻

The phone was picked up on the second ring and a girl's voice said, 'Box.'

'Two nine one.'

A man's voice said, 'Box 291.'

'You free this evening?'

'If necessary. Where? When?'

'Ronnie Scott's. Ten p.m. OK?'

'See you.'

There were people who said that Ronnie Scott used his bouncers to throw people in the club rather than out. And there were people who rated Ronnie as a better jazzman than the well-loved Tubby Hayes. The club was full that night but not overcrowded. And very still as Ronnie and his tenor sax reminded them of 'Serious Gold '77'.

Waring was sitting at a cramped table like a school-desk, with two beers in front of him, waiting for Paul Rimmer. He could see Rimmer standing just inside the inner door to the club. He stood with his arms folded across his blue denim shirt, his eyes going slowly over the faces in the crowd without his head moving.

He and Rimmer had frequently used Ronnie Scott's as an RV when Rimmer was working with Box. He had warned Rimmer when he had said that he was transferring to SIS, that Box, the trade name for MI5, had very different attitudes to the public than the Firm's more tolerant views. SIS wanted to know what was going on and MI5 instinctively wanted to stop it. They were rivals and they knew it. Rivals for the Prime Minister's approval and the Chancellor's cash. They behaved with one another with caution. They had many things in common. A deep dislike of all politicians and most lawyers, and a genuine determination to protect their country and its institutions from the interference of foreigners. It worked reasonably well, rather as a divorced couple grew over the years to more understanding and the memories of shared triumphs and disasters when they had had to comfort together young sufferers of Scarlet Fever and the excessive bravura of a son who had beaten his best friend at chess with a rather contrived Fool's Mate.

When Paul Rimmer eventually settled in beside him, Waring had lifted his glass and smiled as he said, '*Na zdrovye*'. He laughed softly, pursing his lips as he saw the disgust on Rimmer's face. Rimmer's loathing of Russians and Russia had been well-known throughout MI5 and had been one of the reasons why they had not been too reluctant in letting him be transferred to their rivals in SIS, when that organisation was looking for someone who knew what the KGB were up to in the UK rather than in the rest of the world.

Rimmer said, 'Did you have a look at that file?'

'Of course.'

'Go on.'

'She's got lots of contacts but she's a photo-journalist, it's probably just part of her job.' He paused. 'Why the sudden interest?'

'Off the record?'

'Yes, if you want it that way.'

'I started this file on Katya Felinska just before I was transferred. She'd been reported at far too many leftie places. Her father's a Brit but started out as a Pole.' He paused. 'I've got reason to believe, as the fuzz say, that she has contacts in the Soviet and Warsaw Pact embassies far beyond what she needs for her job.' He paused again. 'And one last thing – she and her boyfriend met while they were in college at Cambridge. And you know what I think about those bastards.'

'What is it you're looking for exactly?'

'Enough to nail her. Not in court, they're far too smart for that. But enough to show her that if she's up to something we'll get her – one way or another.'

'What first got you going about Commies?'

Rimmer shook his head. 'Some other time. Some other time.'
He looked at Waring intently. 'Will you do it – unofficially?'

'Yeah. We'll see how it goes.'

'And you'll keep me in the picture?'

'Sure I will.' He smiled at Rimmer. 'And you keep me in your picture too.'

Chapter Thirty-Seven

The receptionist at Professor Brandt's clinic had told him that Dr Falin wanted to see him before he saw the patient.

Falin had come for him and taken him back to his private office.

'Would you like a whisky, Mr Inman?'

'No thanks.'

'Right. I thought I ought to have a word with you before you see your colleague. It's not going to be an easy meeting. He has deteriorated a lot in the last few days. He probably won't recognise you and if he does he won't know who you are. Apart from the effects of trauma he is physically OK. He needs the wheelchair but he's already quite used to it.

'I want you to imagine that the patient is a very old man. In his eighties. The traditional absent-minded professor. His memory is very poor and most of his past life has been wiped out of his mental databank. He gets flashes from the past but nothing coherent. You'll have to remember when talking to him that his mind can be elsewhere. He can take his wheelchair to a shelf for a book but when he gets there he won't remember why he's there.'

'So what's the use of me spending time with him?'

'We've noticed at the hospital that his brain is more active when you're there. We had indicators to measure his brain activity. When you were around the activity increased.' He shrugged. 'We'll have to see how it goes. Don't try to probe his memory. You'd be wasting your time and unsettling him.' He paused. 'Let me take you to his room. About five minutes would be enough this first time.'

Bekker was sitting on an upright chair alongside his bed. Inman was surprised at how well he looked. He walked over and sat on the side of the bed facing Bekker. For a moment Inman wondered what language he should use. They'd always used German when they met and Inman said quietly, 'Hello Otto. I came to see if there was anything you wanted.'

Bekker looked up at him and made a desperate effort to speak but no sound came out. Inman put his hand over Bekker's hand where it lay on the coverlet of the bed and Bekker turned his head slowly to look at Inman's face, his eyes staring as if he were trying to speak. Then Bekker shook his head and looked away to where the curtains at the window were moving gently in the breeze. There was a bowl of fruit and a bunch of green grapes on the window-ledge. It was strangely calm in the white-painted room despite the tension of Bekker's attempts to speak.

Inman stayed for about ten minutes and as he touched Bekker's cheek gently as he stood up, Bekker said quite clearly:

'Books to read.'

'You want some books to read?'

Bekker smiled and nodded.

'I'll bring you some books tomorrow.'

As Inman walked to the stairs outside he realised that they had both spoken Russian, not German.

With more or less complete freedom of movement between the two parts of Berlin it was going to be easier to have his meetings with Josef Vlasov and Inman's place had been the obvious meeting-place.

It would be strange meeting with Vlasov who knew nothing of the doubts and discussions that had led to his exchanges with Otto Bekker. It had all been very tentative and amateurish and Vlasov wasn't a man for doubts and hesitation. Inman smiled to himself as he thought about how he would describe Vlasov. He was what O'Shaughnessey had in mind when he wrote 'We are the movers and shakers'. Vlasov was a mover and shaker. And even Operation Janus fitted in with the last lines of O'Shaughnessey's ode – 'For each age is a dream that is dying, or one that is coming to birth'.

Vlasov arrived mid-afternoon. More subdued than usual and obviously aware that he was now included in something that the Kremlin were watching closely. But there was back history that Inman needed to know about and Vlasov was the only person likely to tell him the truth, or as near the truth as his courage allowed.

'I understood from Moscow that by the time you caught up with Otto Bekker he was already incapable of telling you about our joint operation.'

'Yes. But Abramov and Serov filled me in as best they could.'

'I'd better explain the rules of the operation because we worked as a team. He wasn't batting for the Soviets and I wasn't batting for the West.'

Vlasov shrugged and smiled. 'It seems to have worked very well, so tell me the rules.'

Max Inman had spent an hour explaining the philosophy of the operation and the kind of information they had passed to one another.

'Bearing what I've told you in mind, do you want to clear any of it with Moscow?'

'No. They told me that I should go along with whatever you wanted.' He smiled. 'They made it clear that you were in charge.'

'Any questions so far?'

'There's something been puzzling me. Maybe you know the answer.'

'What's the problem?'

'I kept Moscow fully informed about what had gone on with Otto Bekker and my telephone call to you on his behalf. No problem. But I had stills and a video done of you going to the car at the checkpoint and later at the hospital. They were sent by wire to Moscow to Abramov and in less than an hour I got a priority call from Moscow. I think it was from Abramov. Not about Bekker but about you. They knew your name and they were desperate for me to hang on to you and not let you back through the Wall. No problem except that there must be no rough stuff, no force at all. Use any excuse I could think of but I must hang on to you until Abramov could fly down to Berlin and take you over. Thank God the Wall came down that night and I was able to use that as an excuse to delay you going back. They told me if you raised hell about staying I was to let you go back but to follow you. I asked why all the fuss and they shut me up. Try and hang on to you but not annoy or offend you.' He paused. 'Why all the fuss?'

For several moments Inman was silent and then he said, 'Did you ask Abramov why all the fuss?'

'No way. He's my boss's boss. You don't ask guys like that what's going on.'

Inman shook his head. 'You'll have to ask Abramov, it's not for me to explain it.'

'Have I offended you?'

'Not at all.' He paused. 'Let's get back to how we continue the operation.'

'Before we do that – what did you think of Bekker?'

Again Inman hesitated before he answered.

'It makes me sick, Josef. And ashamed of being part of an organisation that can do that to a man.'

'Wasn't it treason what he was doing?'

'No way. No way. If he was committing treason then so was I.' He paused and his face was serious as he spoke. 'When you look at Otto Bekker you're looking at a man who has done more for the Soviet Union than anyone else you're ever likely to meet.'

'Could you tell me about the kind of information that you passed to one another?'

'OK. Let's talk about that.'

Inman had talked with Vlasov for several hours a day for over a week about how the operation should go. He felt that they were wasting time looking for just an item of information to give to each other. When they talked about what Moscow wanted to know it was obvious that the operation would have to be substantially restructured.

It was Moscow that had the problems. Not only of disintegration but of divided loyalties and indecisions and chaos at all levels. Inman decided to suggest that Vlasov should warn Moscow that he was on his way back for a full briefing on what the various interests in Moscow wanted to know. Abramov had agreed immediately and Vlasov had flown on the next plane to Sheremetyevo. He was back two days later with a sealed letter from Abramov for Inman, and Abramov's approval of the new format.

It wasn't easy adapting to the new regime. It was not only a time of great changes in the Soviet Union but there was little that London wanted to know. They were warned of what was likely to happen and it called for little reaction on their part. Over the next six months the Soviet Union literally disappeared, Russia became an independent state, the Russian Federation, Lithuania,

Latvia, the Ukraine and Uzbekistan declared their independence and nobody in Moscow tried to oppose them.

East and West Germany signed the Reunification Treaty and when East Germany had officially ceded its sovereignty to Bonn the Ost-mark became the Deutsche-Mark, a move that Bonn was to live to regret. Max Inman had written a piece that was widely used under the title of 'Premature Generosity'. He had claimed that Bonn was taking on a debt that would be disastrous for the strong West German economy.

In the following year, February 1991, the temporary allies threw Saddam Hussein out of Kuwait. In the new Russian Federation Gorbachev was President and the new man, Boris Yeltsin, became the Party leader and the effective leader of the Russian Federation.

Visiting Otto Bekker had become part of Inman's life, but it was obvious that it had no effect on Bekker's condition. He was physically much improved, capable of walking in the gardens of the clinic and moving around in his room. It was also obvious that Bekker had no idea who Inman was and sometimes he seemed to think that he was one of the medical staff. Bekker's actual speech improved but what he said was meaningless. He always spoke in Russian which made it difficult for the medical people who were German to assess the significance of what he talked about. For a long time they recorded what he said on tape for Inman to translate but it revealed very little and was merely incoherent ramblings of some vague conversation in his head. But as Bekker survived into the second year, Inman made more effort to make Bekker respond to things he said.

When he arrived at the clinic that day he had brought a few books. Current Russian novels and one or two children's books that Bekker seemed to enjoy. He had also brought an audio-tape of *Peter and the Wolf* in Russian.

At reception the nurse had phoned an internal number and asked him to wait. It was Falin himself who came to see him. Otto Bekker had died in the early hours of that morning after a massive brain haemorrhage. A doctor and a nurse had been with him when it happened. There had been no sign earlier that there had been any change from Bekker's normal condition.

Max Inman had gone up alone to Bekker's room. There were heavy bandages round his head but otherwise he could just have been asleep, and there was a shaft of sunlight through the curtains at the window that lay across the body beneath the white sheets. He stood by the side of the bed looking around the room. It was all so spotlessly clean and white and on a bench at the foot of the bed there were two pieces of luggage. They contained all Otto Bekker's worldly goods. He'd have to tell Vlasov to contact Moscow about where Bekker's body would be buried. So far as he was concerned this was the end of Operation Janus. He'd carry on because that was what they wanted. For the first time in his life he would just be doing a job.

Max Inman couldn't exclude two burdens from his mind as he looked again at Bekker's body on the bed. Foremost was his awareness of the fact that what had been done to Otto Bekker had been done by the people he had always sympathised with. The Brits and the SIS were frequently accused of acting outside the law but he couldn't imagine anyone he knew in SIS authorising or allowing the kind of brutality that Bekker had suffered. The only extenuating circumstance was the fact that it had been done by a rebel group who were now languishing in various Gulag camps and would never be released. They too would claim that what they had done was done for what they saw as the good of their country. But Max Inman knew that there was no weasel excuse that would allay the feeling that he was in some way responsible for what had happened.

After phoning Vlasov Inman tried to apply his mind to how the operation should be organised in future. Once again he was aware that he had nobody else to talk to about Bekker's death. He wondered what Katya would do in his situation. But he knew exactly what Katya would have done. She'd have raised hell with everyone, called in old favours and threatened exposure for all concerned. But you had to be internationally famous and beautiful before you could do that. And get away with it. Maybe you should do that even if you didn't get away with it. He couldn't even give some money to Bekker's girl at the club because he couldn't explain where Bekker had disappeared to or why. He sighed. All they had wanted from Bekker was for him to identify his Brit contact. Abramov told him that Bekker hadn't said a word.

Inman had walked back slowly towards the Ku-damm, crossing the wide street at the junction with Tauentzienstrasse. Out of habit he walked across to the Europa Centre and up to the café. He had some soup and a couple of cups of coffee and tried to think of something he could do to lift his depression. His table was alongside the window that looked down at the people in the *platz* below. The lights were just beginning to come on in the shops and apartments. It was a fine evening and it was mostly families and teenagers. Teenagers inevitably disrupting the peace with skate-boards and loud portable radios. He wondered what their reactions would be if he told them about his life in Berlin. Disbelief in most cases and suspicion in others. But these were the people that Otto Bekker had died for. Trying to save them from their fates. Trying to ensure that their tomorrows were just like today. They had no idea what went on in their names and they would have been shocked if they were told that there were men in London and Moscow actually working out what their fates were likely to be. Who was he and Cooper and Abramov and the others to influence the lives of millions of people just getting on with their lives? The daily round, the caring, the family responsibilities, the disappointments, the stress of modern lives. Who could prove whether he and Bekker had preserved a single soul with their complicated attempts to prevent another war? This wasn't what he had wanted when he had fallen in love with the Russians all those years ago.

He could see the lights in the windows of the cathedral built to commemorate Kaiser Wilhelm, just a jagged empty tooth of masonry alongside its modern replacement. He had always argued that there wasn't much difference between Communism and Christianity but Christianity seemed to be surviving what was undoubtedly the end of Communism. He thought fleetingly of catching the evening plane to London the next day. But he knew that if he talked to Katya about his feelings he would be cheating because he could only tell her half the story. Maybe someday he could tell her all of it and just telling her would be relief enough.

He walked back along Kant Strasse to his place and made the unmade bed, washed up and poured himself a neat whisky. He'd go to Bekker's funeral if it was in Berlin.

In bed he turned to Karl Popper's comments on his two paradoxes. The 'paradox of democracy' which means that if the majority vote for Fascism or Communism you have no moral grounds for active resistance. And then the 'paradox of tolerance'. If a society extends unlimited tolerance it is likely to be destroyed. So a tolerant society must be ready in some circumstances to support the enemies of tolerance. Max Inman closed his eyes and went to sleep still holding the book. The phone rang just after midnight but he didn't hear it. It rang again at 2 a.m. but he still didn't hear it.

Chapter Thirty-Eight

Over the next six months Inman's relationship with Vlasov developed but the operation itself had run out of steam. Moscow discovered that even its forays into Chechnya and Afghanistan were costly mistakes with losses of men, weapons and prestige. If Chechnya could give Moscow a bloody nose then military wars against the larger independent ex-Soviet states were just pastimes for thwarted generals who hadn't yet found a rôle in the new system.

The Duma still voted and the Kremlin still ignored the results. With the army and the other services unpaid for months they were the only real problem for the West. The disposal of weapons and equipment was as haphazard as a boot-sale but London and Washington were beginning to be really worried about what was happening to nuclear weapons. At least three countries were known to have taken delivery of nuclear war-heads and were searching frantically for means of launching them. The indications were that even if launchers were obtained the countries concerned would almost certainly not risk using them. But fanatical dictators and turbulent regimes were quite capable of ignoring the facts of life and the inevitable consequences.

More and more of London's questions were military rather than political and this was an area where both Inman and Vlasov were totally ignorant. They were becoming messengers rather than analysts and neither of the two was competent in this area or willing to be part of it. Vlasov was not, as Inman was, in such a secure position with his colleagues as to be able to suggest closing down Operation Janus. So it fell to Inman to raise the subject with SIS. To his surprise the Operation Janus committee shared his views. They thought that his talents and experience were being wasted. They would leave it to him to tidy up what was left of the operation so that his contact was not offended by the closure. And they saw no reason why he shouldn't give the other side a frank explanation of why they felt Janus had changed to a matter of military rather than political intelligence.

They had one more suggestion to make to Inman. Joe Shapiro was retiring, and he was being offered Shapiro's desk with responsibility for overseeing all intelligence covering the new Federal Russia and the newly found independent states. He was flattered by the offer and the praise for the years of Operation Janus and he had agreed to start in his new responsibility in a month's time.

They had gone to their Italian place in Frith Street and she smiled as he ordered their meal and a bottle of Chianti. He usually stuck to spaghetti and the house red.

'Are we celebrating something?'

He looked at her quickly. 'What made you say that?'

She laughed. 'A real meal. Real wine and you looking relaxed.'

He smiled. 'You should be doing my job.'

'So tell me. What's going on?'

'I'm leaving Berlin and coming back to London permanently – or as near permanently as no matter.'

'Are you happy with that?'

'I'm so relieved, Katie. You've no idea. Berlin and the work just drained my batteries. It's like recovering from some ghastly illness.'

'Will it be the same kind of work?'

He shrugged. 'Not really. I'll be more concerned with analysing what other people have produced.'

'What happened to the guy who was doing it before?'

'He's retired.' He looked at her, smiling as he realised why she had asked. 'You don't trust them do you?'

'Of course I don't.'

He seemed to hesitate as he opened his mouth to speak and then, looking at her intently, he said, 'Can I make a crazy suggestion?'

'Carry on – whatever it is.'

'How about we give up our two flats and move in together with something a bit more comfortable – and a bit more space?'

She was silent for long moments and then, looking at him intently, she said, 'Are you sure it would suit you? You wouldn't feel we were on top of one another all the time?'

He shook his head. 'No. I'd like it with you there all the time – well, most of the time.'

She smiled. 'You'd have to remember where the salt was left and how to work the micro and the dish-washer.'

He laughed. 'Are you trying to put me off?'

'No way. Let's start the move tomorrow.'

'You're quite sure it's OK with you?'

'Very sure.'

They had finally settled for a maisonette in Kings Road, Chelsea. Two floors of a Victorian building over the Scotch Wool and Hosiery Shop below. A short walk to Sloane Square and an even shorter walk to the river if you went through the Royal Chelsea Hospital gardens.

They had agreed to take a few days' holiday and she had been amused and asked him where he would like to go.

'Let's have a long weekend – in Vienna and you show me the places you grew up in.'

She was delighted and surprised. They booked return flights to Vienna and four nights at the Deutschmeister Hotel in the city centre.

What really amazed her was how easily Max Inman fitted into the easy-going ways of Viennese life. She had been recognised as they landed at Wien-Schwechat airport and the first night their suite at the hotel had been full of people she had grown up with or people wanting to interview her. So far as Vienna was concerned Katya Felinska was Viennese. The difference to parties and such-like in London was in the laughter and compliments. There were two singers from a local theatre who sang one lilting Viennese song after another. Max Inman had obviously enjoyed himself and the attentions he got from pretty women. The fact that an Englishman spoke fluent German they found almost incredible.

When at last they were alone and the chambermaids had cleared away the debris, she sat down facing him. He still had a glass of wine in his hand.

She was smiling as she said, 'And how do you like your first evening in Vienna?'

'I loved it. I really feel at home here. Everybody seemed so friendly and so . . . so charming.'

She laughed. 'Remember what my Papa used to tell me. Don't fall for all that Viennese hand-kissing – they don't mean it. It's just a disguise.'

He shrugged, smiling. 'I still like it, honey. It's a good medicine. Disguise or not.' He reached for her hand. 'I feel at home here. I really do.'

She laughed and stood up, bending to kiss his cheek. 'There'll be so much of it in the next few days that you'll get sick of it.'

But Katya Felinska saw a different Max Inman in the following days. A man who was enjoying life. It was hard to believe that this was the man from all those years in Berlin. The man who had come back worn-out and depressed, whose only comfort came from knowing that he didn't have to go back to it. The euphoria wouldn't last but there would be some sediment left in his views of the few days in a friendly environment.

Chapter Thirty-Nine

The Operation Janus group gave him a lunch at Cooper's club, the Travellers. A home-from-home for SIS people, past and present.

Cooper was now Deputy Director-General. A waste of a talented man but that's how you had to do it. The only way you could reward his kind was promotion, which meant losing an experienced operator and turning him into an administrator. Usually not a very good administrator.

Inman was now seeing reports or summaries from SIS men at embassies and diplomatic missions, GCHQ, Military intelligence (MD) and SIS agents in the field. Reports from undercover SIS agents came to him direct.

He was surprised to find out the vital importance of GCHQ and its association with the USA's National Security Agency at Fort George Meade, Maryland, USA. No radio signal of any kind anywhere in the world was immune from GCHQ or NSA monitoring, and few telephone communications escaped the network.

Max Inman's weekly summary went 'Eyes Only' direct to the Foreign Secretary. The Director-General of SIS has a one-to-one meeting with the FS once a month.

Inman now had a wide view of what was happening in the new Russia and the newly independent states. And he covered not only the KGB's operations in the UK, but in the whole of Europe and the United States. Despite the new responsibilities Inman was still haunted by Bekker's death and the brutality that had caused it. And all for a piece of information that didn't matter all that much anyway. But that was ignoring the fact that once they could identify Inman there was nothing to stop them from doing the same to him. There were people in Moscow he dealt with who were angry at what had happened to Bekker. Angry, but not shocked or ashamed. Discussing like some business problem the limits to the financing of Bekker's medical treatment and his financial support for an unknown period until he died. No thoughts of compensating his parents for their ill-treatment. And these weren't the usual KGB thugs. They were well-educated and well-informed about the world in general. You didn't get to their ranks unless you were something special. And they had wives and children and mistresses who loved and respected them. These weren't psychopaths, they were the men who read modern philosophy, both official and underground. Even poor Bekker had read Karl Popper.

Strangely enough he found that, despite his responsibilities being so extended in his new job, he seemed to have more time for himself than he had had before. He and Katya had recently gone to see a new version of *Hamlet* at the National and he had suddenly realised the significance of Shakespeare's words – '. . . perchance to dream; ay there's the rub . . .'

They saw more of Katya's parents now that Max was permanently in London. Her father was starting on a film about a man, a Roman Catholic priest, who was about to give up his vocation and was in a turmoil of indecision.

Her mother said, 'What made him start having doubts?'

Jan Felinski shrugged. 'They always have doubts if they're any good. But that's the wrong end of the story.'

Gina Felinska smiled. 'So what's the right end of the story?'

'It's not the end that matters. What matters was what made him a priest in the first place. That's the essence of the film. Looking back on when he was first influenced by the thought of being a priest.'

'There must be dozens of reasons why a man could do that.'

'Tell me some.'

'A need to belong to a group of people who have firm rules about life and living. Perhaps even disagree with the world.' She laughed. 'Maybe it was the chance of hearing Fauré's *Requiem* every other month.'

Jan Felinski laughed. 'What would attract you to being a Catholic, my dear?'

'Oh. Just ordinary things. Saying prayers for actual people, the lovely show-biz stuff. The singing and the costumes.'

'You're not far wrong, dear girl. Very near the mark. There's always some small human thing that tips the balance.' He turned to look at Max. 'You had this great sympathy towards the Russians. Why? apart from all the political stuff.'

Inman thought for long moments and then said, 'It was a photographer, like Katya, who tipped the balance for me with a photograph that I saw in a newspaper or a magazine, I can't remember which.'

Katya said, 'What was the photograph?'

'I remember now. It was in a book. It was a Left Book Club book and it was a picture of the Jarrow marchers. All those men in the rain, not looking angry at losing their jobs. But sad and defeated. I read how they had been thrown out of their shipyard jobs. Thousands of them. No compensation and massive unemployment all over the country especially in the North-east. Most of them would never work again. They'd live on the dole. The dole was fourteen shillings a week for a married man. It really upset me that people could be treated like that. I wanted desperately to do something for them.' He smiled, wryly. 'So I joined the Communist Party.' He turned to look at Katya. 'So don't think that your photographs don't have any effect on people. They do.'

Jan Felinski smiled. 'And what made you leave the Communist Party?'

'I found I wasn't really interested in politics.'

'You . . .' said Felinski '. . . you not interested in politics? I can't believe it.'

Max Inman smiled and shrugged. 'It kind of fades away, Jan. The people matter more than the theories.'

Chapter Forty

When he retired Cooper had moved to a small cottage just outside Chichester. It was not far from Rimmer's place and they visited one another for drinks and a chat from time to time. So he was not surprised when Rimmer phoned him and said he'd like to have a word with him. They had arranged to meet at Cooper's place the next day but he had felt that Paul Rimmer was being a bit evasive when he'd asked what it was all about. 'Something about the Firm, Frank. I'll explain tomorrow.'

Paul Rimmer had arrived mid-afternoon in an old Morris Minor. Old but immaculate. The kind that was frequently advertised for sale as 'the property of one careful lady-driver.' He was careful to park it in the shadow of the large willow-tree that dominated Frank Cooper's front garden.

When they had dealt with the weather and England's chances of levelling the Test Match series with the Australians, Rimmer said, 'I've got a problem. I'm not sure how to deal with it. I'd like your advice.'

'What's the problem?'

'D'you remember your chap Bennet who was OC the SIS detachment in Berlin?'

'Yes of course.'

'What did you think of him?'

'He was very thorough. Young in those days but coped well. A bit unimaginative – stuck to the rule-book a bit too rigidly.'

'He's been approached by a chap he thinks could be useful.'

'We're winding down Berlin. There's no room for more than a couple.'

'The chap wasn't looking for a berth. I think he saw himself as an informant.' He paused. 'This came to me from an old friend in Box. They could be interested in him.'

'How would they use him?'

'Researcher for their team hunting down alleged war-criminals in the UK.'

'So what's the problem?'

'I've got a feeling in my water that our lot ought to take him on. Not Box.'

'To do what?'

'Let's say as a piece of insurance.'

'Against what?'

'My contact at Box had interviewed the guy to look into his background. Amongst a lot of other stuff he claimed that he'd been involved in an SIS operation based in Berlin.' He paused. 'What was the name of Inman's opposite number?'

'I've no idea. That was part of the deal. But I got the general impression that his contact wasn't a German but a German-speaking Russian.' He paused. 'What's this guy's name?'

'I've no idea.'

'I still don't understand why you feel SIS should take him on.'

Rimmer shrugged. 'I've been around this business for a long time, Frankie. All my instincts say we've got a loose cannon here and we ought to have him under our wing. Soonest.'

'Have you spoken to anyone else from SIS about this?'

'No. I only heard about it a couple of days ago.'

'Go on.'

'I think this guy could cause us a lot of trouble. Not necessarily intentionally. If we take him on and we find there's no problem we can always throw him back or fix him up somewhere else. But not in Box.'

Cooper looked intently at Rimmer. 'There's something you aren't telling me. What is it?'

'I've got a suspicion. I'm not sure about what. But instinct tells me we should take the guy over.'

'Are Box keen to have him?'

'I wouldn't say keen. But they're interested.'

'Who should we talk to about this?'

'Nobody. That's why I've come to you.' He paused. 'I'll find him and get him over here and we'll talk with him. Just you and me.'

'My God. You're really serious, aren't you?'

'Yeah.' He paused. 'I'd like to bring him here.'

'You mean under some sort of duress?'

'No way. Just the two of us chatting to a guy who'd like us to employ him.'

'And then what?'

'Who knows, but we could fix him up somewhere in SIS provided he cooperates.'

'What have you got in mind?'

'I'll fly to Berlin in a couple of days when I've found out enough to be able to identify him.'

'I wish I knew what you've got at the back of that devious mind of yours.'

Rimmer stood up, smiling. 'You will, dear boy, just be patient.'

As Cooper watched the Morris Minor head out into the lane, he wondered what the hell he was doing. He was sixty-two and retired. Living a quiet uneventful life whose high-spots were a visit to the theatre at Chichester and a weekly visit to Sainsbury's and the public library. And what was odd was that he found diffi-culty in casting Paul Rimmer as having the slightest interest in fending off trouble for SIS. He realised as he made tea that he ought to have offered to pay half of Rimmer's expenses. He pinned a note on his corkboard in the kitchen. Rimmer/ Expenses.

When Operation Janus was wound up, Vlasov had been left in Berlin by Abramov who didn't want him hanging around in Moscow. Fortunately Vlasov had wanted to stay in Berlin and Abramov had given him the task of reporting on what was happening to the remnants of the Stasis in Berlin. Also included in Vlasov's brief was anything he could glean of what the attitude was of West German officialdom, particularly the BND, in dealing with the Stasi records and archives.

There were a couple of cafés and two or three pubs patronised by various elements of several erstwhile intelligence services where quite accurate information on current events in the intelligence world was as common as complaints about the prices in the shops on the Ku-damm. It only took Rimmer a day to find his quarry. Rimmer was so obviously a Brit and his German was so bad that he had no difficulty in introducing himself to the man who was sitting alone at a table reading an out-of-date copy of *Der Spiegel*.

'My name's Paul, they told me you speak good English. Can I join you?'

Vlasov looked wary but not unfriendly as he put his magazine to one side.

As Rimmer pulled out a chair and sat down he smiled. And very quietly he said, 'They tell me you're thinking of making a change. A work change.' He paused. 'I'm very interested.'

Vlasov shrugged. 'Times are changing, Herr Paul. We have to change with them.'

'I'm staying at the Savoy, why don't we go over there and have a meal and a chat?'

✳   ✳   ✳

'So tell me . . .' Rimmer said '. . . how did you come across our chap Holloway?'

Vlasov shrugged. 'The word went around that a Brit intelligence guy was looking for somebody who could guide him round the Stasi records. People said he was tracing the records of ex-Stasis offering to work for the Brits.'

'And you were interested?'

'Interested enough to talk.'

'Was he interested in recruiting you?'

'Not until I'd told him that I'd worked with the Brits at one time on a special assignment.'

'What was that all about – the assignment?'

Vlasov shook his head. 'I can't talk about that.'

'Is it still going?'

'No. It was going a long time but I only took over when it was being run down.'

'Who did it before you?'

'Like I said – I can't talk about it. It's still top-secret.'

'And this was with the Brits?'

'Just one Brit. Just the two of us.'

'Who was your boss?'

'He was KGB in Moscow.'

'Name?'

Vlasov smiled. 'No.'

'Are you still KGB?'

'I didn't say I was KGB.'

Rimmer smiled. 'There's more ways of telling than just talking.' He paused. 'Are you still interested in working with the Brits?'

'Yes. If it's reasonably secure.'

'How about you come back with me and meet a few of the people you might be working with?'

'That's OK with me.'

'OK. Book in here at the Savoy for the night. Put it on my tab. I'll tell reception and we'll fly to London tomorrow.'

Cooper had picked up the phone on the second ring.

'Cooper.'

'He's coming back with me tomorrow. Needs working on but my guess is that he played some part in Janus. Maybe not mainstream but somewhere.'

'He's coming voluntarily?'

'Of course. I left my car at Gatwick so I'll pick it up and drive us both down to your place.'

'About what time?'

'Three to four if there's no problems with Immigration that I can't sort out.'

'OK. Take care.'

They had talked around the subject of the operation that Vlasov had claimed to have taken part in and finally Cooper said, 'What I can't understand is why you can't tell us more about it when you say that it was an operation with the Brits.'

Vlasov shrugged. 'They told me that was part of the deal. That neither side would know the identity of the contact man.' He paused. 'You've got to remember that it had been going on for years and when I came into it it was virtually over. After the Wall came down the operation had no purpose. Both sides agreed to call it a day.'

'Why did you come into it?'

Rimmer saw the hesitation and knew that Vlasov was going to lie. Saw him shifting uncomfortably as he spoke.

'My contact became too ill to carry on.'

'What was the matter with him?'

Vlasov shrugged again. 'I don't know.'

'Who was your Moscow controller?'

Again the hesitation. 'A senior guy named Abramov.'

'How did you get on with your Brit contact?'

'He was OK but when I took over he had obviously seen that it was going to fold and it was just a routine relationship.'

'Did Abramov know the identity of the Brit?'

'I don't know. I'm not sure.'

'Why aren't you sure?'

Vlasov sighed. 'I always felt that Abramov and the Brit had some sort of special relationship.'

'Why did you think that?'

'I don't know. It was just a feeling I had.'

Cooper stood up slowly. 'Let's go into Midhurst and have a bite at the Spread Eagle.'

Over the meal they had chatted informally about how things were now in Berlin and probed diplomatically at how Vlasov spent his time. It became obvious that he was bored, with little to do officially and socially. He was obviously interested in anything that would give him some sort of structure to his life.

Back home at Frank Cooper's cottage, they eased their way back into talking about the operation.

'Tell us a bit about Abramov. What was he like?'

'He's in his early sixties. Very shrewd and very tough. Speaks quite good English and German. His new job makes him responsible for all intelligence by the KGB in Europe.'

'Do you meet him at all?'

'Not these days. Once the operation closed down I've not spoken to him.' Vlasov half-smiled. 'I think he wasn't impressed.'

'With you, you mean?'

'Yes. The operation was his baby. It had been a great success but now it was just a low-level thing to keep me occupied.'

'Would you be interested in working for us to put together the research for a book about the history of the Stasis? From the start to the present day.'

Rimmer knew that he had diagnosed correctly as Vlasov leaned forward eagerly.

'That would suit me well.' He smiled. 'When can I start?'

'In about a month's time. You don't need to give up your KGB job unless you want to. We should treat this as you being a freelance historical researcher.'

'We could see how it goes.'

'Of course . . .' Rimmer said '. . . going back a bit, you said the man you first had contact with about joining us was a Brit named Holloway, yes?'

'Yes. Alwyn Holloway.'

'Interesting.' Rimmer smiled. 'But not the right set-up for you.' He stood up. 'I don't know about you guys but I'm ready to sleep.' He looked at Cooper. 'Can I borrow that couch, Frank?'

'Sure. I'll show our friend here up to his room and grab a couple of pillows for you.'

It was ten minutes before Frank Cooper came back downstairs hugging two pillows and a blanket. As he tossed them onto the couch he said quietly, 'We'd better talk while we've got the chance.'

He pointed at one of the armchairs and took the other one for himself.

'What do you make of it, Paul? You seem to be getting ahead of the script. Why?'

'You realise that Holloway is Box, MI5?'

'Of course I do. So what?'

'So there's clearly something very wrong in this whole set-up, Frank, and if it concerns internal security inside the UK that makes it the clear responsibility of Box.'

'So what for God's sake? Let them get on with it if there is anything.'

Rimmer looked across at Cooper. 'Even if it means Box looking over an SIS operation and SIS offices.' He paused. 'They'd love it, Frankie. They'd love it. I can see the headlines now.' He paused. 'So can you.'

'Are my headlines the same as yours?'

Rimmer shook his head in anger. 'I don't *know* more than you do. But I've been in this game one way or another for nearly thirty years and I know when I can smell trouble. And believe me there's trouble at the back of all this. Way back trouble.'

'Tell me what you're concerned about.'

'No. You'd say I'm crazy. And if I'm right I'm not sure I know how to handle it.' He paused. 'If it gets to that stage I'll put you in the picture.'

'And in the meantime?'

'What do you know about this guy Abramov?'

'Nothing. I vaguely remember hearing his name mentioned but I don't know in what context.' He shrugged. 'Check the files, Paul.'

'I'll do that, Frankie. Cover for me until this time tomorrow but keep Vlasov happy. Make him feel important and respected. That's what he needs right now.'

Rimmer didn't use the couch, he drove up to Guildford and then took a train. He took a room at the Special Forces Club and checked his notebook for two numbers and four addresses.

At 2 p.m. Paul Rimmer picked up the package that had been flown over from SIS Berlin and he put it in the leather case that housed the documents that were the result of the rest of his evidence, and headed back to the cottage.

He had to wait until Vlasov was watching a tape of *Zhivago* on the TV/VCR in Cooper's small study before they could talk.

'There's nothing definite but there's enough to make my concern more credible. First of all – Abramov. Abramov was at the Soviet Embassy here in the UK for five years. His cover was

Press Attaché but like most of them he was actually KGB. The press liked him because he was easy-going and reasonably cooperative.

'Apart from that I've got the video tapes covering Max Inman's visit to the checkpoint, going off in an official Soviet car and visiting the hospital. We can show that to Vlasov.

'All we want is what the hell was Inman doing and why the operation folded from then on. Who was the original Soviet contact. There's a lot to be explained.'

'By whom?'

'I guess by Max Inman or Vlasov, or both of 'em.'

'Why should Max Inman, a serving senior SIS officer, agree to being cross-questioned by a couple of retired has-beens from the same service?'

'We don't ask him to do that.'

'So what *do* we do?'

'We arrange for a chat with him, arranged by the Director-General. Nobody's accusing anybody of anything. Operation Janus is over, we're just tidying up so that it can be officially put to bed. Just part of the archives.'

'You think Sir Brian would go along with this?'

'I'm sure he will.'

'Why should he?'

'Because he knows that if we don't nail it down it will leak over to MI5 and they'll turn it into a cross between Moscow Circus and *Oklahoma*.'

Cooper stood up and walked to the window and its old-fashioned geraniums in terracotta pots. Maybe he should just pull out. Wish Rimmer good luck and let him go it alone. But Rimmer seemed so sure that something was seriously wrong. He turned and looked at Rimmer who was sitting there with his arms folded, waiting for a response.

'We'd better see the D-G together. I can fill in about Janus and you can explain your doubts.'

'OK. How about you contact him? You know him better than I do.'

Sir Brian had listened carefully as between them Cooper and Rimmer gave a rather rambling version of their thoughts. When they had finished, Sir Brian said, 'Are you two suggesting that we should hold an internal investigation into a senior serving SIS officer because you, Paul, have an instinct, an instinct not proven, that something was wrong with the Janus operation which is now a closed file? Is that it?'

'Not quite that, Sir Brian.'

'Tell me what it is then.'

'We need to know why Frank wasn't given a true picture by Max Inman of what was going on in Berlin. Why no mention that his Soviet contact had been changed? What was he doing in a KGB car at Charlie and why was he visiting an East Berlin hospital?' He paused. 'And I didn't envisage an official enquiry. Just an off-the-record chat with Max Inman so that he could show that it was all above board.'

'And that's the lot?'

'No, sir. I should want to know a lot more about what went on in Moscow when they abducted Max Inman.'

'If I remember rightly they apologised profusely for an administrative cock-up.'

'After they had had him for over three weeks. Why the sudden change of heart?'

For several moments Sir Brian said nothing, then he said, 'I'll think about it, gentlemen. I'll contact you, Frank, later this evening. You'll be at the cottage, yes?'

'Yes, sir.'

Chapter Forty-One

Sir Brian's PA had said that they wanted some confirmation from him before they closed the file and passed it to Archives. The meeting was at 11 a.m. in Sir Brian's conference room.

Sir Brian had waved his hand at the people already there.

'No need to introduce Frank Cooper and Paul Rimmer, but I don't think you ever met Tony Bennet. He was OC the SIS detachment in Berlin when you were there. We had to drag him into helping us trying to track you down when you went missing.'

Max Inman nodded acknowledgment to Bennet and sat down. Sir Brian looked across at Cooper.

'Perhaps you could act as Chairman, Frank, and lead us through the various points.'

Cooper looked at Inman and said, 'A few missing pieces in the jigsaw, Max. We're hoping you can throw some light on them.' He paused. 'First of all, do you feel free now to talk about the other side?'

Inman smiled. 'Ask me the questions and I'll do my best to answer.'

'Right. Your Soviet contact, could you identify him for us now that it's all over?'

'I did give an undertaking not to divulge his identity.'

Cooper said quietly. 'Was it by any chance a man named Vlasov? Josef Vlasov?'

Inman was silent for long moments and then, obviously reluctant he said, 'Yes.'

'But Vlasov was only your contact when Janus was being closed down. Who was your contact before Vlasov?'

'Let's move on a bit and come back to that.'

'OK. Let's do that. When SIS Berlin were dragged into the search, one of their undercover officers got hold of some video tape. Either Stasi or KGB. We aren't sure which. Were you aware that this was being done?'

'No. Why was it done?'

'It showed you getting into a car at Charlie. A car with diplomatic plates. Actually KGB. You appear to have got in the car voluntarily. There was further video tape of you in a hospital and of the car parked outside. Does that all seem possible to you?'

Inman shrugged. 'I'll take your word for it.'

'What was going on, Max?'

Inman looked around the faces at the table.

'You aren't tidying up, are you? You're digging it up – why?'

Sir Brian said, 'We need to know, Max. We need to know. You surely don't expect that when there's something we don't understand, that we don't ask the person at the centre for answers to our questions?'

'You mean answers to your doubts.' He turned to Paul Rimmer. 'Don't think I'm not aware of Katya being harassed by your old friends in MI5.' He looked around at the others. 'The Inland Revenue have been going through her accounts for months. I've had my people sweep our place for bugs once a week. Two phone mikes. One voice-activated tape machine on the top bookshelf and they've even got an approval for a blanket monitoring of our home phones and our mobiles.' He paused and looked at Rimmer. 'Maybe it's you people who should be answering the questions.'

Sir Brian looked at Rimmer. 'Do you know anything about this, Paul?'

'I've no interest in that sort of stuff, Sir Brian. I *am*, after all, retired.'

'So why are you here, my friend?' Inman could barely control his anger. 'Both of you are retired but you're still playing games.'

'What games, Max?' Cooper spoke quite calmly.

'Reds under the beds, and all that rubbish that gives you no time to think about what the world's really all about.'

For a long time nobody spoke and then Sir Brian said, 'Let's stick to the matter in hand for the moment. We can look at your complaints afterwards.' He paused. 'I can't understand why you didn't inform us that you had changed your Soviet contact. Why didn't you?'

'I didn't feel it was London's business. You didn't know either man. It was I who worked with them.'

Cooper intervened. 'Why *did* the contact change?'

'The original man became seriously ill and couldn't carry on.'

'So how was the successor chosen?'

'They chose Vlasov as a temporary operator and then when it was obvious that there would have to be another full-timer, he was the one they chose.'

'Was it the original man who you visited in hospital?'

'Yes.'

'Was his name Chebrikov, Alexander Chebrikov. Also known as Otto Bekker?'

Inman sighed with apparent boredom. 'Yes. Yes. Those were his names.'

'And you'd worked with him before Janus, hadn't you?'

'Yes.'

'So you judged that he was a real asset?'

'Yes.'

'But you had no experience of Vlasov? He was just dumped on you by Moscow?'

'Janus didn't call for inspiration at that stage. It was nearly over.'

'And Chebrikov had inspiration?'

'Yes. We worked out Janus together. He contributed just as much as I did.'

'What was his illness, Chebrikov's?'

Inman shrugged. 'I don't know.'

'You visited him in hospital but you don't know what was the matter with him?'

'It was just a formality.'

'And from there you went to Moscow?'

'From there I was *taken* to Moscow.'

'How did you go?'

'By plane.'

'What airline?'

'It was a military plane.'

'Where did it land?'

'At an air-force base near Moscow.'

'Then where did you go?'

'I was taken by car to the KGB headquarters in Dzerdzhinski Square.'

'Go on.'

'I was taken to the office of a senior KGB officer and he asked me things about Janus.'

'What did you tell him.'

'Just generalities.'

'When they took you to the plane in Berlin, did you protest?'

'I don't remember.'

'Did anyone else go with you?'

'Yes, Vlasov went too but after I was taken to the fellow in the KGB Vlasov was taken away.'

'What was the name of the senior KGB officer?'

'I don't remember.'

'Then what happened?'

'I was taken to a room at the Rossiya and a junior KGB officer became my minder – my escort for the rest of my time there.'

'What explanation did they give you for abducting you?'

'I was told it was some sort of administrative cock-up.'

'So why didn't they take you straight back to Berlin?'

Inman shrugged. 'Bureaucracy. And then I was told that there was some sort of negotiation going on with you people.'

'And for all that time, despite the way you lived, more or less, free, it didn't strike you that you could have phoned and told us of your situation?'

'They warned me not to.'

Sir Brian waited for a moment and then said, 'I think we've got plenty to think about.' He looked at Inman. 'Thank you for your cooperation. We'll meet here again tomorrow, same time. Perhaps after some thought you might feel you could take us a little further into your confidence.'

Nobody spoke and Sir Brian stood up and walked to the door without looking back.

On the train back to Chichester where Rimmer had left his car, they said very little. Cooper said only, 'What did you think of it?'

'I didn't believe a word of it. He was collaborating with them.' He paused. 'But I've got a couple more questions I want to ask our friend Vlasov.'

Vlasov seemed pleased to see them. He'd been watching TV all day.

When they were all there sitting around eating sandwiches and drinking coffee, Rimmer said, 'Tell me, Josef, you said you thought there was something odd between Max Inman and the people in Moscow. What do you think it could have been?'

'Not the people in Moscow, just Abramov.'

'Go on.'

'They didn't seem in any hurry to take Inman anywhere. He was stuck with us using the excuse of the Wall. Then they got the video stuff and within an hour they wanted him. And when I took him into Abramov's office Abramov came forward, holding out his hand, and smiling, and he said, "Great to see you, Max."' Vlasov paused. 'Abramov is very senior and he's not given to smiles and welcome speeches. Just seemed odd to me. As if they both knew something that I didn't know.'

Rimmer looked at Cooper. 'It's always the thing that's bottom of the pile when you're looking for something.' He paused. 'Let me go and check my file.'

Ten minutes later Rimmer shouted down the stairs, 'Can you spare me a minute, Frank?'

When Cooper got upstairs Rimmer was sitting on the bed in the small spare bedroom with papers littered all over the coverlet.

Rimmer beckoned him over. 'This is a rough report on Abramov and his career. Just look at that . . .' Rimmer pointed with his finger '. . . Abramov was First Secretary at their London embassy from 1973 to 1978.'

'So?'

'Don't come the innocent, Frankie. That's when they first met and that's when Max Inman was recruited. All in a good cause of course, but once you're in, you're in for life. No wonder he was so welcome in Moscow. Abramov had recognised his young "mole" from the video tapes. The only problem there was how to get him back to Berlin without rousing Brit suspicions. But luckily Katya Felinska raised hell at the embassy and that was excuse enough.'

'This is serious stuff, Paul. You're accusing a senior SIS man of having been a mole since he was at Cambridge.'

Rimmer shrugged and smiled. 'Wouldn't be the first one, my friend, would it?'

'So what next?'

'No accusations of anything. Not even saying what we know. But leaving him in no doubt that it's over. Just one carefully worded question. Leave it to me.'

Inman had arrived five minutes late at the meeting and Cooper had wondered if he'd backed out.

Sir Brian said amiably, 'Well, gentlemen. Has anybody had any bright thoughts overnight?'

Rimmer said, 'I've just got one more question, Sir Brian.'

'Then go ahead.'

Rimmer looked directly at Max Inman and said, 'Max. When did you first meet Yevgeny Abramov?'

There was a long silence and then Inman said, 'I'm not prepared to answer any more questions and I'm not prepared to continue this farce.' He stood up. 'I'd like to see you privately, Sir Brian.'

Sir Brian had taken the point but he said amiably enough, 'A good idea. Have a bit of lunch with me at the Reform. I'll get us a private room.'

The waiter had laid out cold-cuts and salad on two oval dishes and there was a thermos of tea and another of coffee.

Sir Brian's usual amiability was no longer on show. There were no ground-rules for dealing with double-agents who are eventually exposed. The essential is to negotiate so that the experts can do what the CIA called 'walking back the cat'. Trying to find where wrong decisions had been taken because the enemy knew more than you did. You may loathe the treachery but you mustn't scare them off. For the moment they were valuable properties.

As he reached over for a beef sandwich, Sir Brian said, 'I'd like to settle how we deal with this problem today if possible. Just the framework. 'He looked at Inman. 'Who else knows?'

'Nobody.'

'What about Katya?'

'She knows nothing. If we come to some arrangement she'd have to be left out of it.'

'I thought that we could go through the motions of you taking over a new assignment. Something you could do away from SIS. Then a slightly early retirement.' He paused. 'If this suited you I should want you to cooperate fully with Frank Cooper about your dealings with the KGB. Right from the day you signed on. What you provided. Means of communication and all the rest of it. Is that agreeable to you?'

'Yes. I'm sorry about all this . . .'

'Neither side wants it publicised, agreed?'

'I certainly don't.'

'And we get the truth and the whole truth, OK?'

'Yes.' He paused. 'What happens after that's done?'

'You'll officially have an early retirement on full pension.' He paused for a moment. 'Can I ask you just one question, a personal question?'

'Yes.'

'What on earth made you do it? You spoke the language, you'd seen the set-up, and you were bright. Why?'

Inman sighed. 'I was a fool. I was critical of how they treated people and they listened and seemed to take notice. I thought I could help them build a better kind of world.' He paused. 'It sounds so naive and pathetic when I say it now. But it seemed real and possible in those days. And when I started I wasn't in SIS. I hadn't been recruited.' He shrugged. 'I was just a sympathiser.'

'How will you spend your time when Cooper has finished with you?'

'I thought I might get a job as a genuine freelance journalist and maybe some translations.'

'I hope you realise that we're letting you off very lightly. If you wonder why, it's because you did such great work on Janus.'

Sir Brian stood up and Inman stood up too. He held out his hand which Sir Brian took reluctantly.

Chapter Forty-Two

———◆———

She was looking at a contact sheet of black-and-white photographs. He could see the halo of light from the table lamp at the edge of her hair.

'Are you very busy, Katie?'

Without looking up she said, 'Nothing in particular. Are you hungry?'

He sighed heavily. 'I've something to tell you, something serious.'

She looked up quickly. 'Are you ill or something? What is it? Tell me.'

'Way back I did something that was stupid and it's caught up with me.'

'How far way back?'

'About four months before I met you.'

She smiled. 'Don't tell me you've had a secret love all this time.'

'Don't laugh, sweetie. I could end up in prison.'

'For what?'

'For treason. For assisting the Queen's enemies.'

'Oh come off it, Max, you were what? About twenty-three or four. What the hell could you do that's treason?'

'I agreed to act as an agent for the KGB, even after I joined MI6.'

'I thought that sort of thing had ended when they collared Philby and Burgess and the other one.'

'It still goes on, Katie. Same old game.'

'Did they pay you to do it, the Russians?'

'No. I just wanted to help them establish a socialist state.'

She shook her head slowly in disbelief. 'For God's sake, Max, you don't agree to become a traitor just because you see a lot of poor wretches repairing the cobbled streets of Moscow while you're on a school exchange visit.' She paused for breath. 'There are poor wretches like that in every country in the world. Socialists, fascists, Marxists, Buddhists, Muslims, and raving Tories. They're all the same. That's what all politics are about – power. Just power – nothing else. And you – my boy – ain't going to alter it by selling the secrets of our artillery to the Reds.' Again she shook her head. 'What an idiot. I suppose your people have discovered what you were up to?'

'I'm afraid so.'

'And what are they going to do to you?'

'I've got to tell them the things I did for the Russians and I retire early on full pension.' He paused. 'Are you ashamed of me now you know this?'

'No way. Surprised but not ashamed. You're still you and I didn't love you for being a patriot.'

'Will you stay with me?'

'Of course I will.'

'I couldn't go on without you.'

'Let's go to the Italian place and eat a bowl of spaghetti bolognese.'

As the months went by she never mentioned the matter again and asked no questions about what was going on. He was conscious of the feeling that while she may not be ashamed of what he had done, she saw it as sheer stupidity on his part and typically unscrupulous on the part of the people in Moscow who had controlled him.

Frank Cooper was the one who was shocked as he cross-questioned Max Inman and heard how he had provided Moscow with regular reports on SIS operations against them. And it explained a lot about why many of those operations had failed. What angered him most was the fact that Inman took no real risks in his treason. If he had been uncovered the most that would have happened was a prison sentence. No wonder the death of the self-styled Otto Bekker had left its mark on Inman's conscience. But in his more rational moments Cooper was aware that this fool of a man had not only devised but operated successfully a collaboration with the KGB that had benefitted both sides and which the Soviets would never have agreed to had it not been run by Max Inman. Poor Otto Bekker had paid with his life and although Inman didn't yet seem to have realised it, his old life was over. Cooper wondered if Inman had told Katya, and if he had, what her reaction had been. Even Rimmer had concluded after hearing Inman's sorry tale that Katya Felinska probably knew little or nothing about what Inman was doing. They hadn't even met when Moscow originally recruited him. But could Operation Janus have gone ahead successfully if Moscow hadn't reckoned that Max Inman was their man?

Katya Felinska had not been shocked by Max Inman's revelations. It was what politics was all about. The struggle for power that never counted the cost because other people paid. Paid in misery and subjugation where survival was the best you could hope for. But her affection for Max Inman was not affected. For her he was a victim. One more victim of the men in smoke-filled back-rooms and their stooges with the AK47s. Men who always talked about 'our people' and 'the new politics'. The Brit politicians hadn't yet got to the AK47s, they used the media instead. They'd turned politics into a soap opera.

Chapter Forty-Three

They had the final meeting at Sir Brian's London apartment and what they were talking about seemed in strange contrast to the sunshine coming through the tall French windows. Sir Brian had put the file with Cooper's report on the floor beside his chair. He looked across at Cooper, but Cooper was waiting for Sir Brian himself to speak first. Which he did, very testily.

'This is one of those Judgment of Solomon situations. If it wasn't for Janus he ought to go in the slammer. He cost people's lives with his arrogance. Who did he think he was – deciding that we were the villains and Moscow should be forgiven everything because they were building a true socialist state? What rubbish.

'And then on the other hand we have Janus. His initiative and his influence with Moscow who seem to have been as divided on the issue as we were. Undoubtedly Janus prevented mistakes being made by both sides. Mistakes that could have cost a lot more lives than his treachery did.

'If we ignore Janus it would be a terrible injustice.' He shrugged. 'But that's our privilege. And to ignore the damage he caused over the years as their man in SIS would equally be an injustice. An injustice to at least a dozen men and to the service itself. What is this wretched man – a hero or a traitor? What do we do?'

Cooper took a deep breath. 'We don't really have any choice, Sir Brian. We gain nothing if we expose him and probably do more damage to SIS than he has done. I suggest that we call it a day and hope to God it never gets exposed.'

Sir Brian pointed at the file beside him on the floor. 'And what do we do with this? Destroy it?'

'We could rightly be severely criticised if we destroyed it. I think I could dispose of it where it could be found if we needed to find it but where nobody else could find it.'

'Are we both thinking of the same place?' He paused. 'The — for want of a better description — the French Connection?'

'Yes. Shall I deal with it?'

'Yeah.' He stood up. 'Thanks for your help on all this, Frank. I won't forget.'

Built-in to the fabric of the structure of the Eurostar tunnel are several dozen lockers that house fire-fighting and medical equipment. They are never locked and are opened by turning a metal handle. There are four similar lockers that appear to be part of the fabric of the tunnel and without any indication that there is anything abnormal about them. The four can only be opened with a smart card whose code is changed on random dates.

Cooper stood watching as the Intelligence Corps Major placed the taped-up file inside and closed the well-oiled door. It clicked smoothly into place.

Chapter Forty-Four

They had gone to the open-air concert at Kenwood and were sitting on the grass in front of the lake. There had been enthusiastic applause for the orchestra's *Walk to the Paradise Garden* by Delius and there was an interval before the Dvorak fiddle concerto. Max had walked over to the house and brought back ice-cream wafers and tea in plastic cups.

She licked round the sides of the ice-cream and then turned to look at him.

'When will they be finished with you?'

He looked at her, surprised. 'What made you ask that?'

She shrugged. 'Just curiosity.'

'But why this moment?'

'I've no idea.'

'They finished with me today.'

'What happened – do they break a sword on your shoulder or what?'

'It was Frank Cooper and Sir Brian. Both very frosty. I signed a piece of paper about non-disclosure on either side. There was an official letter accepting my resignation and confirming the stuff about my pension. There was a slight hiccup when I pointed out that officially I was still employed by *The Economist*. But they waved that aside.' He paused. 'As I was going to the lift

Frank Cooper walked alongside me for a few steps and said, "It was Janus that saved you, Inman." Then he turned and walked away.'

'Your ice-cream's melting, lick it up.' As he licked the wafer she said, 'When will you start writing?'

'There's no point, Katie. Nobody will give me work. When these situations come up they put out the word. They don't give any reason. They don't need to. Just recommend extreme caution.' He shrugged. 'That's enough.'

'Use a pen name.'

'I hadn't thought of that. Why not? A good idea.'

'Maybe you could do the words for my book on the two Germanys. Not much politics. Not much economics. Just ordinary people with vices and virtues.' She paused. 'I've got really good pictures. Let's talk about it when we get back.'

The invitation from the Soviet Embassy was for 'Katya Felinska and partner'. The party was to celebrate the appointment of the new ambassador, His Excellency Yevgeny Abramov and his wife Svetlana. She tore it up angrily after she had shown it to Inman.

'They never stop trying, do they?' she said.

He felt that there could be several quite acceptable reasons why they'd sent the invitation but he said nothing. They would have heard on some grapevine or other that he'd been thrown out of SIS. And for Abramov Operation Janus would now be no more than just a small, half-forgotten item of history.

A small para in the *Daily Telegraph* and another in *The Times* recorded that Frank Leonard Cooper had been awarded a knighthood in Her Majesty's Birthday Honours List for services to the Foreign and Commonwealth Office. Hobbies, model trains OO gauge. Sports, bowls.

* * *

SIS set up Vlasov with a freelance translating bureau. He had a nice apartment near the British Council Offices in Berlin and was making a very good living which included a Mercedes-Benz convertible. However, old habits and attitudes prevailed and he developed a side-line that became even more profitable as the representative in Berlin for the disposal of technical equipment sold by officers of the Red Army, who had not been paid for over six months. The goods he could supply ranged from binoculars and radios to highly technical items like range-finders for sophisticated artillery and working drawings of high-technology items still at the design stage.

He had been carrying on this trade until he was being offered parts for devices capable of launching nuclear war-heads. At that stage he was negotiating with high-level operators from third-world governments and was out of his depth. Inevitably he was arrested by the German intelligence service, the BND. His claim to have connections with British intelligence was checked, denied and dismissed. He offered to do a deal and work for the BND but that was declined. He was sentenced to five years imprisonment on tax-avoidance charges.

Paul Rimmer lived reasonably comfortably off his pension, voted Conservative and was a Magistrate at the local court in Guildford. But he valued rather more the fact that he was voted to be the chairman of the cricket club for which he had always played. A stylish batsman and medium-paced bowler. Both his son and daughter are at university. His son reading computer science at Birmingham and his daughter on a creative writing course at Brighton.

* * *

Katya was sitting with her mother on the grass by the Serpentine lake. It was the hottest day that year so far but there was a breeze across the water that cooled them with the summer smell of mown grass.

'I heard you on Woman's Hour about adopting the little girl from Mogadishu. Was that really true that they wouldn't let the couple who wanted to adopt her do it because they were coloured?'

'Absolutely. They said the little girl is coloured and she would not learn how to survive from a coloured couple.'

'But why not for heaven's sake? I should have thought being coloured made it a perfect match.'

'The Social Services said that the couple had learned how to survive being coloured and they wouldn't be capable of appreciating what the Somali girl's problems were.' She paused. 'They also wanted pictures of the little girl's home and the town where she lives.'

'Is that a problem?'

'Yeah. Several problems. Her family was murdered by the "*shifta*" at a place called Bulo Burti. It's about fifty miles north of Mog. The road ends there. That's the only road for four hundred miles. There is no town. There isn't even a village. All Somalis are nomads. They follow the rains with their goats and camels and carry their sticks of homes on their backs. They move on when the rains move on. Even if there had been no war, the girl would not have belonged anywhere nor have what you could call a home to photograph.' She paused. 'When I told them this they told me it was none of my business and they would not even consider the application for at least a year.' She paused. 'I told them that the little girl was so under-nourished that she was unlikely to last a year.'

'What did they say to that?'

'Just dismissed it. The rules are the rules. I said I didn't believe that those were the rules. And she said I had no status in the adoption, she would speak only with the couple.' She paused. 'And all the time I was tape-recording all this. Quite openly but they didn't give a damn. They don't like people who argue or query what they do.'

'What's going to happen now?'

Katya smiled. 'You know me. The local MP is seeing the PM. A press release goes out tomorrow telling the whole story and naming names plus the fact that the Somali ambassador here in London is arranging for the child to be brought over by the Red Cross next week and will be backing the application.' She grinned. 'The Red Cross and the Red Crescent Committees have already assured me that the adoption will go ahead immediately. The media are going to have a field day.'

'It sounds like a crazy dream, doesn't it?'

'It's what happens when bureaucrats take over. Those are the people Hitler wanted. And the stooges loved it. A new set of rules for the "good of everyone". If you speak up against the phoney rules you're an enemy of the state. It's all right for people like me who've got influence or can raise hell, but most people are helpless. Who do they turn to for help – their MP – Parliament – the courts – the police – forget it? They have nobody to call on. The state talks of equality and freedom, fairness and justice for all – but they have no intention of disturbing what their underlings are doing. Their bit of power over people is part of their reward. They don't want people who argue at any level.'

'So what can we do about it?'

'Nothing. That's what makes me so mad. I used to think that education was the solution. But it isn't. When you get down to it and look at the facts, it's simple. The fact is that half the world's population are selfish, cruel bastards and the other half – are women.'

Her mother laughed and changed the subject. 'How's your fellow coping with retirement?'

'I'm not sure. He never talks about it. Spends a lot of time reading and writing and I guess that some day it will bear fruit.'

A year later they moved to Cambridge. Max Inman had been offered a post as lecturer on 'Philosophy and Politics' at King's and had been a great success. Academics admired his ability to argue the perfect solution to any political thought and then argue equally tellingly against it. And the students loved his sweeping lack of approval for any kind of politics. SIS had vaguely wondered about sticking the knife in to his appointment but by the end of the first term it was too late. Max Inman had found his niche in life and strangely enough it had suited Katya too. She listened to him lecturing and wondered why she hadn't really appreciated what she'd got from this strange man.

He had been lecturing for five years when he died. In Berlin, of a heart attack, and appropriately enough at the end of a talk he had just given at the Bertolt Brecht House.

Katya moved back with her parents and is still with them. She appears quite often on talk shows, fulfilling the role of quota intellectual and quota woman. The bone structure and the Polish-Italian genes have left her with a face that some say is even more beautiful than when she was younger.